From the
STREETS TO THE SHEETS

NOIRE

Noire presents

From the
STREETS TO THE SHEETS
Urban Erotic Quickies

One World | Ballantine Books | New York

A One World Books Trade Paperback Original

Copyright © 2008 by Noire

Published in the United States by One World Books, an imprint of The Random House Publishing Group, a division of Random House, Inc., New York.

ONE WORLD is a registered trademark and the One World colophon is a trademark of Random House, Inc.

LIBRARY OF CONGRESS CATALOGING-IN-PUBLICATION DATA
From the streets to the sheets : urban erotic quickies.
p.   cm.
Title appears on item as: Noire presents From the streets to the sheets
"A One World Books trade paperback original"—T.p. verso,
ISBN 978-0-345-50848-5 (trade pbk.)
1. Erotic stories, American.   2. American fiction—African American authors.
3. African Americans—Fiction.   I. Noire.
II. Title: Noire presents From the streets to the sheets.
PS648.E7F76 2008
813'.01083538—dc22 2008006686

Printed in the United States of America

www.oneworldbooks.net

2   4   6   8   9   7   5   3   1

This book is dedicated to the hard-body writers
who jumped on board to take a long ride
on my Urban Erotic Train.

Andrea, Eric, Euftis, K'wan, Aretha, Jamise, Gerald,
Plea$ure, Gerald, Joy, Kweli, and Thomas . . .

You are some of the hottest urban authors on the
shelves today. You brought style, eroticism, and
originality to your slammin urban quickies, and not
many out there can match what you do.

Every fan of mine should become a fan of yours, too,
because each of you talented writers has
pure fiyah coming out of your pens.

CONTENTS

From the
STREETS TO THE SHEETS

NOIRE

THAT BITCH JUICY
Noire

"Make that money-money! Make that money-money! Make that mothafuckin' money-money, honey!" The heat meter was spiking off the chain in the G-Spot. Dicks were swollen and the scent of hot pussy was blowing through the air. Big-money ballers chanted along with the bass of street music as they watched the solo act being performed onstage under the filtered spotlight.

Playas and hustlers near the front of the stage grabbed their dicks and hollered, and niggahs toward the back of the room started standing up on tables to get a better look at Money-Making Monique as she bent her blooming onion over and inched a pair of fishnet stockings down her thick, shapely thighs.

"Take that money-money! Take that money-money! Take that mothafuckin' money-money, honey!!"

Cash was sailing on the stage like green leaves falling off a tree, and the other strippers in the Spot were calculating how much bank they could squeeze outta these horny niggahs before the night was over. They stood onstage behind their girl, clapping their hands to Monique's spicy hot beat. "You workin' that cake, girl! Making all these niggahs feen for a slice!" They cheered her solo act because even though Monique was the one spiking up the heat with her bomb booty and make-a-niggah-cum moves, she damn sure couldn't slide her one pussy up and down every hard dick in the house. All the fuck rooms in the Spot were about to be occupied tonight, and the cleaning staff was gonna have to work overtime just to keep fresh sheets on the beds.

Up onstage, Monique ignored the noise from the crowd as she did her nasty thang like she'd been born with a golden pole wedged between her legs. She slipped her hips and popped her spine the way she had practiced a thousand times before in the mirror, and it was that kind of dedication to her grind that had made her the Spot's top money-maker for the last two years.

Monique didn't mind the fact that all kinds of niggahs wanted to fuck her. She was proud to be the kind of freak that men just couldn't resist. And yeah, her body was simply fuckin' stunning. Damn right they was feenin' for her, because what good was having the best shit on the shelf if you couldn't make a niggah cry for it?

Tonight Monique was doing one of her new ill na-na routines. She had about thirty dance acts she worked, switching the moves up every other night, and every last one of her routines kept niggahs digging deep in their pocket stash, producing guaranteed cash results each time.

Some long-legged hustler sitting right up front screeched like a bitch as Monique squeezed her firm cantaloupe-sized breasts in her hands and let her red-polished fingernails flick her inch-long nipples seductively. He screamed again as she lowered her head and licked that stiff little nipple that sat smack in the middle of her upper chest, the one protruding from her tiny third breast that was round and perfect, but sat up closer to her neck than her normal breasts did, and was much, much smaller, like a twelve-year-old's.

Yeah, she thought as niggahs started whistling and wildin' at the sight of her tongue swirling around that little tiny titty. Everybody loved a freak. And of all the things Monique could claim to be, she was a true freak-a-leek above all else. She turned her back on the crowd and popped her hips, letting her chips dip and her backbone slip.

Ya'll niggahs take a good fuckin' look at all this chocolate birthday cake, Monique thought, clapping her thick booty cheeks and showing them flashing bits of her pink pussy and her sweet asshole. *'Cause a bitch is gonna be off this stage and paid in a minute. Straight fuckin' paid.*

Niggahs moaned out loud and nutted in their drawers, but Monique couldn't care less about their sexual satisfaction. She had thoughts of retirement on her mind, and if shit went down the way she and Pluto planned, she was about to give up the poles and become the number-one bitch at her very own strip club down in B-More.

Harlem is too hot. It's time to get the fuck out, she thought, her body undulating with movements on its own. She'd been working the G-Spot for over two years now, and she couldn't believe how fast her luck had suddenly changed. That dumb bitch Juicy had fucked around and betrayed G by getting caught on camera suckin' off his very own son, and right now Granite McKay's main bitch was downstairs chained to a bed in the Dungeon, beat down and fucked the hell out.

That left all the room in the world for Monique and Pluto to take over the G-Spot2 when it opened in Baltimore, the same joint that G was fronting all the money for and had been planning to hand over to his son, Gino.

Monique was down on the floor now. Laying on her side, her right leg doing a wide scissor dance as niggahs drooled and tried to push their eyeballs up into her uterus. She rolled over on her back and slid her body around the long way. She knew how delicious she looked from the side. Bodacious titties rising into the air like two firm brown hills, each one with a shiny little cherry on top. Her shoulders were pressed back and her waist arched up high, a gap of light showing between her lower back and the stage floor due to the thick mound of ass she was packing. She waved her legs in the air. They were shapely and in perfect proportion.

Already Monique could see herself flossin' down there in

B-More. She'd step up in that brand-new territory like a bad-ass bitch for real. She'd shop for some fly New York gear before she left, then take all her banging fashions right down I-95 along with her. Of course she'd come back to Harlem to get her hair whipped all the time, but no more poles and stages and fuck rooms for her. She'd be too busy managing her own stable of strippers and hoes. She'd be pushing Pluto's Porsche and staying iced the fuck out seven days a week.

The excitement of her thoughts had Monique moving her body on the floor like a snake, slithering and shivering as her nipples hardened and her pussy began to leak. Just imagining herself as a classy bitch running a high-powered joint kicked her sex-o-meter into automatic. Her heat was turned up extra-high, and every niggah in the room was dying to stick his tongue in the pool of hot juices that were bubbling between her thighs.

Monique closed her eyes and tuned out the noise of the crowd. C-notes fluttered down on her body, some of the green bills sticking to the dampness of her skin. She bounced her ass to the beat, then shocked them all by spinning around on her butt until she was facing the crowd with her curvy legs gapped wide open.

A sexy grin spread over her face and she stuck her fingers between her legs, pulling back her pussy lips and exposing herself to their greedy eyes, then began masturbating herself slowly, then faster. Monique knew just what to do, and she couldn't wait to teach some of her old tricks to the new bitches she was gonna hire when she got to Baltimore.

Monique had the wettest pussy in the whole wide world, and she tossed her head back and worked herself with three fingers, sloshing them around inside of her slit, but making sure she pulled them out every so often so niggahs could see the thick juices that dripped from her fingers and splattered down onto the stage floor.

The screams coming from the crowd drove her into a frenzy, and she fucked herself deeply, squeezing her clit, stroking her breasts, and licking that third nipple that mighta been tiny, but was sensitive as hell and sent sparks shooting through her pussy that felt like electric perfection. The moans rolling off her lips wasn't fake no more, and this is what the crowd had been waiting for. Her plump ass splashed around in the pool of juices she was creating on the floor, and she was concentrating on her orgasm like it was the last one she would have in the world.

Her shit was for real, and them niggahs in the G-Spot knew it and loved it. Some of the bitches right up onstage loved it too, and had even tasted what Monique had to offer a time or two themselves. Monique screamed as her clit swelled and throbbed like a mini-dick. She parted her swollen pussy lips so everyone could see her pearl, then whipped it back and forth with her wet fingers, pressing down and massaging it until her legs shot straight out and her back arched in a C. She started trembling and whimpering as cum rushed from her body, her pussy squirting and ejaculating on the floor in spurts just like a man.

Monique floated back down to herself and opened her eyes. Security was having a real hard time keeping them niggahs from rushing up on the stage and fucking the shit outta her, and she smiled real big at the hot ballers as they strained against Greco's armed crew and tried to reach her. She knew she was safe, but she made sure each and every one of them got a good look as she rubbed her spilled sugar all over her mound, and even all down in the crack of her ass.

Ten minutes later Monique had picked up her money off the stage and was repeating her performance in fuck room number eight. Some high-rolling hustler from Connecticut had paid premium dollars to keep her on lock for two hours, and right now he was tickling her tonsils with his tiny dick as his woman buried her pretty face in Monique's still-wet pussy.

I ain't gone be doing this shit much longer, Monique told herself as she humped her hips, even though the chick between her legs was eating her pussy out deliciously. She opened her legs wider, getting bomb-ass head and getting paid for it at the same time. Shit, this bitch was fine as hell too. She had stripped naked and was laying on her stomach, her face buried in Monique's snatch. Monique moaned and pushed her hips up off the bed, holding the back of the girl's head and pressing her tongue deeper inside her. She shivered as that hot tongue probed her spots and lapped at her clit. She gazed at the female nestled between her legs and liked what she saw. Monique loved dick, but she also appreciated what a woman could offer her, and this one here had a better-looking ass than any ho in the house, except her of course. But best of all, the girl was licking Monique's pussy just right, concentrating on that clit so good, that Monique had to force herself not to let go of the dick she was bobbing on and grab the girl's head and cum all over her face.

Instead, she rode the beat that was thumping deep inside her coochie and concentrated on giving this playa his money's worth. His pockets was deep and his dick was little, so the next two hours was gonna be a breeze. Hell, after tonight, the rest of her life would be a breeze. And she didn't have nobody but that stupid bitch Juicy to thank for all the good tongue, and the good fortune, that had fallen right in her lap.

•   •   •

Monique never could stand Juicy's ass.

She'd known her from 136th Street, and used to tease her retarded brother Jimmy in school all the time. Juicy's grandmother was sanctified, and used to look down her nose on Monique's mother because she had ten kids by ten different daddies and couldn't control none of them.

Monique had moved across town in the ninth grade and forgotten all about Juicy, but years later here that bitch came, strutting her shit up in Monique's territory like she was special or something. Monique had felt herself fill to the top with envy when G brought virgin-ass Juicy up in the Spot, then shut down his whole operation and took her up on the stage and asked if anybody had fucked the bitch or even sucked her.

"Who does that bitch think she is?" Monique had fumed to her girl, a stripper called Honey Dew. "I shoulda raised my hand and screamed, 'Me! Me! Me! I sucked that phony bitch out and I fucked her too!' " Monique laughed hard at the thought. "G woulda dropped her so-called virgin ass so quick she would still be wandering around Harlem trying to find the train station."

"Who cares?" Honey Dew shrugged. "G don't fuck with no hoes, and don't no real bitch wanna be pinned down by an old head like him no way. That niggah is grimy and cold-blooded, and I'm glad he won't touch nothing but a virgin. That means my ass is safe. So you can dead all them thoughts you been thinking about you and him, Monique. Your pussy meter been clicked too many times, because just like the rest of us, your ass been *run through* up in this Spot."

"Who said I wanted G's old ass? Yeah, that niggah's paid, but shit. So is Pluto. I'm straight with what I got."

"Bitch, don't front. Everybody can see how hard you trying to be down on G's dick. And since he's the one feeding your stankin-butt boo Pluto, you might wanna watch that shit. I hear Pluto's funky ass can be a bitch-buster too, you know."

Monique let Honey Dew's warning bounce off her. Yeah, Pluto could get stupid with his hands sometimes, but every ho working the Spot, including Honey Dew, would have slit Monique's throat if it meant they could get closer to her man. Stank drawers or not.

But Monique had really been steaming inside the night G pronounced that Juicy was gonna be his new woman. Her young, dumb ass had stood up on that stage grinning like she was the shit. Like she was the prize that had been chosen by the king. While Monique, who was G's top stripper and big-money flatbacker, had to stand there and watch that bitch get the kind of top billing that should have been hers.

But Monique wasn't no damn fool. And she had to give it to Juicy. The bitch was fly. She had killer curves, good hair, and a real pretty face. But she was square and too damn stupid for her own good. A playa like G needed a real bitch who understood the game and could watch his back. He needed a bitch who could contribute to his empire and make shit happen for him on all levels. A trick like Juicy wasn't good for much more than sitting up on a bar stool looking tight all night, and although Monique knew she was one devastating bitch herself, she was working with a real brain too, so she was much more valuable to any niggah's hustle.

So for two years Monique hated on Juicy and mindfucked her every chance she got. G's money was being well spent because that trick stayed draped in fly, expensive rags, with her hair and nails done to perfection every day. Monique made damn sure she kept right up with her too. She had always made sure her shit was whipped butter from head to toe, but with Juicy on the scene she put even more effort into her style, sauntering up in the G-Spot with so much pussy-appeal that niggahs stopped in their tracks and pulled out long bank just to watch her step out of her panties.

But Juicy had done fucked up now. She'd gotten with that broke sherm Gino and let a little young dick go to her head. Monique had laughed her ass off when they dragged that ho through the doors looking like a shit-on rat. They tossed her *and* that fine college-boy Gino down in the Dungeon and fucked them both up real nice.

She knew Juicy's X had definitely hit the spot when G ordered his boys to bring her upstairs so she could work the poles. Monique's face almost split in half from laughing so hard, especially when she saw Ace and Pluto dragging that bitch around the corner smelling like old piss and sporting a black eye, a busted lip, and a big red noogie on her forehead.

"Damn, Juicy!" Monique laughed. She had just gotten herself powdered, pressed, and dressed, and she knew she was looking like a cotton candy dream. "Your shit is fucked *up*! I always knew you wasn't nothing but a low-profile ho!"

That bitch had the nerve to stunt.

"Fuck you, you three-titty bitch!"

"Oh, but ya niggah loves 'em," Monique taunted her, squeezing her own breasts. "And while your stank-ass pussy is getting scuffed and plunged tonight, he's gonna be sucking on all three of these titties!"

If she hadn't hated Juicy so much, Monique mighta felt sorry for her. The girl had been humiliated as fuck dancing up on that stage, but she slid her pussy and legs up and down that pole just like she was told, because she knew better than to fuck with G.

Later on that night Monique got the good news from one of the other girls. Every ho in the house was gonna have a light night, because Juicy was in hot demand. Monique caught up with Pluto and Greco as they were dragging Juicy toward fuck room number nine, and Monique skipped over happily to tell her the good news.

"Juicy, you my motherfuckin' girl! Them niggahs out there just LOVE you! Your fine ass got twelve chips and a whole line of cash niggahs waiting on you. It musta been that 'ass thing' you did that freaked them all out. Whatever it was, thank you! You giving all the other hoes up in here a break tonight!"

Monique had wanted to scream with laughter at the look on Juicy's face. The high-maintenance bitch looked terrified as shit. As if fuckin' fifteen or twenty stank-breath niggahs with hard dicks was gonna kill her or something.

"Here," Monique said, taking some pity on her and passing her a pill from her personal stash. "After the first ten dirty-dicked niggahs screwing and slobbering all over you, you're gonna need this to help you get through the rest. Later, hater!"

* * *

"What the fuck is going on around here?" Monique caught up with Honey Dew in the dressing room a couple of days later. "Pluto didn't bring his fat ass home last night. Some shit is up, girl. I can feel it."

"I'on't know," Honey Dew whispered. She pulled her shirt over her head and her butterscotch titties with thick chocolate nipples stood straight out from her body. She cupped them in her hands and thumbed her stiff buds.

Monique eyed them hungrily, but she'd already fucked Honey Dew more than once. The girl was a squirter and had some real soft pussy, but right now Monique was much more interested in whatever news Honey Dew might be able to put her up on than she was on tasting her juice.

"I heard they did Gino, girl. I heard Moonie telling Greco that they took him out by the airport and deaded his fuckin' ass."

Monique nodded and smiled. Good. With Gino gone, that meant the path was all the way clear for her and Pluto to slide right into position. G had already fronted almost half the money for the state business licenses and shit, and him and Pluto was gonna ride down there together in about a week so he could pay off the cops and the people who signed off on liquor licenses. After that G said he'd drop a bucket load of bank on Monique so she could hire some girls to work the stage and the back rooms too.

Monique couldn't wait till they were heading south on the Jersey Turnpike. She'd been fucking Pluto for years, even though he smelled like a dead man and beat her ass and treated her like shit whenever he felt like it. But so what. The niggah was a loyal soldier. He was way up there on G's team, and rolling with funky power was better than rolling with a fragrant wankster. She'd stick close to Pluto and put up with his shit-streaked drawers and nasty breath until she could get with a strong niggah like G. Maybe she'd find herself one down in the B-More. She was damn sure gonna be looking around.

But shit veered off course for her the next evening when Pluto called her cell phone and told her the G-Spot was closed and to stay home for the night. Monique was suspicious. She knew that amateur-ass Juicy had fallen off on her shit a few days ago, and was too worn out to work the rooms anymore. Niggahs had been tossing their room chips back at Creco and refusing to fuck her 'cause her stank pussy was bleeding and she was talking out of her head.

So vacation time had come to a close for Monique and the other hoes, and niggahs was so full of cum that she'd been forced to take on a double load the night before. Ballers had been horny and wanted to fuck, so Monique had performed all of her little tricks to get them to nut as fast as possible, and Pluto's call had caught her soaking her sore pussy in a hot tub of water and going over her pole routines in her mind.

"Yeah," Pluto told her. "Stay the fuck home. We closed to the public for the night. Ballers only. So keep your ass at home."

Monique was too suspicious! What kinda private party could G be having that didn't involve his hoes? She didn't even like the way that shit sounded, so she had to let a niggah know!

"What up like that? What kinda private fuckin' party? Why ain't nobody invite me?"

"Jawn," Pluto growled in her ear. "I'll snap your motherfuckin' neck! You better remember ya goddamn role. Don't be asking me no fuckin' questions. Especially on the air. Just do like I said, and stay your ass the fuck home." *Click*.

Monique had looked at the phone for a second, then threw that shit up against the wall. That stank niggah better not be trying to roll nowhere without her! Just the thought that Pluto might try to shake her off and leave her in Harlem made her face sweat as she sat in all that hot water.

She thought about that shit for a second, and decided it was best to regroup.

Jumping out of the bubbly water, Monique let the stopper out of the tub and dried off real quick. Then she sprayed cleanser all around the bathroom, especially the nasty-ass toilet that Pluto couldn't seem to aim his dick into, and cleaned it until the room was sparkling and smelled like roses and vanilla. She had already cursed the landlord out and told him they were leaving and not to look for another fuckin' penny in rent, so she hated to waste her energy cleaning an apartment she was about to vacate, but she had to. She had stepped her ass outta pocket with her man, and there had been a killer edge in Pluto's voice when he set her straight that told her there was more to come. She knew that niggah had a temper, and she knew he had a memory too. If she wasn't careful he could either ride down I-95 and leave her ass stuck in Harlem, or walk through the door swinging his fists and punching her lights out. Unless she got his mood right.

Monique spent the next few hours preparing for her man to get home. She was gonna butter his ass up like a piece of toast. No, like some corn on the cob. He'd walk in the door and find a clean house, a hot meal, and best of all, a docile bitch who knew her proper place and how to keep her fuckin' mouth closed.

But when Pluto shot through the door around three o'clock in the morning his mood was too crazy. Monique had planned on holding her nose and sucking the membranes out of his fat, nasty dick, but he wasn't having it.

She'd been lounging on the sofa in a lavender silk robe,

makeup in place and smelling real nice, but when she looked up and saw the expression on her man's face she lost all of her cool and jumped to her feet because what she was seeing was truly impossible.

"What's the matter, baby? Baby, what's wrong?"

Pluto's eyes were red and swollen like he had just finished crying or something. He must have wiped some serious snot from his nose because crusty green streaks had dried up all across his cheeks.

Monique couldn't imagine what could have her man looking so bent, but whatever it was, she was gonna make it go away. "Don't worry about nothing, baby," she cooed as Pluto pushed past her. She followed him into their bedroom. "Monique got you, Big Papa. And I'm here to make you feel good."

Pluto stopped in the bedroom doorway and cursed, then rushed over to the dresser and began throwing shit out the top drawer.

Monique beamed as she looked around the spotless room that just hours ago had looked like a hurricane hit it. She had folded every stitch in all of his dresser drawers too, so there wasn't shit he could complain about. "I did a good job, baby. Didn't I?"

For the first time since he entered the apartment, Pluto actually looked at her.

"Gimme my bitch."

"Huh?"

"My burner. My piece. It was in the fuckin' drawer, Monique."

"Oh," she said, rushing over to the closet. She flung the doors open and felt around in her shoe bag and took the gat out of a pair of bloodred pumps.

"Here you go, Papa. I just put it up for you, that's all."

Pluto snatched the burner from her and walked into the bathroom, slamming the door behind him. Monique hadn't liked the deadly look in his eyes, and she stood outside the door listening as he plopped down on the toilet and took a piss. She stood there running her mouth a mile a minute and praying he wouldn't fuck her up after he shook his dick off and came back out.

"You ready to take over Baltimore, Big Papa?" she yeasted him way up through the door. "Your shit is gonna be large! Prolly larger than what G has going right here in Harlem! I mean, his game is tight and all, I'll give him that. But he ain't you. He can't handle no business like you can, and he definitely ain't got a pocket-bitch like me clocking for him, ya know? Yeah. Let G have Harlem. This shit is played anyway. B-More is where it's happening, baby. It's a whole new grind poppin' off down there, and we about to drop a big bomb and make all kinds of noise."

Monique heard some funny sounds coming from the other side of the door, and if she didn't know no better she woulda thought Pluto's fat ass was farting and crying. She dismissed that notion because her niggah mighta been hefty and stank, but he was one of G's fiercest soldiers and his reputation spoke loud for him and proved that he was harder than a brick.

"I fried you some shicken," she sang brightly, damn near

stepping on Pluto's heels as he stomped out the bathroom without flushing the toilet or even washing his nasty hands. "Some shicken thighs and shicken wings. I got some shickcn nccks in there too."

Monique didn't mean to, but she peeked in the bathroom behind him and had to force herself not to choke—both from the smell he left lingering behind, and the two fat turds that floated around in the nasty water where there wasn't a single sheet of toilet tissue to be seen.

Nasty motherfucker, she thought. *Learn to wipe your fuckin' ass!*

But all shc said as she followed him in the kitchen was, "You know you like my fried shicken, Daddy-o! Can't nobody fry no shicken the way your Mo-Mo do. First thing I'ma do when we get down to Baltimore and buy us a phat crib is fry my Big Papa a whole pan of shicken!"

Pluto was tearing up the broom closet that she had just straightened up. He came out with a half-empty box of garbage bags, some rubber gloves, and a large jug of Clorox. Monique ignored the look in his eyes, and watched curiously as he threw everything in a plastic shopping bag and headed toward the front door.

"You leaving out again?" She followed behind him whining. "C'mon, Big Papa. You just got here. I got a whole pot of lima beans boiling on the stove too. Fatback all up in the pot just the way you like it. Come on and sit down and eat with me, Daddy."

She grabbed his thick arm and pulled, then shrank back in surprise as he whirled around and shot her a look of intense hatred.

"Dumb trick!" Pluto grabbed Monique by the back of her head, winding his fat fingers in her hair weave and snatching her back toward the kitchen by her sewed-in tracks.

"Wait!" she cried weakly, wobbling across the floor in her purple stilettos. "I fried you some shicken, baby! I got you some beans—"

"You got you a big raggedy fuckin' mouth is what you got! Don't know when to keep that shit closed neither!" He dragged her into the kitchen by the hair, slinging her painfully from the wall, then into the refrigerator, then slamming her into the table and knocking over salt and pepper shakers and two chairs.

"I'ma fry something in here, bitch. Fry your shit up real nice and crunchy for you."

Monique felt his hands grip her neck and squeeze until her breath caught in her chest and her eyes bulged outta her head.

"Yeah." He sweated above her. Monique yelped when he pushed the whole pot of beans off the electric burner and forced her face down toward the hot spirals that were glowing orange-red.

"Help!" Monique tried to scream, praying her nosey-ass super was listening through the pipes and would at least bang on the door to distract Pluto and save her ass. She tried to fight him, but Pluto used his body weight to pin her against the stove as he inched her face closer and closer toward the hot coils.

She was screaming and crying and trying to push herself away from the stove. Her thumb skidded across the burner and she shrieked as heat shot up her arm. Pluto had both thick hands on her now. He squeezed her neck with one, and used the other to push her head down so low that Monique felt scaring heat on her cheek. Her gold hoop earring heated up immediately, sending fire shooting through her earlobe. A thick lock of her silky Chinese weave hit the burner and sizzled like melting plastic, and pee ran down her legs as her eyebrows and eyelashes started to singe.

"Please . . . please . . . Pluto, baby. Please . . ."

Her face . . . Oh, her *face*! Her right ear was burning like shit and her cheek was being scorched, and Monique was powerless to get away as tears fell from her eyes and hit the hot coils, sending little puffs of steam back up toward her. She closed her eyes and gave up, unable to bear it as her face loomed closer and closer to the orange burner. And just when she was braced to feel her flesh sizzle and her skin stick to the glowing coils, that niggah let her up and flung her across the room. She crashed into the microwave cart, then yelped as she twisted her ankle, fell onto one knee, and then crumpled to the floor.

"Ain't gone be no fuckin' Baltimore, you stupid-ass bitch," Pluto growled as he picked up his plastic shopping bag and headed toward the door again.

"Not for me or for you."

.   .   .

My fuckin' face!

Monique snatched off her hot earring and jumped to her feet as soon as the door slammed. She kicked off her shoes and hobbled over to the freezer and took out a frozen can of grape juice. She held it to the right side of her face, then ran in the bathroom to check out the damage Pluto had done.

Aside from being really red and tender, her cheek didn't have any burn marks or blisters yet, but the ends of her weave had fried and so had some of the fine hair around the edges of her face. Her ear was straight burnt, and it hurt like hell as she splashed cold water all over her face, then caked a mixture of melted butter and Vaseline on her earlobe, and then spread it around on her cheek and eyebrow.

Monique didn't know what the fuck was going on that had set Pluto off bad enough for him to burn her, but she'd heard one thing loud and clear: no B-More. Whatever it was that not only had Pluto crying but had changed all their plans was too big for her to imagine. But she knew one thing. There was no way in hell she was just gonna sit up in that apartment and wait for him to come back and deep-fry the other half of her face. She was gonna get out there on the streets of Harlem and find her some fuckin' answers.

She changed into a pair of pants and a thick sweater, then grabbed her coat and her keys, and with Vaseline still caked up on half of her face, she jetted from the apartment and jumped in her whip.

Monique drove in the snow straight past the G-Spot and parked two blocks over. She'd gotten a pretty good look at the windows on her way past, and even though Pluto claimed they were having a private baller party, the Spot looked dark and deserted and there wasn't a single hustler or pimped-out ride to be seen sitting outside.

Monique got out of her car and trudged through the snow back toward the Spot, hugging the buildings and staying in the shadows. She turned left at the corner, then ran across the street and slipped down the alley behind the Spot where she saw G's Benz parked and waiting.

It was cold as shit outside, and steam was coming from the tailpipe as the car idled. She walked in the tire tracks, then ducked behind a small garbage Dumpster when she saw Pluto, Moonie, Cooter, and Ace come out the side door, carrying something big that was wrapped up in plastic.

"What the fuck!" Monique muttered under her breath as she watched them dump whatever it was in the back of the Benz, then fling a small plastic garbage bag in there along with it. Moonie slammed the trunk and all four of them went back inside the Spot, leaving the car running. Monique waited a few minutes then crept out of the shadows of the Dumpster, and keeping her feet in the tire tracks, inched her way over to the car. Whatever the fuck was in all that plastic had looked soft and heavy, and curiosity gnawed at her as she imagined what it could be.

She was halfway between the Dumpster and the car when the door popped open again. Monique scuttled back to the Dumpster saying fuck the tire tracks, and dove behind it just as the four gangstas appeared once again.

This time they were carrying something else. Something wrapped in a red sheet from one of the fuck rooms, and when Moonie yanked the trunk open and then slid the bundle halfway in, Monique gasped out loud at what she saw under the trunk lights.

A hand and foot were sticking out. The hand hung from an opening in the sheet and something glinted in the darkness that Monique had seen a million times before. Gold and onyx. A special-order twenty-thousand-dollar ring. G used to twirl that shit constantly, like a bad habit. Especially when he was mad. Monique noticed that the foot hanging out was wearing a fly leather shoe. Italian leather, probably. The kind of shoes that paid niggahs like G had imported from overseas.

Monique sat down on her ass in all that ice and snow. Her heart wanted to stop beating and she could barely believe what the fuck her eyes were telling her.

Her dreams were dead.

Pluto was right. Wasn't gonna be no fuckin' Baltimore for neither one of them. She was ass-fucked. Just out there. She'd already told her super and her landlord that they could go eat each other. She'd run up all kinds of bills in Pluto's name in stores all over Harlem that she hadn't planned to pay, and she'd double-crossed folks and burned bridges like a motherfucker too. Skipping out of Harlem hadn't been just a wish, it was a fuckin' requirement, and now somehow all of that shit had been canceled. Monique didn't know what the fuck had gone down, but if G was bodied then the future she had planned for herself was bodied too.

Monique hid, pressing herself deep into the shadows of the Dumpster as the Benz backed outta the alley. Moonie, Pluto, and Ace were in the whip and Cooter had gone back inside the Spot. She was dying to know who or what had been in that first package they put in the trunk. G was in that second package. She knew that shit for a fact 'cause she'd seen it with her own eyes. And she knew something else too. Whatever the fuck had gone down that ended up ripping all of her dreams apart, she was willing to bet her sexiest fuckin' thong that it had something to do with that raggedy bitch who was chained to a bed downstairs in the Dungeon. That bitch Juicy.

•   •   •

Monique sat in her car watching the front door and the alley of the G-Spot. She had moved to a better parking space after the Benz rolled out, and she kept her engine running, even though her lights and heat were off.

It was cold as shit outside and in the car, but it didn't bother her at all. In fact, her right ear was now cooling to a dull throb, and the icy air felt damn good on her burnt skin. Every now and then she peered into the overhead mirror and stared at the welp-like blisters that were beginning to rise on her cheek and shuddered inside, even though her face was now the last damn thing she was worried about.

Monique sat there running details through her mind, wondering who had merked G and why the fuck Cooter was still inside the Spot instead of rolling out with Pluto and them.

Monique waited, and about fifteen minutes passed before Cooter came back out. He walked out the front door of the G-Spot like everything was everything, and put his hands in his pockets and strolled calmly through the snow toward the bright lights up ahead on the avenue.

Monique just didn't understand that shit but before she could figure it out, the front door opened again and a girl ran outside.

"No this bitch ain't butt-ass naked!" Monique screamed out loud when she saw who it was. "No her stank ass ain't wrapped up in no motherfuckin' sheet!"

She watched with her mouth hanging open as Juicy ran barefoot through the ice and snow with a sheet around her waist, then staggered over to the curb and flagged down a bootleg taxi and disappeared into the night. Monique cut her lights on, then pulled out into traffic and headed in the same direction. She knew exactly where that skank bitch was probably going. Straight to that Puerto Rican bitch Rita. The same bitch who had threatened to get one of Monique's brothers locked up over her hot-in-the-ass little sister last summer. She followed the cab down the slippery streets and a few minutes later Monique sat boiling outside of Rita's house. She sucked on her burnt thumb and watched as Rita opened her front door and Juicy jumped outta the cab and ran her ass inside the apartment. *That bitch is gonna get hers,* Monique promised. She didn't need to know all the little details in order to know what time it was. G was gone and so was all of Pluto's front money, his muscle, and his pull. Every ounce of their bad fortune was tied to that bitch Juicy, and that burned Monique up worse than the hot stove.

If it's the last fuckin' thing I do in this world, Monique swore to herself again, *I'm gonna get her ass back.* And if Rita and her ho-ass fuckin' little sisters wasn't careful, they could end up getting some too.

＊　＊　＊

Shit was hot all over Harlem for weeks.

The po-po was outta control, and hustlers was getting knocked every day. As soon as word hit the streets that G had got took down, Harlem was on fire with chaos and turmoil. Moonie did the fuckin' bird and nobody knew where he had gone. Some young hustler named Flex called himself taking over G's project operation and got popped with a quickness.

Ace and Pluto both got bum-rushed by the police.

They caught Ace coming outta his grandmother's crib and when he pulled out his tool and started firing, they shot out every window in the joint, catching Grandma with a bullet through her forehead as she sat in her rocker.

They got Pluto about four o'clock one morning when they kicked the door down and maced him and Monique right in their bed. About twenty cops rushed in and beat the hell outta Pluto, cracking him down to the floor with their night-sticks and digging their boot heels all up in his soft stomach.

Then them motherfuckers stood around laughing as they made Monique lean up against a wall ass-naked as they admired her from behind. They took turns patting her down even though she was all skin, like she mighta had a gun stuck up in her pussy or under her firm coconut titties. One of the white cops jammed two fingers up in her pussy and inserted his thumb in her ass, but Monique took that shit with her mouth closed. All of the others got them some too, squeezing and rubbing, digging in her hole. One of the young heads pressed his dick against her ass and moaned and yummied against her neck. He pumped against her softness, breathing hard, then grabbed her breasts and squeezed them gently, fingering her nipples until he shuddered, wetting up his drawers. Before he left, he bent down and bit her softly on the meatiest part of her ass cheek and thanked her for her civic cooperation.

They could only keep Pluto and Ace down for thirty days, but that was long enough to do even more damage to Monique's situation. By the time her man was free, Monique had gotten put out on the streets and was sleeping on a love seat in Honey Dew's apartment.

Of course, Pluto had some bank stashed away, but when Monique finally got hold of his cash and tried to pay the landlord the back rent and the current rent all at once, he just laughed and threw her money back in her face and told her he already had the necessary paperwork required to put them and all of their shit out in the street, and that's exactly what the fuckin' po-po did that next morning.

"You wouldn't be trying this shit if my man was here!" Monique screamed as they tossed all of her shit on the sidewalk. She grabbed some plastic bags and started pushing her clothes inside them, and Honey Dew rushed over to help her.

"Well that motherfucker *ain't* here," the landlord said, "and I hope they keep him locked up forever and throw away the fuckin' key. That way, I'll never have to see neither one of y'all trifling asses again!"

Monique was happy when they released Pluto. They didn't have enough shit on him to keep him, and as soon as he got out he swung by Honey Dew's apartment and picked her up and took her to get her hair and nails done, then they hit the stores and shopped for all new shit.

"Fuck all that stuff," Pluto said when Monique told him Honey Dew had had to help her put the contents of their apartment in storage. She was glad she'd held on to his money, though. Too much had gone on for her to even think about crossing Pluto, especially since she knew he wasn't gonna be locked down forever.

"We'll get new shit, girl. G is gone, but we gone start this shit all over again."

That night they checked into a phat hotel in midtown Manhattan and fucked like rabbits, then ordered room service and filled each other in on the details that had caused their world to go dark.

"It was Jimmy," Pluto told her. "That niggah capped G, then did himself. Fucked my head up. That fool little niggah popped himself."

Monique lay there crying quietly inside. Not for Jimmy, and not for G's ass neither! She was crying for her damn self, and for what Juicy and Jimmy, that retarded-ass sister-and-brother team, had cost her.

"G didn't deserve that shit," Pluto went on, and Monique could hear the pain that was still in his voice. "He was my niggah, straight up. A real motherfucker who was out there handlin' a real fuckin' world. None of us saw that shit coming. All of us slept that night and it cost us our boss. And that's fucked up."

Monique sat up and rubbed Pluto's fat stomach. The funk coming off him told her he probably hadn't washed his ass the whole time he was on Rikers. But so what. She let her hand wander down between his legs and started to jack his gummy dick anyway.

"Yeah," Pluto repeated sadly, ignoring her fingers. "That shit was fucked up."

No, Monique thought. *What was fucked up was the fact that Juicy got away.* That bitch had dipped outta New York with that niggah Gino and all of G's money too. Ace said he had gone by G's crib to get a key outta the safe, only to discover the key was gone and so was all the bank in G's crib and in all his other stashes too.

"What's fucked up, baby," Monique went ahead and spoke her thoughts out loud, "is how that bitch Juicy got away. We got left hanging while she got to roll outta here with her life intact and all of G's money too. That trick shoulda got popped for real. Right along with her brother in the G-Spot."

Pluto nodded, and Monique could tell he was thinking real deep because his dick wouldn't even get hard.

"Don't worry. I got this. Me and Ace gonna find that bitch and get her back to New York. And when we do, she ain't never gonna leave again."

"Yeah," Monique said, excitement surging through her at the thought of getting her some revenge on the bitch she hated the most. "I know just how to make that happen too,

Papa. Remember, she's real tight with that trick named Rita who tried to get my brother Maurice locked up. We can use that bitch and her little sisters as bait. Get next to them, and we can get next to Juicy. I guarantee it."

Monique squealed with glee as Pluto nodded in agreement, then she dove under the covers and put his sticky dick in her mouth and started sucking him off like a pro. She was too excited to be bothered by the rancid smell coming off of his body or the shit stains she saw on his side of the sheets. Fuck all that. She had a plan coming together in her head right now, a foolproof way that was guaranteed to work.

And if it was the last thing Monique did, she was gonna get Juicy-Mo Stanfield.

She was gonna pay that bitch back.

AIN'T NUTHIN' SWEET
Plea$ure

Last Week . . .

I watched her ass dance in the air, jiggling from one side to the other as she straddled him doggy-style, hovering her naked-ness above Whisky's. Candlelight glowed on the moist droplets of sweat coating their bodies, making their skin glisten in its light. The scene was beautiful; dark chocolate arms gripping creamy caramel, legs candy-caning swirls of brownness in a sexual intertwine of readiness. With juicy lips, she switched up and traveled south, sporadically kissing and licking down the deep groove between his abs. Whisky threw back his head in anticipation, bucked his groin, and closed his eyes. Every move they made suggested they were going to get their shit on and poppin' tonight.

"Here, baby?" I heard her ask, zooming in on his thick pole before nibbling on its head.

"Ooh, damn! Yeah. Right there. Swallow it," he replied, gripping the back of her head as it bobbed up and down, lips greedily taking his entire dick into her mouth.

She sucked, slurped, gurgled as she deep-throated him. Ass see-sawing in tune with her head, she bounced to a beat that couldn't be heard, but it was definitely there. A rhythm that said she and Whisky had jigged together before; their moves were effortless, prac-ticed. Too knowing to be new.

Her cheeks nodded again, teasing me while I hid in the shadows. I gripped my tool as hard as I could when she slid her titties north, lining up her midsection with his, preparing to swallow Whisky's dick with her pussy.

But she wasn't the only one prepared. I raged, watching her reach between her legs, spread her lips with two dainty fingers, then cap the tip of Whisky's hardness with her moistness. Before she could slide down his pole gunshots clapped through the silence, shatter-ing the quiet, the custom headboard and their sense of safety as I slipped all the way into the room with my tool aimed.

"Suck it again, bitch! And you bet' not turn around!" I yelled to her now stiff and quivering back. "Now!" I cocked the burner, hear-ing the cling of a bullet move into the chamber.

She bawled as she backtracked. Her café au lait breasts dragged down Whisky's chest, then stomach, before she reached her final destination: a flaccid piece of meat that no longer saluted or wanted her mouth.

Whisky reached for the lamp on the nightstand, yelling, "What the hell?"

"Not a fuckin' move, Whisky!" I threatened, waving the burner from him to her. "You want me to splatter yo bitch? Huh?"

Grabbing her waist, he tried to push her off him.

"Uh-unh," I said, walking closer to them. "You enjoyed her doggy-style. Now it's my turn to get a taste."

With her back to me, she begged. Pleaded. Prayed for someone to save her when I stuck the barrel of my gun in her asshole, then rammed it as far up as I could.

"Ya better suck like you ain't never sucked before. Matter of fact, tea bag him!"

Whimpering, the chick pulled Whisky's soft penis in her hands. Lifting it skyward, she rested her head between his thighs, cocked open her mouth, and dunked his nuts in and out of it.

"Slurp, bitch. Ya betta moan like you love it."

"Come—" Whisky began.

"Oh, don't worry. I am. Y'all got yours off, I'm gonna get mine off too," I said, letting loose three shots in her ass, literally blowing her back out.

This Week . . .

A bunch of pretty mu'fuckas walked by vying for attention as I threw back a double shot of Courvoisier and chased it, upping the game two bills. 12 o'clock, the niggah I'd held down while he'd rocked a baker's dozen in the bing before springing on an appeal, sat opposite me. He nodded and called my play, slapping a couple hundred on top of the stack. Reading the other gamblers, my eyes stopped on Lil' Lee. I knew there was going to be trouble. He was a diesel, blue-black brutha who snuck up on people like nighttime. Down ten Gs, he gripped the edge of the other side of the table while his lower lip twitched—a sure sign that he was frustrated, ready to explode. There was an excess of pussy buzzing around and too much money on the green felt for him to get down. Weak-ass niggahs like him were always distracted by fat asses and the possibility of riding them. That's one of the reasons I'd gotten in on the game. No way was I going to walk away with less than I came in with. Especially in my own spot: Sweets Treats, an all-night bakery that served up confections in the front and offered every kind of sweet a person could imagine in the back. Drugs, liquid, down-low hoes, and gambling, with a little money-laundering added in for extra flavor.

"Hurry up, yo. We ain't got all day," Runner, my brother and right hand, who'd outrun the police more times than any of us could count, rushed me.

I swept his tall ass with an icy glare, saw he was slipping. He had his dough in front of him where everybody could see. "Shut the hell up. Five men gotta roll before you even touch the dice."

"Yo! Who the fuck you talkin' to?"

I snatched the money out of his hand. "Why not just buy you some ass, that's why you holdin' your paper up, right?" I winked. "Hoping one of these sack chasers bow down to it?" I asked, knowing that taking his stack had gotten his undivided attention. Kicking him under the table, I tapped my foot twice. Our signal that he should pay attention to the man in the two o'clock position—the one who stood two places over from 12 o'clock—Lil' Lee. He was too jumpy, eyeing the money on the table like a child tempted by candy.

Runner gave me a slight nod of approval. I tossed his stack to Lil' Lee and aimed my burner at him under the table in one swoop. If he wanted to play underhanded, we could both get grimy. "My fault. Pass that to 12."

"*Word?*" 12 o'clock asked, taking the money from Lil' Lee and laughing in his grill. He shook his head, pocketed Runner's dough. "American's Express, baby," he said, coding the nickname he'd given his gun because in our part of America the streets demanded you have at least one. "Nevva leave the crib wit'out it. Call it!" He sat back and crossed the lumberjack arms he'd choked out plenty of bruthas with.

Shaking the clickers, I threw in my last shot, and came up on the come-up.

Lil' Lee smacked the table. "Aw, hell nah! Them dice's loaded."

"What the fuck you tryin' to say, niggah?" I barked. I wasn't in the mood for his shit. Not tonight. Just hours ago, I'd been less than five seconds away from catching a body after I'd caught my *main* piece with someone else. If it weren't for a busy intersection and swarms of witnesses, my burner's chamber would've been smoking and the coroner's dinner would've been interrupted. Again. "If it's any lead in these dice, you put it in'em. They yours, right, bitch-ass?"

"You the only bitch at the table, Sweets," he shot back, looking around. "Last time I checked."

The table quieted, and the other players turned to stone. Everybody knew there were two things I didn't allow anyone to play with. My money. And calling me outta my name. "Bitch," in particular, just got under my skin.

12 o'clock leaned forward with a Desert Eagle in his hand, turned it on Lil' Lee. Runner grinned and opened his jacket, revealed he had enough steel on him to start a mill. The other players cleared. Even Lil' Lee's phony cronies, who only rolled when his paper was thick, bounced.

Lil' Lee held up his hands. "Come on now, Sweets. You don't really want this. Do you?"

I swept my arm across the table, raked the money into my bag. "Damn right, I do." I strutted over to him, kissed him on the cheek and slapped his ass. "What, baby? You were going to sneak-thief us, or just take the money?"

Lil' Lee's stutter ran from his mouth to the south. He quaked in his boots. "N-nah. Y-you know me betta than that. I ain't no cr-crab-ass niggah. What I look like h-holdin' up a wo-woman, Sweets?"

"Thought I was a bitch." I dug my long, French-manicured nails into his firmness, gripped his ass. "Ain't nuthin' wrong with sticking a *bitch* for her paper, right?"

Lil' Lee threw me a sideways glance; pleading masked the scowl I knew was hidden underneath. He'd kill me quicker than I could make two cents if he could. Fuck me even faster. And I was hella paid, churning out paper faster than the U.S. Mint.

"Say ya sorry," I whispered, moving my grip from his ass to his jaw. "Make nice, niggah."

Lil' Lee hung his head. His rep used to precede him around the way. He'd been a tough sonuvabitch who'd taken no slack, stacked his chips as high as his bitches. Dime-store pimp, player, triple-momma baby maker, he'd made himself a millionaire before his twenty-first birthday. But now he'd have to ice my cake—if he wanted to live past the stroke of midnight.

With a nod of my head, 12 o'clock laced him up—dragged him into the back office—patted him down, shook him for all his weapons.

"Sit'im down, 12," I instructed.

He sat Lil' Lee down on one of my hot-pink chaises, then took his position, blocking the office door. He cocked his burner, made sure one was in the chamber.

Lil' Lee nervously looked from 12 to me. Confusion furrowed his brow before he bitched up. "Can't we talk about this, Sweets? Y'know I ain't mean no disrespect, Ma. All kinda shit is said when niggah's gamblin'. It was game."

"Still is, baby," flowed out of my mouth as I licked my lips. I was going to have some fun with Lil' Lee. As dirty as I knew he'd wanted to do me at the craps table, I couldn't help but notice that he was a pretty mu'fucka. His blue-blackness, beating tunes like an African drum, made my pussy throb. With just one look I knew his ancestors hadn't been as violated as mine, and that shit turned me on. He was a Mandingo brutha if I'd ever saw one.

Leaning against my desk, I spread my legs, let my skirt ride up my thighs, expose just enough of my amber flesh to tempt him. Lil' Lee fidgeted. Gave me a look that said if

12 o'clock wasn't in the room he'd try to push up. But 12 was there, and no one moved inside of my groove unless I said so. Except one man. Whisky.

"Come get you a taste of Sweets," I beckoned, pointed to my moist spot, then slid out of slick fabric, kicking my thong his way. Looking at 12, I smiled. He was going to get off just as much as I was. Spread-eagling my thighs, I propped my feet up on either side of me, gripped my knees so close they kissed my shoulders and made my lower body resemble an M.

Lil' Lee looked from my exposed poonany to 12, then back again. 12 nodded his okay.

"Serious?" He needed confirmation. Most of them did, having never been in a situation like the one I'd put them in.

"As a murder charge," purred from my mouth.

Lil' Lee stood, gripping his dick through his jeans. Licking his lips, he swaggered my way like he had no problem performing in front of another man. Opening his pants, he released his hardness, and I saw why the brutha was so confident. Baby was so blessed he made my lower lips smile.

Positioning his body so his flesh touched mine, his dick bounced against my navel. The thickness made me shudder, and its warmth caused my clit to blush. I wanted to feel him inside me. But I couldn't. He was here to pay, not play.

Face-to-face, his breathing was sporadic, lustful, and intoxicating. Inhaling me like perfume, there wasn't a doubt that he wanted me as badly as I craved him.

I looked at him, nodding. "Want some?"

Lil' Lee bit down on his lower lip with the answer in his eyes.

My toned legs lifted me until his face met my moist spot. Spreading its thickness open for him, he flicked his tongue against my clit, then he took it into his mouth and suckled it like a newborn. Heat pooled between my legs, reminding me of the game. This was my show, not his.

Raising myself to my full height, I spread my legs as wide as I could, then lowered myself back onto my elbows, and pointed at my snatch.

Lil' Lee paused.

"Ass," I demanded. "Lick it."

Silence for a moment.

"*What?!*" His response was laced with shock. "Ya know a brutha don't get down—"

Clearing my throat, I gave my cue.

A round clicked as 12 cocked his burner again, spitting the previous bullet housed in the chamber to the floor. A reminder—a warning—for Lil' Lee.

Less than a second passed before Lee's large hands were all over me, spreading me like melted chocolate. Nervously he looked at 12, then me. Flicking my tongue at him, I winked.

"Lick your way to forgiveness."

Lil' Lee was a liar. He was a pro. Gripping, he cupped my ass and lifted it in the air until it met his mouth. With a long tongue, he parted my cheeks, then dug in like it was a holiday feast, burying his face between the firm softness. He ate the bottom like most men eat pussy. Savoring it, he sucked, dipped in and out of it, lingered on the spot that made me jump and buck, all while playing with my clit. He was a nasty nucka, and I was two heartbeats away from letting him push in my bush.

Panting, I pushed him off me. He had to go. I couldn't be in charge of *anything* if I was succumbing to his wicked tongue.

Before Lil' Lee could tuck his bobbing hardness into his pants, 12 snatched him up and deposited him on the other side of the door. Turning the lock, he signaled Runner on the walkie-talkie to put his ass out. Brutally.

I sat up, heat still throbbing. "Enjoy the show?"

"Not as much as you did. You was gonna break him off. I could tell," he said, walking toward me.

"Now why would I do something like that?"

He stuck his long, thick finger deep inside me, swirled it around, then took it out and licked it. "I can't tell . . ." he replied, dropping his pants and boxers, revealing the biggest dick I'd ever laid eyes on, ". . . not when I got all this here."

My heart dropped to my knees at the sight of him. As many times as I'd seen him naked, I still couldn't get used to his size.

"Fill it, 12. Give this fat, juicy poonany sumthin' to hold on to," I whispered in his ear, wrapping my legs around him as he carried me from the desk to a chaise.

"Homeboy got it ready and wet for me, Sweets?" he asked,

positioning my ass on the cushion and putting my legs on his shoulders.

Nodding, I closed my eyes and gritted my teeth as he pushed his weight on the back of my thighs, making my knees touch my shoulders.

"Watch," he demanded.

"No," I replied breathlessly. 12 knew I wanted to feel the experience, not see it. Fuckin' one of my boys wasn't right, but it was necessary—needed—after I'd had my ass blessed.

The body heat between my legs cooled when 12 removed his hands from my legs and his midsection from above mine.

"Gimme what I want, you'll get what'chu want," he said, crossing his arms.

I shook my head in disbelief. 12 was strong-arming me, and he knew it. We'd gone through this before, but he'd never pulled away. This time he was serious. And I was in desperate need of feeling his hardness penetrate my softness. So although my mind said no, my body told it to shut the fuck up.

"A'ight," I gave in, knowing I'd regret it later.

Again his weight pressed against my flesh as he grabbed my ankles, spreading them as far apart as he could. Searching my eyes, he told me to put him inside my wetness—another thing he knew I didn't do.

Cupping my hand around him, I swallowed my rules as I tried to wrap my fingers around his girth. Excitement veined throughout me when it proved impossible. His dick was just too big. But huge or not, I gently grabbed it, put the head onto my wetness, and tried to calm my pulsing coochie. Up and down. I rubbed his pole between my wet slit, teasing him and tantalizing myself. I needed my form of foreplay to relax—open up—so he could fit that chocolate monster inside me without damn near splitting me in two like the last time.

"I got it," he said, releasing my right ankle from his grip, placed it on his left shoulder.

My breathing labored when I realized that he was putting me in the twist. Right ankle opposite shoulder. Left leg splayed toward the floor, as far as his arm extended. 12 had rotated my landing strip, and was going to work me in a sideways V. I damn near fainted at the thought.

In and out, he dipped the head of his thickness into me. My wetness voiced its yearning as it snapped, crackled, and popped with each tease. My pussy was talking to him, begging him for a taste as he continued sliding his head up and down my split.

"Fuck me . . . I want every inch."

Biting down on his lip, he lightly pinched my clit, then softly kneaded it with his thumb and index finger. Euphoria moved through me, pushed me to the edge. But I refused to jump. No way was I going to cum without his dick riding me over the rainbow.

"Ya sure you want to do this, Sweets?" He slid a couple of inches in me. "Ya know the other reason I go by 12, right?" he asked, teasing and warning me. Baby had damn near a foot-long, but I had my own sweet weapon.

"Yeah," I panted. "Same reason my name's Sweets."

Holding my lower lips open, 12 worked his way halfway in. Creaming myself, I couldn't contain my excitement. That niggah had a way of hurting me so good. I wiggled, tensed, and met his thrust when he fit his long thickness inside me. Clawing at the chaise, his chest, anything I could get my hands on, I gripped. Had to bear down on something to keep myself from screaming as I felt my poom-poom stretch until it burned. His actions said he knew he was doing me in, and he was going to make me suffer. Pounding, he man-handled my pussy—beat it up—made me take all of him. And I came. Came. Then came some more, wetting my walls for him to slide and glide in my hotness before pulling out and erupting on my stomach.

Two minutes later, we were both panting. He was on the floor, I was still spread out on the chaise with gapped legs.

"Why you keep givin' me the pussy, Sweets?"

I turned to him, shook my head. He was my boy, but he was fuckin' up my flow. I wanted to bask in the moment, and he wanted to ask questions. Quiz me on a subject we'd agreed never to discuss.

"I'm saying, yo. You got Whisky. So why you keep breakin' me off?"

It was my turn to bite my lip. 12 knew just like I did that Whisky wasn't up for discussion. There was just some shit I didn't talk about. My man was one of them.

"Come on, Sweets. It's me," he coaxed. "We go way back— you know you can trust a niggah. You trust me to fuck you and not tell . . ."

He had me.

"A'ight, you got me on that one." I sat up, straightened myself out. "But you gotta give me your word—"

"Sweets, ya know my word is my bond. If it wasn't, you'd a did a bid up north, not me. I ain't know the first thang about launderin' no damn money."

I looked at 12 and bitched up. Tears welled in my eyes as I thought about him doing a dozen for me. Yeah, I could trust him.

"I gots love for Whisky. I do," I assured 12 and myself at the same time. "He's always buttered my bread, made sure I *felt* like I came first. But he does his own thang. He comes first in his world."

"So, you fuckin' me is your way of gettin' back at him?"

I sat silent because I really didn't know how to respond. On one hand it was true; banging 12 was just a needed fix after I punished those who crossed me. It was hard to get licked without gettin' sticked. On the other side of it was loyalty. Whisky had put me down and taught me how to grind the game. And once upon a time, he'd fucked and sucked me 'til I couldn't see straight. I stayed true to him until I found out that he'd been giving other hoes dick lashes *and* money— *my* paper I'd refused to share. I'd had to knock a couple of persistent ones off, but I'd calmed down. Promised not to body another bitch over my man. Until I caught him in the act.

"I need to know if you love that niggah."

"Why, what up?" I asked, noticing the seriousness in 12's eyes.

He cleared his throat, steepled his massive hands. "Ya know Quita, right? My wifey?"

I nodded even though it was a lie. I'd had no idea 12 had a girl, let alone a wifey.

"Well, she died—caught one up the ass. I found out Whisky dropped her."

I flinched. 12 took it as a different kind of shock.

"Yeah, they was fuckin' around. Her sister told me after the fact, *and* she'd dropped her off at one of Whisky's cribs he's got tucked away somewhere."

Jumping up, I paced. Cum juice running all down my legs. "*Word?* Whisky was fuckin' your girl? My Whisky?"

12 cracked his knuckles. "Nah, not just my girl—my baby's mama." He got up and walked over to me, grabbed me by the shoulders. "Look, Sweets. A niggah got a lotta love for ya, but I gots to handle it. You know this. So what's up?"

Damn. He was asking me what I thought about him putting Whisky down for a dirt nap. All I could do was shake my head. Until he hit me with the rest.

"Either he clapped her, or had some grimy mu'fucka do it for him. Keila—Quita's sister—told me that Whisky was going to take Quita away, move her up outta the hood so they could play house. She said Quita wasn't wit it, had changed her mind. You know Whisky doesn't entertain rejection."

A new heat moved through me. Fire of violence and jealousy. I couldn't believe that Whisky planned on bouncing on me for the next bitch. Not after all I'd done for him, the years I gave him. "Do what you gotta do," I gave my permission, knowing that the trigger finger that blasted Quita's back out was attached to my hand. But I rationalized it. Me and 12 had both been crossed. I'd done my part without his knowing. He'd finish it off. There were just certain things I didn't talk about. I'd already gave him a pass by discussing Whisky. I didn't see a need to give him two by telling on myself. Hell, I was a hustla, not a fool. No way I was going to be on the receiving end of my boy's Desert Eagle.

This Weekend . . .

Whisky rested his head on my lap, giving me a look I'd never seen from him before. Looking deeply into his cognac eyes, I massaged his temples, kissed him deeply to make him feel like the man he'd no longer be after 12 dirt-napped him.

"What's on ya mind, Daddy?"

"Thinkin'," he said, and sat up. "You'd never cross me, Sweets." It wasn't a question, it was a statement. An order.

Blushing like the nineteen-year-old girl he'd once turned out, I agreed with him. He'd always needed loyalty confirmed for him, so I wasn't sweatin' it. "Got that right. And you'd never do me in, would you?"

"How you holdin' down for money," he asked, ignoring my question. "You straight?"

I stood, crossed my arms over the ice-blue silk robe covering my titties. "You know I am. I gets mine, Whisky. If nuthin' else I stack chips. I sell cakes in the front of the bakery and make dough in the back." I paused. "You ain't answer what I asked you. You'd never do me in?"

Whisky laughed. "Don't come at a playa like that. I put you on—you'd know if I took you off. Ain't nuthin' sweet about mines. Except you." He kissed me. "What'chu think about letting Runner or somebody hold down Sweets Treats for you, and you and me bounce. I found a house you'll like."

It was my turn to giggle. Crack the hell up in his grill. Whisky had pegged me for a fool's fool. He must've, thinking I'd relocate to the house he'd planned to tuck his side-bitch in. Had to be outta his rabbit-ass mind if he thought I'd let someone hold the reigns and run the show where *I* made dough, legally and illegally. "Give me a minute to think about it. It ain't easy parting with ya cake," I said, sure that 12 would cradle-to-the-grave him before I could say boo, yet I already missed him because he was my cake. And I hated to lose money.

•   •   •

My body ached from stress and the dick whipping 12 had put on me a couple of days ago. I sat at the bar going over my *real* books as music pumped through the speakers, and patrons buzzed around the back of the bakery. I was in the midst of it all, yet I really wasn't there. I hadn't been anywhere mentally since I'd found out Whisky had planned on trading me in for a new model.

Sucking my teeth, I added up how much I'd lose because of Whisky. Ten to twenty grand a month, depending on income. "Fuckin' niggah," I hissed, realizing how much losing him was gonna hurt me. He'd been the one who dished out the payouts to the po-po.

"Ya a'ight, sis?" Runner asked, his breath smelling like a garbage bag full of weed.

"Haze or Chronic?"

With a big Kool-Aid grin, he laughed. "Shit, maybe a lil' of both. Want me to roll you a blunt to go with that tall-ass glass of yak? What, you guzzlin' gallons now?"

"Nah. Just a little stressed. What'chu gettin' into?" I asked, hoping he was on his way out. I didn't want him playing me too close until 12 had knocked off Whisky.

"A chicken-head if she calls me on time. A hood-rat if the chicken don't call first. Unless you need me."

Laughing at the truth, I handed Runner the keys to my whip and a wad of cash. "Do yo thang."

"Word? Money *and* the ride? Must be a niggah's birthday."

I gulped my yak. "It's cool. 12 got me, he'll make sure I—"

"Get to the crib safe," 12 cut in from out of nowhere.

"Cool," Runner said, then answered his celly. "I'll check y'all later." He pointed to his phone. "Chicky, chicky," he mouthed, disappearing in the crowd.

"Sweets, I hate to do this to you. But there's a problem." 12 put his hand on my shoulder.

My legs were splayed in an M again, mounted on my desk as Poochie, a big bouncer of a brutha, stared at my naked and still swollen poom-poom. The phatness of it made his eyes dance in his head. Turning to 12, he got the same confirmation as Lil' Lee did: It was cool to move forward.

"How you gonna push your shit up in my place? Ya knows the rules, Poochie. I don't give a fuck how big your ass is.

Three hundred and fifty pounds of muscle or not, can't nobody flip weed in my spot. Now lick your way to forgiveness," I said, then closed my eyes when I heard 12 cock his burner.

Poochie was all up on me in five seconds flat. Lids still closed, I shuddered at the thought of his tongue all in my groove when he spread my booty cheeks apart and fingered the rim of my ass. Heat consumed me again, and I moaned—a sign of weakness as far as I was concerned. I looked at 12 to see if he heard. He just nodded, and I closed my eyes again, cocking my legs open an inch wider as I felt Poochie near my domain.

He licked one thigh, then the other. "You want this, huh?" his deep voice asked, trailing his tongue toward my bottom.

"Just make nice, niggah," I shuddered, enjoying the longness of his lasher.

Poochie gripped my thighs hard, and my eyes shot open. Bending over me, he had his dick in his hand. "I'm gonna give it to ya, a'ight."

I tried to sit up, but he pushed me back so hard I thought I'd cave the desk in. He pinned me with the weight of one of his arms, but it felt like I was being held down by five niggahs. He was that strong. I looked for 12, but was greeted by the click of the door closing behind him. That niggah had left me. Straight up bounced while a sistah was naked and vulnerable.

I cried out when Poochie parted my pussy with calloused hands, but no one answered. The bakery had grown completely quiet of the voices normally blending in with the tunes. But now all I heard was the music. Loud. Blaring. Drowning out my calls for help.

"Can't nobody help you, Sweets," Poochie said, inserting the tip of his dick inside my tunnel. "No . . ." he plunged the rest of it in me ". . . fuckin' body!"

Lying there helpless, I squirmed as he fucked me hard and fast, beating my already beaten and sore pussy, and prayed he was a two-minute niggah. And he was, I realized when he pulled out suddenly, then shot his cum into a Big Gulp cup I didn't know he had.

The door opened, spiraling freedom through me. I knew I was saved.

"Finished?" 12 asked.

"What the fuck do you mean, 'finished'?" I yelled. "Do you know what this niggah—"

"Yeah," Poochie answered him, cutting me off. "Was some sweet pussy too. Just like you said."

I'd been set up. "What?!"

12 grinned at me, then turned and looked behind him. "Forty, you next." He turned back to me. "Funny how much a niggah can tell when a pistol's in his mouth. Whisky dropped dime on you." He closed the door after Forty walked in with his dick out.

Poochie held out his hand, and Forty slapped it. An official sign of tag-teaming. Pushing my ankles over my head until my knees pounded my shoulders, he almost cut off my oxygen when he climbed his big ass over me and held me in position from the other side. "I got this, dawg. But you gone have to hold her down for Ray-Ray and them."

Tears threatened to fall, but I refused to cry. Running a train on me or not, I wasn't gonna give them dirty niggahs too much of my energy. So I sat there—like I had a choice—and took that shit like a pro. Five of them switched up, battle-ramming my pussy like they'd never had ass before. All of them spilled their cum in the cup.

A loaded gun to my head was how the gang bang ended.

"Had enough?" 12 asked with a big, doofy-ass grin on his face. "Sit up."

I looked into the nozzle of the same Desert Eagle that'd had my back for years. "Why, 12?"

"Told ya, Sweets. Ya man sang like a bird."

"You gonna believe that niggah over me? After he was fuckin' your wifey?"

12 laughed. "Nah. I'm gonna believe the tape that the hidden cameras produced. The same cameras that had night vision."

I'd fallen for many things, but never the okeydoke. He was tryin' to pull my card—make me tell on myself. I shook my head. "Wasn't me, 12. We go way back, you can trust me."

12 held the cup of cum out to me. "You always tryin' to play a niggah. I know what I saw, Sweets. And it was you. Point blank."

Tears fell now. "No it wasn't."

He cocked his burner. "You got two options. Drink this cup of cum or join ya boy Whisky."

I pushed the cup away, squeezed my eyelids closed.

I'd die tonight. Because the last time I checked, when it came down to the taste of cum, ain't nuthin' sweet about it.

GRIMIER
Euftis Emory

Damn! All the women I had on constant rotation had already made other plans. Seven numbers deep on my "to fuck" list and I was horny as hell without a pool for Monster to swim in. I was left with one other option: my alternate call list. Women who were still being evaluated until I could determine whether to push them out the door or bang them on the floor.

It was Friday night, and I damn sure wasn't going to be stuck at home playing with myself. Real playaz don't get down like that. Don't have to when there's a side chick waiting to be slid to the front. For me, that was Rasheeda. When all else failed, whenever I needed a hit at the last minute, I could always depend on her.

Rasheeda had been promoted to the top of the alternate list, but hadn't graduated yet because she'd gotten on my last fuckin' nerve. Her ghetto ass had gotten a PR job, and she'd tried to put the B in bourgeoisie because her paycheck was legit and mine was legitimately counterfeit, until I'd flipped that ass over and leveled the field and made her take every inch of my swerve. But the real reason I kept her around was because she gave good head.

Hitting her up on the home number, I hung up after three rings. She'll see my name on her caller ID and get back to me later, I thought, powering up my computer and logging onto www.aroundthenati.com. There had to be something going on in the city. If I couldn't get some ass from one of my girls, I had to find something to distract my mind from sex.

Before I ran up on something, my cell rang. Rasheeda's name flashed on the screen and her phat ass flickered in my mind. "What up?" I answered.

"You! I just got in from work and saw that you called. What's goin' on wit you?"

"Nothing much. Just wondering if you were interested in a brotha this evening."

"You know I am!" she replied, excited. "I would love to tickle you again!"

I frowned. That was another reason I hadn't moved her ass into rotation. She played too damn much. Instead of just giving me the pussy, she was always trying to tickle me.

Acted like that shit was foreplay. Don't get me wrong, a little sex play here and there is nice. But tickling me off and on until I rolled around on the floor screaming like a bitch was downright irritating.

"I got something you can tickle . . . with your tongue."

"But you're so cute! I love to see you laugh," she said as I sighed heavily.

"I know another way you can make me smile . . ."

She giggled softly. "I bet you do. Tell me what you have in mind."

"I was thinking . . . you . . . in something form-fitting. A couple of drinks and your fireplace."

"Ummmmm, I can do that," she purred.

"And no tickling! Just you and me, one-on-one, rolling around on the floor."

"I can't promise that. But you're going to get the pussy, baby. Don't worry."

I was in my ride in an instant.

Turning onto Gilbert Avenue, I skirted scenic Eden Park as I headed toward Hyatt Park, where Rasheeda lived. I clicked on my CD player and jumping to track four I grooved to Reem Raw's cut "A Day in the Life." Not only was it a gully driving song, the lyrics were appropriate for me.

Bad bitch in the bed from the previous night!
All I remember was the head, she was treating me right.
  Right!
I'm a beast in the sheets, feelin' me heavy,
I give it hard to a bitch whenever she ready!

"Hell yea!" I banged my fist on the wheel, and bumped to the rest of the track as I passed the Greenwich, a Rasta bar and poetry club. Rolling up on one of Cinci's better ho strolls, a woman standing in front of Rent-A-Center snatched my attention. Big titties stuffed in a T-shirt and a phat ass tucked in teeny jean-shorts made me slam on my breaks. I swerved my car, then parked in front of her.

Scanning her, my HUD (heads-up display) opened up the database of information that I'd learned from Tariq Nasheed's book *The Art of Mackin'*. My onboard systems then queried the database.

[Query : Female categorization?]
{Hood Rat x Round Way Girl Hybrid}
[Query : Approach style?]
{Thug Methodology}

Tailoring my demeanor and speech pattern appropriately for the type of woman she was, I engaged her. "What up?" I asked, staring hungrily at her body, then her smooth, brown face framed in Egyptian braids.

Soft eyes gleamed as she quickly scanned me and my car. A big smile spread across her face as she pushed herself from the wall.

"What's . . . up! Come here!" I demanded.

She looked back at me nervously and hesitantly walked over to the passenger side of the car. Leaning forward, she stood back a little, checking me out as if I was the po-po or a killer who'd snatch her.

"What up?" I asked again, trying to determine if she was just out looking for trouble or if she was 'bout it.

"Nothin'," she finally answered, smiling.

"Wanna get into somethin'?" I asked.

She shrugged her shoulders.

"Get in."

She hopped into the car, and I did a U-turn and headed back toward downtown. I was determined to take her—and that ass—home.

"I'm E."

"I'm Kianna. Where we goin'?" she asked, eyeing me suspiciously.

"To my place. Unless you want to go somewhere—"

"You *better* take me somewhere," she stated seriously, cutting me off.

I laughed. "Oh, so it's like that!"

"Yea, it's like that!" She gave me a "what the fuck do you think" expression. "So now what?" she asked, frontin like she didn't know from the door.

"Let me see what you're working with." I reached over, lifted up her T-shirt, and squeezed her titties. They had to be at least a D cup.

I unzipped my pants and stuck her hand between my legs. She rubbed Monster hungrily and then unleashed him. "Damn. How far we goin' again?" she asked in a rushed whisper like she couldn't wait to get there.

"The West End."

"They got some stank crack hoes down there." She switched up quick, looking like she had a piece of rotten fruit in her mouth. "Do you fuck wit any of them?" she asked, again looking at me suspiciously.

"I don't fuck around in that hood."

"Good. 'Cause they are some ugly, stank hoes. We look much better up here," she remarked, lifting her chin haughtily.

Inwardly, I laughed. A universal concept was at work. Everyone needs someone else to look down upon. Whites look down on Blacks. Japanese look down on Koreans. Straights look down on gays. Saved folks look down on sinners. And the hoes on Gilbert Avenue looked down on the hoes on the West End. "Can't we all just get along?" I thought sarcastically.

"Ya ain't from 'round hure," I said, imitating my Memphis relatives. "I know a southern, cornbread-fed sista when I see one. Where you from?"

"A-Town."

"Hotlanta. I knew it! They don't make 'em like you around here."

"Thanks. You're okay, E. You know that?"

"Why do you say that?"

"You're not trying to lecture me."

"Lecture you about what? Selling your ass? Baby, I can't talk about what I'm tryin' to be about."

"Well most times when I do this the guy wanna start lecturing me. They tell me I'm too pretty to be hoeing. But that don't stop them from taking me somewhere so I can suck their dick or finding something to bend me over so they can bang. One old guy even asked me to go to church with him . . . *after* he fucked me."

"Wanted you to go to church with him? After the nut, huh?" I said, laughing.

"Yes! Can you believe it?"

"Now *that's* some funny shit. I despise hypocrites. Like I said, I definitely wanna hit it. So I'm not about to trip on ya, baby."

I escorted Kianna to my home office and opened the door.

"What do you want me to do?" she asked, standing in the middle of the room.

"I want to get some pictures of you. Then you can suck my dick," I told her as I picked up my digital camera from my desk. Walking over to her, I handed her a twenty-dollar bill. She took it without protest, so I sat on my couch and began shooting pictures of her. Slowly, she started stripping, pausing between garments to give me plenty of photo opportunities. Turning her ass toward me, she slid her hands into her shorts and peeled them off enticingly.

"Damn!" I moaned at her wonderful roundness. She smiled, stepped out of her shorts, and did a little booty clap. Leaning back against the couch, I unzipped my pants and unleashed the beast.

Watching me, Kianna got on all fours and crawled along the floor until she was between my legs. She inhaled Monster, taking long, slow, sloppy drags along the length of my shaft, making him swell to his full length and width. It was heavenly. I allowed her to suck it for about five minutes, all the while staring at her huge ass as her head bounced up and down on me.

"You know what," I began. "I need to hit that."

Loudly slurping her drool off my dick, she pulled Monster out of her mouth, then looked at me mischievously. "You wanna hit this?"

"Yea, I think I wanna hit it. You gonna charge me more?"

"No," she answered, spinning on her knees and crawling to the middle of the floor. On all fours, she laid her head on the carpet and reached back, spreading her ample ass with both hands. Her perfectly round ass and open wet slit beckoned me to tap her. "You can have it. You don't have to give me more money. You're an ass man. So you probably want it like this."

"Oh, got-damn," I sighed. "Hold up, baby. Keep it right there. Let . . . me . . . go get a condom . . ."

•   •   •

After doing the nasty, I took my new friend back to where I found her on Gilbert Avenue. "My car is parked over at Kroger. Would you drop me off there?" Kianna asked.

"No problem," I said as I drove up Gilbert the additional block and dropped her off at her car in the Kroger parking lot.

Kianna got out of my car and then hesitated, leaning down and sticking her head back into the vehicle. "Save this number in your phone . . . 241–0813."

Pulling out the cell, I dutifully saved the number she recited. "What's up?" I asked.

"That's my mama's number. Call me sometime," she said as I cocked my head and raised my left eyebrow. "Not to fuck . . . I mean . . . we can fuck . . . but on a . . . personal . . . tip . . . not . . . professional. Call me if you wanna kick it. Or if you just want to chill. I can cook dinner and we could watch movies. I get bored and lonely sometimes sitting at the house watching Mama all day."

"Oh . . . so . . . now . . . it's like that!" I remarked sarcastically, grinning from ear to ear.

"Yea . . . now . . . it's like that!" Kianna replied, imitating me, smiling even broader.

•   •   •

I got to Rasheeda's apartment complex a little after midnight. After fishing for my cell phone under my car seat I checked my call log to ensure that she hadn't called. She hadn't. "Good," I said aloud. I didn't have to think of an excuse as to why I didn't return her call.

Some of the chicks on rotation had finally hit me back, so I called my voice mail to listen to my messages. As soon as I got past the automated voice mail message my phone beeped once loudly . . . very loudly . . . in my ear. "Fuck!" I exclaimed as I quickly moved the phone away from my ear. Two seconds later, the phone beeped loudly again and then promptly went dead. "Goddamn Sprint!" I cursed. Only Sprint would make a phone that gave you a low-battery warning right before the battery went dead.

"'Bout time you got here," Rasheeda said in a sleepy voice as the loud buzzer buzzed.

She opened the door with a thin blanket wrapped around her and stared at me with a blank expression on her face. Her bone-straight hair was wound in a tight wrap, and her beautiful, juicy lips were poked out, making me want to rub my dick on them. Scanning her body, I tried to see what kinda sexy panties she had on but the damn cover was cock-blocking. My eyes traveled south to her legs. I smiled. She had oiled up all that good dark chocolate for me.

Turning her back to me, Rasheeda walked into the apart-ment and disappeared around the corner. "Lock the door, Euftis." Her words wafted around the corner.

Stepping into the dimly lit apartment, I took off my shoes and held tight to the gym bag I'd brought along. Walking into the living room, a twinge of guilt assaulted me. She'd illumi-nated the room with scented candles and a romantic, crack-ling fireplace. A bottle of Pinot Grigio was on the table, and Rasheeda had uncovered her package. Her goodies peeked through a tight black lace teddy.

I felt so damned guilty. Rasheeda had gone out of her way to get ready for me, and I'd just finished fucking a ho. Even worse, she was gonna suck my dick after it'd been all up in Kianna. I'd done some dirty shit in my life, but this was grimier by far.

Rasheeda sat on the couch, then rolled onto her stomach, showing me that thick, oiled, dark chocolate ass. Tossing the bag, I unbuttoned my Rocawear jean shorts and let them fall to the floor, then pulled off my matching shirt. She smiled, flipped onto her back, and spun around with her feet facing me. Her little maneuver caused the bottom of her teddy to unsnap between her legs, revealing her thick bush. "Oops," she exclaimed, spreading her legs, causing her lower lips to open.

Falling down on top of her, I squeezed her tight in a bear hug. Her body was hot. She burned with that special inner heat that women are blessed with every month. I held her tighter, relishing her body's warmth. "You're ovulating," I said, filing the date away in my mind so that I could add it to my Horny Girl Calendar. I tried to keep track of my hos' cycles to know when their hormones inspired them to fuck.

She reared back against the couch, staring at me wide-eyed. "How do you know this stuff?" she asked me in awe, confirming what I already knew.

"You learn a thing or two about people if you spend enough time around them," I said, then fell to my knees before her. Pulling her ass forward until her crack was level with the edge of the couch, I snuggled my face with her thick bush and buried my lips into her moistness, slowly licking circles inside her slit.

"Hmph . . . and you said you weren't going to eat this pussy unless it was shaved," Rasheeda remarked arrogantly.

"I lied," I replied as I stopped licking, and slid up her torso until we were face-to-face. My rigidness was pressed against her wet opening.

"Don't stick it in without a rubba!" Rasheeda whispered, and rubbed her moistness on Monster.

"Chill, baby. I'm not going there," I said, reassuring her that I wasn't going to attempt to get any of her love without a glove on.

"Better not!"

"Wanna taste your pussy?"

"Gimme that tongue," she instructed, then sucked it like it was a dick. Pounding my fingers inside of her, I brought Rasheeda to her first orgasm of the evening. As she came, she sucked my tongue like she was trying to swallow it, then released it when her orgasm subsided. She fell back on the couch, panting.

"You sure you don't eat a little pussy on the side," I mumbled, turned on by how ravenously she'd sucked her pussy juice off of my tongue.

"I'd eat mine if I could get to it."

"Get on the floor so I can fuck it!" I ordered as I stood up.

"Don't you want me to suck that dick, baby?" she asked, giving me a sexy smile.

"That'll work," I replied, sitting down on the couch and spreading my legs as far as I could.

Rasheeda got on all fours and licked the insides of my thighs, getting closer to my dick with each repetition.

"You know you're teasing the fuck out of me?" I said through gritted teeth.

Her answer was biting down hard on my inner thigh. Sucking in my breath, I tried to move away, but she stayed locked on. After leaving a passion mark, she began to sloppily lap at my balls, making them bounce.

"That's it, baby! That's it!" I yelled out as she finally began to give some oral attention to my dick, which had begun to drip that salty, yet curiously sweet stuff. Licking up the shaft, Rasheeda got a little taste before making my dick disappear with her humongous lips. Deep-throating, she held her head still.

"Don't play, baby. Get the dick," I pleaded, urging her to suck it.

Rasheeda finally took her mouth off my dick, leaving a trail of saliva on it. She laughed sexily from the depths of her belly. Grabbing her by the wrists, I snatched the gym bag off the floor and pulled her into her bedroom. Pushing her against the wall, I ripped the top of her teddy down to her belly and held her by her shoulders as I licked her titties. I fed on them, greedily, hungrily. I was nasty. So very nasty, I thought, tossing the bag of tricks onto the bed. Slobbering on her forty-inch D cups, I took each nipple into my mouth and sucked.

"Oh . . . God!" Rasheeda yelled as I attempted to swallow her juicy titties. She begged, wanting me to bury my rock-hard tool inside her and fuck her standing up against the wall.

I dipped two fingers inside her pussy and rubbed my thumb on her clit. "Bring it here," I told her, stepping away from the wall and pulling her along. Slamming my hand savagely and repeatedly inside her, I fingered her in the middle of the floor.

"Oh," she moaned, then slid to the floor in a sitting position as I continued to finger her.

"Get up!" I ordered, but Rasheeda just stared at me with her legs and mouth open. I was so turned on by her wetness and reaction, I snatched her up by the arm and threw her on the bed. Monster was as hard as platinum and I was gonna make her beg for him.

Reaching in the bag, I pulled out a bottle of baby oil. Popping the cap, I liberally sloshed oil on her booty, asshole, and punany. She squirmed as the cool slickness hit her body. Turned on even more, I spread the oil evenly on her ass, and slapped her right booty cheek with a resounding slap. To my surprise, Rasheeda arched her ass in the air without protest. My hand whooshed through the air again with greater force on her left cheek.

"Ooooohhhhhhh," she sang, slowly rotating her hips.

"Is that right?" I asked, tapping that booty again.

"A bitch might like a little pain," she replied, lifting her hips, signaling she wanted some more.

"Is that a fact? I got some more tricks for you then. Didn't know I was dealing with a closet freak. But a brotha came prepared," I told her, reaching back into my bag and pulling out my anal starter kit. Rasheeda was an anal virgin and had run scared every time my dick got anywhere near her ass.

"What's that!" Rasheeda blurted.

Ignoring her, I applied a liberal amount of oil to the four-inch anal vibrator, then turned it on low. Slowly, I rubbed the tip of it up and down her asshole.

"Don't . . ." she began, then contradicted herself. Wiggling her ass and warming up to the probe, she moaned and nodded. "Ready?" I gently inserted the toy in her ass and worked it all the way in.

Rasheeda buried her face into the pillow, and gripped its

edges. Moving her delicious chocolate in rhythm with the vibrator, she loosened up.

"This tight ass of yours is getting something it never had before. Didn't know you would like it, did you?" I asked, as I slowly stroked her with the toy.

Rasheeda didn't respond, just continued to muffle her pleasurable cries with the pillow. Reaching back into my bag of tricks I pulled out a seven-inch vibrator and turned it on. She was oblivious to the new toy until I pushed the tip of it against her engorged clit.

"Euftis!" Rasheeda blurted out, lifting her head up as far as she could.

"It's okay, baby. It's okay," I coaxed, slowly inserting the vibrator inside of her pussy. No lube was required. She was dripping wet. "Daddy is just gonna fuck both your holes real good," I said, soothing her again as I began fucking her with both toys.

"Ooooohhhhhhh . . ." she moaned.

"Yes, baby. Give it to Daddy."

"Oooohhhhh," she yelled out as her body began to shake. She was cumming.

"Yessssssssssssssssss . . . that's it. That's it!" I said as I tossed the toys on the floor, and buried my face between her legs.

I flicked the tip of my tongue across her vagina.

"What are you doing to me!" she exclaimed, gripping my head.

"Spelling . . . my . . . name," I told her innocently.

"Oh shit!"

"See . . . watch," I told her as my tongue drew an E on her pussy.

Rasheeda trembled when I tongued a U. Twitched after the F. Bucked when I crossed the T. Shivered from the I. Came when I snaked an S between her slit.

Suddenly Rasheeda turned the tables on me.

"Whose dick is this?" she asked, grasping and holding my dick.

It ain't yours! I thought.

"You don't know her," I replied coolly.

"What?" Rasheeda was shocked. "Awwwww . . . I see a bitch is gonna have to . . ." She walked over to the nightstand at the side of the bed and retrieved a small metallic container. She got back between my legs and opened the container. A can of Altoids.

"Awwwww shit!" I exclaimed.

"Uhhhhh-huh!" she replied as she put six Altoids in her mouth and a few cubes of ice she took from a cup.

"Awwwwwww shit!" I yelled out again.

Rasheeda attacked the dick. Holding it firmly at the base while going up and down on it at a frantic pace. Monster felt as if he was burning and freezing at the same time. I had never felt a sensation like that before and my mind fought to record everything I was feeling from my numb dick.

Rasheeda kept at it as she dripped melted ice and liquefied mint out of her mouth. It ran down the length of me, leaving hot/cold sensations on Monster as it trickled down between my legs.

"Whose dick is this?" she asked again.

I looked down and deep into her eyes before I replied, *"You don't know her!"*

Holding my dick, she inched off the bed until her knees were on the floor. Since she held my most prized possession hostage, I had no choice but to follow her. When my butt was at the edge of the bed, she got on all fours, looking up into my eyes as she prepared to suck my dick in the position where it could be done best.

She stuck her tongue out and licked my balls in an upward motion to the very tip of my love muscle. My body shuddered uncontrollably after just the first lick.

"Whose dick is this?"

"You . . . don't . . . know . . . her!" I grunted through gritted teeth. Monster was so hard that he pointed at the ceiling.

"Dick," Rasheeda said simply.

I pushed the tip of Monster down until he was pointed at Rasheeda's full lips. She rocked forward on her knees and slurped at the tip of my dick.

"Ohhhhh fuck!"

Sluuurp! "Whose dick is this?"

"Ohhh fuck! I'm . . . gonna . . . cum . . . all ova ya face . . ." I breathed, warning her.

Sluuuurp! "A bitch might like—"

The *second* I knew Rasheeda didn't mind me cumming on her, Monster threw a bolt of pearl white lightning onto her face.

"Uuugghh!" I groaned as Monster flexed.

He flexed his muscles again, casting another bolt of white lightning. Rasheeda moaned loudly as my liquid heat dripped from her face. Monster cast another bolt and her eyes snapped open.

"Damn, baby!" she exclaimed, aroused by the abundance of semen splashing on her. She cooed and took my dick back into her mouth, absorbing the rest of my liquid bolts down her throat.

I growled loudly then fell back on the bed, spent.

Rasheeda stumbled into her bathroom, laughing as she went to wash her face. The fitted sheet had been pulled off the bed and her pillows, linen, and comforter were on the floor. I didn't have the energy to make the bed, so I got on the floor and pulled the sheet over me.

Rasheeda came out of the bathroom and straddled my body. She palmed my forehead with one hand and forced me to look up at her.

"Wanna taste your *dick*, Daddy?" she asked me enticingly.

My response was a long, sloppy kiss. Rasheeda got under the sheet behind me and hugged me around the waist. I pushed back closer to her and closed my eyes, cummed dry and ready to go to sleep.

"Euftis?"

"Yea."

"What took you so long getting over here tonight?"

I thought about Kianna, the Gilbert Avenue ho, and grinned.

Rasheeda just didn't know. When it came to getting a nut off, my big Monster wasn't just grimy.

He was grimier.

THUG LOVIN'
Andrea Blackstone

"Damn, Daddy. How much longer I gotta suck this dick? How about some pussy now? My knees getting tired."

I snickered out loud. Some whore done been in my boss's office for the last thirty minutes, sucking that fool off like a Hoover vacuum cleaner. I'd started hearing those steady slurping sounds when I went to knock on his door to ask him a quick question, and after I found out that Mr. Nasty was getting his "head delivered on heels," I decided to press my ear to the door and listen to the action.

I almost laughed as he started going off on her.

"Your knees tired? Standing at five foot two you should stay on your knees! If I want to be hassled over pussy I'll call that bitch I just divorced! What kind of whore are you anyway? Who in the hell did Butch send over here? If you want that quick money I better keep feeling all tongue and no teeth. Now keep this shit rock-hard like your life depends on it! I likes my head and today I wants my head! It's been a stressful morning. Suck up! I don't want no used-up, loose pussy on my dick neither. I want what I want, so stop the bullshit and get down to business like you know the rules! I don't have all damned day! "

"Don't play so mean, Daddy. I don't mind staying on my knees. I was just asking, that's all," the woman said.

"I'm not paying you a hundred and fifty dollars for conversation, I'm paying you to *suck*! Don't stop until you suck this dick bone-dry at least twice. I paid for multiple pops, so don't act like you forgot! Just do what you said you do, or you and Butch will both be owing me some cake. Don't let this corner office and suit and tie fool your ass. I'm still that brotha from the hood!"

"No need to get upset, Daddy. Honey can do it. You chose right. I'm the best these D.C. streets got, and I'm worth every dime. Shit, I love my job. And right now, my job is sucking this dick some more. I want you to be as comfortable as possible, so lie back in that chair and just relax. They don't keep my pimp's phone ringing for nothing. I promise I'll leave a smile on that chocolatey, handsome face. Honey just thought you might want a little variety in the mix, that's all. Most men want me to beat around the bush before I take them 'round the world. I guess it makes them feel like they getting something extra outta the deal. Please don't get me in trouble with Butch. He'll beat my ass black 'n blue if you give him a bad report. You one of his best customers. I'm sorry—I'll make it up to you real quick, Daddy."

"Work your neck and prove it then!"

"First, I'ma kiss it real sweet and tender. Do you like that?"

"Kiss it? Young whores like you don't know shit about shit. A man needs a good—a-a-a man needs a good—" my boss stuttered. I began hearing an extremely loud and clear slurping noise again. "Aaah—that's better. Mmm. Mmmhmm. That's what I'm talking about. Yes, Mommy!" He moaned slow and long. "That's what I want! Don't stop sucking. Aaaw shit! You *do* know what you're doing," he added. I could hear Honey begin to moan right along with her paying customer as she gave him a sloppy, wet blow job. My boss had one helluva sexual appetite, and this latest whore was making his cranky ass eat his own words and shoot them straight outta his black dick!

"I'm about to bust! Come closer and open your mouth, bitch! Open it wide. Drink yo daddy's nut, Honey! Be a good girl and drink it all."

I had no idea that my boss was so damn freaky, but now I knew the real deal. When I heard Mr. Nasty about to cum, I broke down outside his door like a tired-ass hooptie, and couldn't manage to stay strong. My boss man's dirty little secret had me so hot I couldn't just stand there anymore. Instead, I pulled my ear from the door, ran into the ladies bathroom, and played with myself until my pussy lips were red and swollen.

About ten minutes later, I returned to my desk with a dripping wet and finger-sore pussy. I pretended as if I didn't hear a damn thing, although I continued to hear muffled moans and groans for another twenty minutes. Shit, I guess that nigga did bust that second nut! Honey definitely made homeboy do a 180 and made his doubting ass a believer in her oral skills!

Not long afterward, a petite little whore opened the door and left carrying some phony package like she'd been sent to pick up something for the mailroom. About two minutes later my boss made an appearance. He glanced over my shoulder, and I fought to pretend as if I didn't know shit. I began tapping away on the keyboard, acting as if I'd been typing an important correspondence to some high-government official the entire time.

"How's the document coming, Yani?" he asked in a professional voice.

"Fine," I answered. I squeezed my legs together tight like I was doing some fitness exercise on a thigh-toning machine. I knew he saw my legs quiver and make my skirt bunch up in between my gap. His whore/work/break session went down three days out of every work week, and I suspected he called the same pimp to send him different girls who were known for their various "talents."

Hell, I didn't know how much longer I could take keeping my horny ass in the background. The last time a paid pussy came around, she jerked him off while he was taking a conference call. The one before that brought a "co-worker" along to give him the best damn sex show a pair of high-priced hoes could offer. They both got fucked and sucked for two full hours—lucky hoes!

"Yani, your blouse is open," my boss said. I'd forgotten to fix my clothes after I groped and licked on my fat melons in the bathroom.

"I guess you're right. I did miss a few buttons. Oops—excuse me," I said, flashing him a warm smile. I stuck my left hand inside of my shirt and arranged my big juicy titties in my bra before buttoning my blouse. My boss was busy taking notice and I could feel his eyes burning my cocoa skin, despite the silence. I got so nervous I buttoned it up crooked and had to start over again because of the way his eyes were wandering all over my cleavage. By my second attempt, I buttoned it correctly.

"Do you need me for anything else?" I asked, smoothing the fabric down.

"No, that'll be all for now, except I should let you know that I'm headed out for a meeting," he answered, still staring at my chest.

"Okay."

"Then again, there may be something else." My boss looked me up and down.

"Yes, sir. What is it?"

"It's recently come to my attention that there may be some reasons that *could* justify giving you a raise," he said. "Think of some good reasons to convince me, Ms. Parker."

I just laughed a little and let his comment leave when he did. As soon as he walked away I squeezed my twenty-six-year-old thighs together again and grinned. The next time his fine ass flirted with me I planned to let my boss know that I'd file a *reverse* sexual harassment suit on him if he didn't stop letting me overhear him getting down. If tongue, lips, and swaying hips was what he needed, he just shoulda asked me! I am still the baddest bitch on this block and I could've fucked and sucked his horny ass to complete satisfaction! I don't mind getting on my knees to suck a dick, and getting a nice raise for it would be even better!

I took typing in high school, and it paid off rather lovely. But if the truth be known, the reason I beat out a long list of college graduates to get my job was because some wrinkled-up white man in Human Resources liked looking at me during the interview. When I realized he was getting off on my chocolate treats, I batted my eyelashes a lot and used my sex appeal to my advantage, until he offered me the job—on the spot.

Since I was all hot and bothered now, I was going to have to fight to concentrate on my work the remainder of the day. After my boss left for his meeting, I called my man, Smooth Willie, and tried to get something popping with him.

"Smooth, it's me. I was thinking that maybe we could hook up tonight and have some fun between the sheets. It's been a while, you know."

"I hear you, Ma. The thing is, I can't make it tonight."

I sucked my teeth and sighed.

"And why would that be?" I snapped.

"I got some critical shit to take care of."

"Again? You sure you can't reconsider? The streets ain't going nowhere. What I'm trying to tell you is I really need to see you. I got needs, ya know."

"I got peeps in town on business. What'chu want me to do? I gotta make that bread."

"Why I gotta make an appointment and get penciled in to get some dick these days? You just aren't freaky like you used to be. I don't turn you on no more or sumthin', huh, Smooth? You always used to make time to break off your girl, no matter what."

"Since you asked . . . you done picked up about ten pounds. I guess I been feeding you too good 'cause you ain't model thin like you used to be. I luh you and all, but you just don't hold my attention as much. But that don't mean Smooth don't still want you, Yani. I still got luh for you. You know you my girl."

"Forget you, nigga! If you want skinny, get with one of your crackhead bitches! I don't have to take your shit!" I yelled. I slammed the phone down in Smooth Willie's ear.

I tried to calm my hot self down. Something just wasn't right about me having all this daily tension collecting in my back. Probably because I wasn't getting served properly at home.

After such a frustrating day at work I decided to make some solo moves. I was gonna take myself out on a date and party all night in the city—Chocolate City. I predicted there had to be at least one pretty nigga that could turn my head and give me some respect.

I'd spent enough time fucking myself at work, so I put on some tight jeans trimmed in pink that showed my butt crack; a black Las Vegas top; pink boots; and a pink rabbit fur jacket that I'd purchased on sale from Wilson's Suede and Leather. As for the perfume, I grabbed the first thing that I could find on my dresser. Ironically, I ended up squirting on one of Smooth's favorites, but so what!

I decided to bump and grind at one of the most popular nightspots in D.C. I paid the parking attendant, parked the car, and crossed the street armed with a sense of adventure. As I paraded by an assortment of onlookers, men stared at me like I was some strange color, like blue or green. I felt like a fuckin' Martian who'd just touched down. At first, I didn't know what to think.

"You see dat? That's one phat-ass motherfucker! Gooot damn! I'd like to hit that from the back!" someone re-marked.

"I'm wit you on this one—she damn sure is a dime!" an-other man answered, twisting up his face and making it ugly in the process.

Other men cussed at the sight of my curves and tried to hand me business cards, and some even followed behind me like a pack of wild dogs in heat. I laughed, but inside I wasn't sure that shit was amusing. Truthfully, the ruckus I was causing on the sidewalk embarrassed me and made me wonder why Smooth Wille kept treating me like some second-class bottom bitch. Shit, maybe I had gained a little weight, but I didn't have to be runway model thin to turn a man's head. I thought most hood niggas like plenty of tits and ass anyway!

I ignored every comment until I heard one particular voice.

"Excuse me, sweetheart. Can I talk to you for a minute?"

I stuffed my hands inside my jacket pockets, then turned around to face the guy. He was a straight thug and I was definitely attracted to that type. His Timberland boots, baggy jeans, black North Face coat, and fresh cornrows made him look sexy as hell. But when he opened his mouth, no gold flashed from his grill. He didn't sport a Caesar haircut, or a gold bracelet or gold chain either.

Still, I ignored his fine ass because his whole package reminded me of the nigga who had me out on a dick hunt tonight in the first place. Instead of acknowledging him, I got in line and waited to be admitted into the club. Although I liked his urban flavor, I pretended as if he did nothing for me and quickly dismissed him like a buster.

When I got inside the club I paid the cover charge and found the coat check. I roamed around the club feeling free. Although I knew that a lot of business professionals hung out at the club, I wasn't interested in a brotha who sat in a cubicle pushing a pen for a living. All of them seemed to want to escape from their 9-to-5 worlds and were stressed out just like me.

But at the same time, I wasn't in the mood to find a carbon copy of Smooth Willie. I had a taste for something and someone else. Someone speckled with spice, edge, and sexual openness. Someone with strong hands and a talented tongue who wasn't ashamed to admit his love of gritty, hot sex. Someone who would tell me bluntly that he wanted to fuck the shit out of me, and make me scream each and every time we had hot sex, then hold me until dawn. But I also wanted more of something that I couldn't quite put my finger on. When I touched that spot, I'd know my finger was laid down right on it.

As sensuous R&B beats and killer rap lyrics played, I roamed around the club and kept running into the anonymous thug, exchanging looks with him. I rolled my eyes at him with mega-attitude, convincing myself that he was probably a drug dealer or menace to society, just like my Smooth. Yep, Smooth was pushing weight up and down the East Coast. Dope was his mistress, although I had begged him to end that relationship. He always asked me how could a man with a ninth-grade education do that if he was making paper so long, he'd put my boss's check to shame. Smooth was addicted to the hustle, and it would take a miracle to change his outlook.

As I pushed my way through the thick crowd, I felt someone gently pull at the bottom of my shoulder-length curls.

"You wanna dance?" he asked.

I looked up at him. My Thug. He was a sexy, tall 'n thick big daddy, and was holding a fat cigar in his right hand.

"Sure. Why not?" As we grooved to "Lean Wit It, Rock Wit It," by Dem Franchize Boyz, the energy of the crowd became electrified. People were emptying champagne bottles, drinks were flowing at the bar, and women were scanning the room for ballers. The place seemed packed to its maximum capacity, and that didn't even count the VIP room.

I noticed how the scandalous chickenheads arched their backs to make their breasts poke out and their asses appear bigger, as they whispered to their girlfriends.

"This part right here is my shit!" I yelled out when the second verse began. I swung my hips, dropped to the floor, and got low, then sprung up, passing his crotch. I became wet and longed to fondle myself—or better yet, his nice hard dick. Instead I pretended as if the sexiness of the nightlife didn't shake my libido up too much.

My plump breasts pressed against his chest and he grabbed my hand while I fantasized about him. When he pulled me toward the edge of the crowd like he knew me, I followed him.

"What I gotta do to get you to take my number?" he asked.

"Who said I *want* your number? I have someone at home," I replied. "I never said I was available, thank you. Just to be clear, I'm taken," I added as my attention-starved pussy throbbed.

"Why you acting so rude to a brother?"

"I'm not. Your opinion is yours, and mine is mine."

"Look, I don't want to hold you up—I just wanted to holla atchu. Maybe talk with you later. Is that a crime?"

I tried to ignore the fact that my panties were soaking wet in the crotch. I told him my cell number and he pulled out his and punched it in. I nodded when I felt my phone vibrating in my purse.

"Now I got your number," I said like I really hadn't wanted it.

He laughed. "You know you really wanna call me, so just use the number and stop fronting."

I thought he was going to keep on pressing me, but he walked away and disappeared into the crowd. A few minutes later I realized I could no longer curb that craving I had. I sped home and pleased myself in my typical way, thinking about him the whole time.

• • •

The next morning I was bored. I scrolled through my received-calls log, found the number I was looking for, then pressed SEND. He didn't answer, and I called back two more times. Each time I hung up after a few rings. I saw no point in leaving a message when I hadn't even gotten his name at the club. Besides, he had my number too. I'd already kissed Smooth's ass for years. I didn't want no new nigga to get any ideas.

But something told me to try again anyway, and this time he answered.

"Yo, what's up? I knew you would call," he said.

"Shit, I didn't know I called you. Maybe I hit the wrong button. Sorry, 'bout that."

"Girl, stop lying. You hit up the right person, all right. The number showed up on my caller ID several times. No one makes a mistake that much. You gonna tell me your name now?"

"Like I said, calling you was an accident. I made a mistake. My name is not *perfect*, it's *Yani.*"

"Well, I'm Life. I see you got some sass in your blood, Yani."

"Maybe. And what if I do?" I answered.

After a few awkward moments we laughed and joked for hours.

Soon, every time Smooth let me down, I began calling Life for my nightly fix. Life stimulated my mind and body with his dreams. He worked at a record shop, but was trying to negotiate and lease his beats to major rap labels, while shopping record deals for independent artists at the same time. Life was passionate about his craft, and I definitely was feeling that.

"So why do they call you Life? I thought you were a straight thug when I met you. Is Life your real name?" I asked.

"Nah, but life is what I'm all about. My biggest fear is becoming a statistic out here 'cause someone else is playing street games that don't got nothing to do with me. I used to be in the drug game, but I left hustling a long time ago. I reevaluated a lot of shit after I lost my little brother to a senseless act of violence. That's when I changed my name to Life. Through me, he lives—he still has life. Yo, my biggest wish is to put my bid in in the music game and have a queen standing right beside me when I make those millions. Shit is pointless if I ain't got a wife and some kids to love. My dreams and goals are what keep my nose to the grind and help me stay on point. Ya feel me, Yani?"

My heart fluttered. Life was so down-to-earth that I felt like I'd known him for ten years. He was about much more than Smooth. It finally hit me that Smooth had no dreams, except chasing dollars and poisoning our people. Smooth had a selfish, shallow streak that didn't bother me when I was younger. But as I grew older, that shit grew stale.

Life had goals and ambition. He never cut me off like Smooth often did when he had to leave to handle his business on the block. Hell, Life even helped me admit that I dabbled in poetry. When I did admit it, he asked me to read him some of my work. I dug in my closet and pulled out an overstuffed binder that Smooth Willie knew existed, but had never cared to inquire about.

"Read somethin' to me, Ma. Got anything wit hotness for me?" Life asked.

"I do but I changed my mind about reading it. You'll laugh at what I've got to say."

"Ain't nothing funny to me about you having an artistic side. As you know, I'm an artist myself. Stop acting shy and let me check you out. Now go ahead and do what you do."

"Okay," I said. "I do have something new." I inhaled, then began my poem.

I cry for love—
My tears of blue pouring all over you.
What to do? What to do?
I call your name in pain, but don't you hear me fighting to be
*   heard above this beating rain? You don't see me. You no*
*   longer complete me.*

You don't feel me licking, touching, tasting, rubbing, thrusting,
  craving your fucking while feeling your hands, my hands—
  us feeding each other in a frenzy in these foreign lands?
Our bodies pressed together, wet with sweat, clinging and
  singing praises of ecstasy as we drift from the motherland to
  the beaches of Brazil, then from one continent to the next?
Are you still there? Are you aware, that it was divine when
  we were intertwined once upon a time?
Then along came that sun; that thug who opened my book of
  thoughts and read every line, one by one. He took his
  time—in winter and spring.
Divine sunshine. Diviiiiiine sunshine. All because he took his
  time.
Now I pry him from the shadows of my mind. At night, in the
  morning, when dark shadows fall. Now it's his name I
  call when my heart is still moving in unison with the way
  he is freeing me.
Because he sees the real me, I crave his touch too much like
  my last breath has come.
If we are one, why do I open my thighs and dream his touch
  makes an orgasm rise?
Why do I fantasize about this urban ghetto poet spitting
  lyrics on his microphone, long after you've come home?
Why do I now pretend he is the one licking, touching, tasting,
  rubbing, thrusting, craving his fucking while feeling his
  hands on my skin—my hands on his skin.
Fill me in. Please somebody, just fill me iiiin.
Life. Life. Life. I cry for you—straight from the heart.
  I . . . crave . . . life, life, life.

"That was the truth! You really should consider doing somethin' with that. Ever thought of putting out a book of poetry? You got my shit standing up and everything!"

After a while, I began caring less if Smooth called or showed up at the crib. Sometimes he did, sometimes he didn't. Fuck him. I yearned to pick up the phone and hear the new voice that made me remember who I was and what made me tick. Life made me feel alive . . .

One Saturday, Life asked me if he could bring some music over to my place for me to hear. I agreed although Smooth warned me never to bring a nigga out the street and into my crib. He *said* it was for my safety. Maybe so, maybe not. Before I knew it, I'd rattled off my home address, and it didn't take Life long to show up with a small bunch of roses. When he handed them to me, I felt weak from his sweetness.

After I put the flowers in a vase, I listened to at least four cuts on Life's CD. I was amazed that his beats were banging—he had mad skills that convinced me he could rise to the top. A slow beat came on and Life broke the ice and asked me to dance.

"Yo, we never got a slow dance in the club that night. How about it right now?" Life said, walking up to me. As we swayed from side to side, I couldn't believe that Life was so tender and romantic.

"Yani, your curly afro smells so good. It's nice to see a natural sista's beauty." He rubbed his full lips against my right cheek, but didn't kiss it. He made my body sway from side to side. I felt his hot breath on my neck, then his lips press against my smooth skin. That was what I was talking about. Life was like that!

I breathed deeply and said, "You smell good too, Life—really delicious. I like it." His cologne clung to my nostrils and made me wet. I exhaled, then suddenly felt a gigantic bulge in his pants. Thankfully, a fast tempo hook began to play again.

"I've got an idea. Let's play a game," Life suggested.

"What kind of game?"

"Let's just say I have a heck of an imagination. Go put on something sexy for me, Ma."

"Like what? Tricks are for kids," I joked.

"Keep your day job, 'cause you ain't no comedian!" Life joked in return. "Now just go put on something sexy. Hurry yo fine ass up," he demanded.

"Oh, now I'm supposed to tip over with happiness just to clap my ass for you?"

"Girl, you are crazy. Pretend we're in a strip club so I can worship that fine ass. Don't make it seem like you ain't down! I peeped you dancing wild at the club."

I headed toward the basement and grabbed a thong off of the top of the dryer. To my surprise, Life was breaking through my resolve. By the time I returned to the living room wearing my thong, a hypnotic beat was pumping. Life's eyes were glued to me as he studied me from head to toe. I walked across the room, then moved toward the center of it. I faced him and began to dance, moving with steady, light gestures. I flashed Life a warm, radiant smile as I worked my hips and moved my arms in fluid motions. I got lost in the hip-hop beat and savored each note as the thong's fabric rubbed between my phat ass cheeks.

My sensuality warmed me up, I was hyped. I let go and really shook my ass and didn't care how crazy I looked doing it! Out of spite to get back at Smooth Willie, I popped my coochie like I was an experienced stripper. I felt like a sensuous woman again. Life confirmed that I still was desirable, even if Smooth had stopped treating me that way.

"You're a good dancer, Yani. A real damned good dancer!" Life commented.

I moved closer to him, stopping a few inches away.

"I know," I answered, while slowly gyrating my hips in his face. Life leaned forward and pressed his soft lips just above my pussy.

"Work it for Daddy!" he yelled. Then he removed a dollar from his wad of money and stuck it on the side of my thong. I placed my hands on my knees, turned around, arched my back, and rubbed my ass on top of him.

"Got-damn, girl! You got some big, fat 'n juicy pussy lips. I bet you taste sweeter than honey. You one of a kind, fo' sure!" Life mumbled as I continued to shake my ass.

He reached out and pulled my thong to the side and gently played with my anus until my pussy was wet and slick. Feeling Life's thumb moving around my erogenous zone made chills run up my spine. As I listened to his music I closed my eyes and imagined him spitting between my ass cheeks, relaxing my sphincter muscles, then letting his tool experience my deep asshole. When Life stopped playing with my ass, my thong string snapped back into place. I shook myself from my fantasy when he began to stuff more dollars in my little thong string.

"Hey! I got enough bills around my waist to make me a money belt! I like this game!" I said, flashing a big smile.

Life's eyes were glossy, as if he had been hypnotized into a trance-like state. I slowly stroked my fingers under his chin, then fondled my bare breasts in front of him. As Life stuffed more dollars in my thong, I stood upright again, then used both hands to open my pussy to show him what I was working with.

"Do something for me, baby," Life asked. "Reach down, stick two fingers inside of that pussy, and suck them juices from your pretty fingertips. Lemme see you do that."

I did what Life asked of me. I felt like a movie star. Before I knew it he pulled his tool out and began stroking it openly.

"Look at what I got for you," he said, working his dick up into a nice thick, long pole.

"Put that thing 'way. That's not a good idea," I told him. The sight of Life's sexy dick made me feel like Jell-O inside.

"You can't even look at my dick. You're nervous as hell. You think there's something wrong with a man stroking his shit?"

"No—I never said that. There's nothing wrong with . . . well. Never mind, Life."

"Before you say no to something, you should at least see what you're turning down," he said, stroking it gently.

I finally took a really good look at Life's dick and my mouth began to water like I smelled good food burnin' at a soul-food spot!

"I'm in a committed relationship. I told you that from day one," I said weakly.

"Yani, the man you got ain't living up to the meaning of a man. He has you hanging your head down and holding back on what you wanna do. If you were satisfied in every way, you wouldn't be writing poetry about me, wondering how I work my dick, or shaking yo ass in my face. So you tryna tell me you half-naked but I'm feeling sparks up in this mother-fucker alone?"

I didn't answer.

"Girl, what you really want right now is a thug nigga like me to hit it like I'm gonna break you in half! From the way you've explained things here and there, the situation you're in is fucked up. I know you need to get fucked, licked, and sucked right—it's been written all over your face since the night I saw you in the club. If you need time, I got time. But don't you think it's about time you just let go, for you? I ain't that nigga that's got you stressin'. If you want this dick, get ready to sit down on it and enjoy it," Life said, tearing open a condom.

I was nearly salivating at the thought of sitting down on his massive dick. But just when I was about to take him up on his offer, something snapped me out of the fuckin' mood. The phone rang.

"Yo, Yani! I'm on my way over. I just wrapped up some business and I'ma come through and holla atchu. Put on some heels and some sexy shit. I wanna see you looking good when I come through the spot for that wet wet," Smooth Willie said.

"Oh shit!" I told Life when I hung up. "That was Smooth!"

"Fuck that nigga. *This* is what you want! You got time to enjoy *my* dick. If this clown gets here before we finish fucking, he can watch me do what he should've been doing all along with a thick mommy like you! If he catches your legs up in the air or my mouth on his pussy, so be it!"

"Life, I don't want any trouble. Please, just get the fuck out, fast!"

"I don't see no ring on your finger, so what's the problem here? Why can't you stand up to this nigga? Just call him back and tell him you don't wanna see his ass tonight. Is that so hard?"

"You don't understand. I don't want to talk about this right now."

"Well I do. What's the deal, Yani? If I don't understand everything, explain."

"Fine. Maybe if I tell you, you'll leave! Smooth's dangerous—he's a drug dealer, and he's not wrapped too tight. Please, do yourself a favor and go home. I don't wanna be with you right now."

"Yani, if and when you get your head together, holla at ya boy," Life told me. He adjusted his clothes and headed for the door.

I wanted to cry when he left. I felt so sad inside for getting so close to something I wanted for myself, and then allowing Smooth to get in the way of it. I picked up the bills that lined the floor and clutched them in my left hand. I walked toward my bedroom and placed the money in a drawer where I kept priceless mementos and souvenirs. After that, I walked toward the bathroom, took my shower, put some sweet-smellin' stuff on for Smooth, before sliding my feet inside of his favorite red Frederick's heels.

A few moments later I heard a loud banging sound at the door. When I opened it, looking my best, Smooth slammed the door and locked it. He was barely inside when he made me open my mouth wide, forced me to my knees, and shoved a glock down my throat.

"Who's been fucking my pussy, Yani? I want the mother-fucker's name and address!"

I shook my head frantically, not understanding what Smooth was referring to.

"Don't play dumb! Word has it that you were at the club letting baller niggas touch on my shit! After all I've done for you, you act up. You get this piece-of-shit job working in some office and now you think you're the shit 'cause you work around some suit-and-tie motherfuckers? You lucky I don't blow your fuckin' head off. From now on, if you ain't out with me, you ain't out! You go straight to work and come straight the fuck home. When I take this glock outta yo mouth, you repeat the last line back to me."

"I go straight to work and I come straight home," I whimpered, shaking on my knees.

"Good. Now get the fuck up and let's go to bed."

I couldn't believe how ruthless Smooth was. The game made him as cold as Alaska—even with me, the person who had tried to be his best friend. I wanted to drift off to sleep, but I couldn't. I prayed that Smooth stayed knocked out and didn't pull out that glock again.

The next morning I got up and made Smooth breakfast while wearing a long, black Victoria's Secret negligee with netted sides that hinted at my dangerous curves.

"You still love Smooth, baby?" Smooth asked as bacon cooked in a skillet.

"Yes," I lied while flipping the strips of meat. What the fuck did he expect me to say after the crazy stunt he pulled? He didn't know it, but I was ready to start plotting my escape from his reign of terror.

"Good. I'll drive you to work," he said. An hour later Smooth drove me up to the curb of the building where I worked and made me sit in the car while he told me again what he was gonna do to me if I ever stepped out on him. After threatening my life, he ordered me to kiss him good-bye. I felt like a prisoner in my own body. He wanted to control my every move, down to my motherfuckin' lips!

I was early, and when I walked into my office I saw a familiar face.

"I came down here 'cause I had to see you."

"How did you know I worked here? You really shouldn't be here, Life."

"I parked my car up the street from your crib. I stayed in it all night because I wanted to make sure you were okay. This morning I followed Smooth's ride here and came inside while y'all sat there talking. I ain't scared of that nigga, but I'm afraid of you being with him."

Life moved closer, softly kissing each of my eyelids. I could feel his hard dick poking at me through my skirt. He roped me in by unzipping his pants and showing me that big, delicious dick again. The minute I peeked at it, I felt like I was standing in quicksand—my ability to continue saying no was sinking fast. I pulled him in my boss's office and shut the door. Life finally kissed my lips once. He moved close to my mouth again and tasted my lips for a second time. This kiss sizzled just as much as the first one. I finally began returning it. I pressed my body firmly against his, sucking his tongue, as we played in each other's warm mouths. I met Life halfway by pulling my stockings down and my skirt off, letting them both fall on the floor. I noticed that his eyes were blazing, full of life, and I finally allowed myself to get lost in those dark pools.

As Life pulled off his shirt, pants, boxers, and shoes, he told me to sit on top of the desk. I did. He caressed my legs, then spread them apart and began kissing the inside of my thick thighs. Next, he took his fingers and began playing with my pussy. My juices began to flow from his persistent fingertip stroking, but that was only the beginning. My new lover dropped lower and stuck his head between my legs. Life licked on my clit like it was an ice-cream cone, until it felt swollen. I threw my head back, finally let go, and began to openly moan. I began throwing the rest of my clothes off until I was completely naked.

Life sucked my juices up with passion. I felt high, suspended above the sun. When I opened my eyes and looked down I gasped. My juices were all over his face and chin. Life's brown skin was glistening, and the sight of his tattoo—a microphone inked over a nasty scar on his neck—made me shake and tremble, as the blissful feeling between my legs took on a life of its own. I closed my eyes and had an orgasm that erupted in one huge creamy wave. I heard a condom wrapper tearing open, and my mouth dropped as he pushed his tool into me and filled me up inside. His warm dick stroked me as he gripped the sides of the desk. I spoke some unintelligible words and Life answered by hitting all my sweetest spots. His focus was completely on pleasing me.

That realization made me jut my pussy back and forth in a steady motion. I became so excited that I wrapped my legs around him and the desk began creaking and moving like a seesaw. When Life noticed this, he looked around for another spot.

"Come on," he told me. He lowered me from the desk and carefully laid me down on my boss's large white rug.

"Get on your hands and knees," Life said. I arched my back sharply and complied, because I wanted to, not because I had to. Life spit between my ass cheeks, then fingered my anus. He began pounding me from behind with powerful and intense thrusts, the way I'd imagined the thugs on music videos did to their hood girls. I gladly gripped my muscles tight around Life's dick. He responded by smacking my phat ass.

"Do you like this shit, baby?" Life asked, burying his dick all the way inside of me.

"Yes. Mmmm," I moaned. "Oh yes!"

"Does that bitch-ass, trifling nigga you got at home make you feel this good?"

"No—never. He . . . Smooth never . . . He never—"

"Then cry for Life, Mommy. If I make this sweet pussy feel good, take it and cry for me," he said, continuing to thrust himself in and out of my pussy.

I began to cry with pleasure as Life caused my ass cheeks to bounce up and down.

"If the dick's good, keep crying. Cry, baby. Cry or I'll take it outta this hot pussy!" Life demanded. I cried until I felt another orgasm swell up inside of me. I tried to dig my nails into the carpet but couldn't hold on to a single fiber of it.

"I'm about to. Damn. I'm—I'm about to cum!" I whispered in a very high pitch. Despite us being in my boss's office minutes before he was due to arrive, Life never stopped stroking me—and I came for the second time.

"Where do you think you're going?" Life said as I tried to crawl away. "Oh no you don't. Keep your ass right here."

I was feeling good and both of our bodies were wet with sweat.

"This dick feels so good! Fuck—what are you doing to me now?" I exclaimed.

"I know what you need. Turn over on your back," Life said.

I did.

"Take this dick!"

Life placed each of my legs on his shoulders. He looked into my eyes as he worked his hips in a rhythmic motion, bending down to kiss me as he kept thrusting himself in my pussy.

Suddenly I was scared. "I think I heard something. We

better stop! This is my boss's office! I can't get caught fuckin' up in here!" I said.

I instinctively lifted my legs from Life's shoulders, pried myself off of his dick, and ran to the glass-cubed wall to see if anyone was coming. My hands shook as I peeped through a small slit in the blinds. Before I knew it, Life had pushed my legs apart from behind.

"But, but—what if—" I complained. Life ignored me and began kissing, sucking, and tonguing my ass like he was getting paid to turn me out.

"Oh shit!" I said. Smooth would never lick my asshole but I loved the way Life did it. The next thing I felt were heavy balls smacking up against me. Life slid into me and began pumping deep while gripping my waist tightly, until I forgot all about my boss and came again.

"Did you like all of that—huh? Did you like that, you freaky office hottie?" Life asked.

"Thank you for fucking the shit out of me," I said. "I needed this so bad. Thank you!" I moaned.

Life dropped to his knees. I felt the most powerful sensation as I dripped into his mouth. His talented tongue persuaded my body to release yet another quick orgasm. He sucked my juicy nectar as he let it pour out of me. When I was dry, Life pulled away from me and began picking up his clothes. I turned around, speechless. I was drained, but also stunned when I noticed his tool was still fully erect. Life had never come, despite all of the nasty things that we'd done in every which way possible.

He saw me looking at it.

"Yea. This brotha got dick control. You betta believe it!" he told me as I put my clothes back on quickly. As Life opened my boss's office door to leave, I still couldn't speak. I wanted to ask him if he wanted a paper towel to clean his face, but he didn't seem to care that my juices were still wet on his skin. I was so turned on by Life's rugged sex appeal that I'd forgotten all about betraying crazy Smooth.

"You real sweet, boo," Life told me before going out the door. "But there are two kinds of thugs on these streets. Thugs like Smooth who are selfish and grimy, and thugs like me who are just rough around the edges. If you get tired of Smooth controlling your every move, you know how to get at me. I would never hurt you. I only want to make you feel good," Life wiped his face with his hands.

As he stood holding the door open I caught a peek of my boss walking into the main foyer. I ran over and shoved an empty FedEx box in Life's hands and tried to pass him off as someone I'd called to pick up a package. I watched Life walk past my boss, wishing he'd move a helluva lot faster, but being the man he was, he maintained his normal swagger.

"Good morning," I said when my boss walked into his office. "I was just getting a few things organized in your office—I hope you don't mind. You told me to give you a reason to consider giving me that raise," I teased.

"I'd say you just earned it for giving me that award-winning performance," he laughed, then cleared his throat. "I came in early today. I was in the restroom when you and your thug friend arrived. You closed the door but you didn't *lock* it, Yani. The only thing I was missing was a jar of Vaseline and a bag of popcorn."

I looked down at the bulge in his pants and said, "Well, *Daddy*, I guess today it was my turn to put on a show for once, not yours. And since you peeped all my action, I'm sure you could tell that my thug baby was giving me the time of my *life*."

PRETTY MF
Gerald K. Malcom

He dug her out. She screamed like someone was committing a murder. His back, full of sweat, housed her hands. Then her fingers. Then her nails. Then her pleasure. He dug her out.

It was that grimy dick he gave her that impressed. It was the way he reached for the sky and came slamming down into her. It was that R&B dick that dug and swirled and stopped and posed and dug again, pressing against her clit. He eased out with a slick grin.

She screamed pieces of his name in between obscenities. His voice was mellow. "Do you like it or love it?" He dug after he questioned. His dick scraped the bottom. He pushed deep and lifted her with his stroke. She touched the air. He asked her to squeeze.

She closed her eyes tight as if that made her squeeze harder. Those muscles had nothing to do with *those* muscles.

She hugged tight. Didn't want to lose the feeling. She closed her eyes even tighter to take the picture. Dark muscular back. Felt like something good to hold on while being pleased. She knew what he liked. She eased him out by sitting up. She ate her mess.

After she cleaned him her spin was slow. She went to her knees and spread her arms across the bed. Her back had arch, two dimples and shape. The color was premium; like she bought the deepest brown they had to offer.

He grabbed each cheek and kneaded them. She needed this. His right hand pressed hard and rode its way up to her neck. He left it there and gripped the back of her neck. He pushed her head to the bed. She couldn't breathe. She would worry about breath later. His hands hurt her neck, but she wouldn't dare move. She would feel any residual pain later, after her body bucked ferociously, her senses emptied, and her world collapsed.

He filled her with one stroke. She jumped. Almost lost her breath. Her body shook violently. It was brutal, almost savage the way he filled her cavity. She wouldn't have it any other way.

He stayed still. Didn't move an inch. She felt every one. She opened her eyes and watched his shadow against the wall. The shadow was bigger, but wasn't as defined. His pumps were smooth against the lightly flickering wall. Her ass looked even bigger. Not better.

He began a slow thrust that popped when he reached her capacity. On her neck, she felt the power in his hand. She wanted to be held down. She wanted to be forced to take everything he knew.

He spoke confidently, "You can keep your money if you don't come when I say." He knew she loved what she couldn't have. She loved the battle, and didn't care who won the war. She didn't care if he knew her body; she was a winner either way.

"You got sixty seconds." His voice was buttery, like he was singing instructions. The bass in it hit her spine. The confidence hit her sex. She wanted it raw, no chaser.

He gave it to her. "Fifty seconds," he barked. He adjusted his hips and spread her ass to the farthest east and west and shuffled himself deep. He felt the beginning of something new when he entered to his max. He swung to the left and pumped slow for three strokes. He listened to her breathing. She hummed like a new car. He needed an older noise. He swung right and dug. It was methodical. His probe was expertly done. Now her engine rattled like a '67 Chevy. "Forty seconds." He pushed himself deeper than she would allow. He consumed her spot. She ran toward the bed. He brought her back, held her head down, and teased her asshole. His stroke was beautiful, like a well-placed kiss. He heard the splatter of her juice as he penetrated. His hairs were saturated and stuck together. Her sex smelled sweet. "Thirty."

She felt her body slump. She didn't care if she failed. She wanted his rhythm. He obliged. Gave her his soul. He never took it all the way out. He knew she needed her spot filled. He knew how. Knew how to give her pleasure with pain. His thumb was not gentle. His grip was not loving. His strokes were distant. She loved it. "Twenty seconds." She blacked out.

He was thicker than most.

He slung dick like dope. Cops frisked him, but never arrested him. He slung dick like dope.

She wandered in from the blackout. Black hairnet cradling her head, and her ass poking out of her panties. She loved purple. Said it reminded her of kings and queens. She stood in the middle of the room, hands on her hips, and her cigarette smoking was far from diva-like. She pushed huge halos into the air like Pedro did when he tried to impress his friends on the corner.

"What do you want me to do now?" Her voice was heavy. Too heavy for some, but not for Pretty. He told her she sounded like Ella. She couldn't comprehend so he told her she sounded like Macy Gray. It impressed her because no one ever told her she sounded like nothing but shit. He sang praises on her alto.

"I want you to do what you do, bitch! You know the rules." He knew she wanted to cuddle and watch a movie. That wasn't his job. She paid for dream music and blackouts.

She pushed the lit cigarette to the ashtray and mashed it. Smoke trailed like a snake toward the ceiling. She mumbled something incoherent and walked out. There was nothing seductive about her gait. It was forced. Her hips didn't know they were supposed to rock with her foot from the same side. He told her it made her appear stronger than most. She trotted to the rear and came back with an envelope. It was standard and full. She fixed him a drink and set both next to him, got her coat and closed the door. She never looked back. His eyes never left his computer. Spirals swirled about the screen, the music blared. His first shift went without incident.

He sipped from his crystal glass. He wouldn't drink from another glass. His lips were accustomed to the finer things in life. He let it warm his throat before he swirled the orange cognac around. He wiped the corner of his mouth like Denzel in *Mo' Betta Blues*. His stance, his sip, and his style were all purposeful. Appearance was everything.

* * *

"Jarvis, can you please come into my office?"

Pretty hated that shit. Fucking Jarvis. Niggas in the hood called him Jay; the bitches on the block called him Pretty. Said he had the prettiest dick they ever seen. Chocolate. Thick like an eclair. Long like a summer day. Tastier than a Krispy Kreme. They ate it like it was going out of style. He slung dick like dope and selected the very few who had the looks and the goods, as long as they came with the right price.

He closed his drawer and nodded at the teller next to him. He lifted his pants and tightened his belt. He shook his tie into the corporate position, and then mashed his cornrows flatter against his head.

He pushed the door open. "You wanted to see me Mr. Patterson?"

Mr. Patterson rocked back in his chair and kicked up his feet. His shoes were black, expensive, and filthy. Dry mud splattered the soles and traveled up the side. He folded his hands and rested them across his stomach. He was at least six months pregnant. "Sit, Jarvis."

Pretty snarled without the facial expression. He peered through Mr. Patterson. He wondered why his boss didn't cut off the three silver strands that lay across his pasty forehead like wet noodles. Each one spread out quite a distance away. They loved their space. His ties never matched. His shoes was always dirty. His double-breasted suits begged at the seams and his suspenders were frayed at the sides. With all that, he still commanded respect. His heavy footsteps introduced his authority. His billowing cough demanded attention. His sky blue eyes mesmerized the crowd. And he always smelled great. All that coupled with being the vice president of the biggest bank in the area.

Pretty sat across from him and inched back slowly, never once letting his eyes leave his boss. His voice was considerate. "You wanted to see me, sir." His "sir" was forced. Almost massa-like.

Mr. Patterson whipped a pack of cigarettes from his suit jacket's inner pocket and began banging them against his fat palms. He unwrapped the package with anticipation. His lips quivered; his squinting eyes helped his hands unwrap his craving. He pulled one out and slammed it five quick times against his desk. He leaned back, opened a drawer and pulled out a lighter. The blue got bluer and he eased his face to it. He blew out smoke. "I need you to do something for me."

Pretty pushed away a cloud that neared. "What is that, sir?" His "sir" flowed easier than the first.

"Are you street?"

Pretty choked on his own air. *"What?"*

Mr. Patterson hustled slowly to the edge of his seat. *"I said,* are you street?"

Pretty put his defenses up. His tone echoed his mood. "Am I *street?*"

Mr. Patterson laughed. His laugh was throaty, loud and full of machismo. "Yeah. Street? Like um . . ." He snapped his fingers to jar his memory. "Fifty coins."

"You mean cents?"

He threw his hand at Pretty. "Coins, cents, it's all the same thing. Anyway, are you street like him?"

Pretty thought about it. He wasn't street like the thugs he knew that sold drugs. Pretty thought of himself as the ultimate individual. He had his own street credibility.

"I'm street enough. Why?" He had no clue what this meeting was about. He made sure his braids were always tight. His edge up was always maintained. His pants sagged a little from time to time, but it shouldn't have been anything to write home about. *Maybe I do present myself in a thuggish manner,* he thought. He didn't want to lose the best job he ever had due to some cornrows and saggy jeans. He humbled himself and steadied for the blow.

Mr. Patterson struggled to lift himself from his chair. His ascent was slower than most, but when he stood he was steadier than a rock. "I bet you're wondering why I had you come into my office this morning, right?" He walked to the door and opened it swiftly, and then shut it just as fast.

Pretty remained cool. His temples throbbed as he bit down. He didn't struggle to stand. He didn't rock when he began his rise. He turned around to face Mr. Patterson. He didn't feel comfortable with someone behind him that he didn't trust. "You can say that."

"I'll tell you. I have a proposition for you, Jarvis." He came back to his seat and flopped into his chair. The cushion held his body like a mother would a fallen child.

Pretty found an antique mirror on the wall adjacent to the door. He pushed his braids flat to his head with one smooth stroke from front to back. He gave the ends a few determined twists to get them proper. He turned his head to the side and practiced his look, and then he straightened his tie again. He never said he wasn't cocky, but arrogant? He wouldn't buy that. That's what women around the way said. They told him that he looked better than most, but he knew it. They always marveled at his skin. They said it was Hershey brown, but smoother than the candy bar. They loved his teeth. He always smiled. He couldn't wait for the summer so he could wear the hell out of his wife-beaters. His arms spoke volumes for his work ethic. He looked back toward Mr. Patterson and wondered if he loved the winter. It was a way to hide all that shit he had underneath his shirt. Pretty checked his watch and cleared his throat.

Mr. Patterson offered Pretty a seat with a hand gesture. "Do you know why you're here?"

"No."

"The ladies love you, Jarvis. You want to know how I know?"

Petty's tone was defensive. "How?"

"I listen. Women rumble like volcanoes when something is hot. That's what they talk about. They refer to you as *Pretty.*" He smiled. "Isn't that what they call you, Jarvis?"

Pretty dusted his pants off. His nerves got the best of him. He was getting a little uncomfortable with the direction the conversation was going in. References like this on the street would've gotten his boss the shank. His foot beat the ground. He closed his eyes and rocked back. It calmed him. He inhaled with strength and blew it out softly. "They do call me Pretty," he said with pride. His eyes opened slowly. "Is there a problem with having a nickname?" He massaged his face and felt anger and heat on it. Two more quick breaths did little to calm him down. He rubbed his hands together and rest his lips on them when they went to mock prayer position. "And they call you?" He paused and laughed. It wasn't hearty. It was a gritty laugh that cut into Mr. Patterson and left him wondering.

Mr. Patterson's thick untamed gray eyebrow shot up.

Phlegm hustled and bustled around inside his mouth; his face showed his distaste for the texture and the comment. His tone was aggressive. "They call me *what*?"

Pretty loved the power of the unknown. Mr. Patterson had never seemed fazed by anything until now. He controlled the whole ship. He stayed in his office and peeked his head out from time to time to scare a few, but if people really paid attention they would know that. He let his pen do the talking. It talked about raises and firings and promotions. Mr. Patterson always remained in control, even when the ship seemed to be sinking.

Mr. Patterson's thick fingers strummed against his desk. Pretty picked up the pattern and bobbed his head every time he heard the thud. He wasn't going to answer automatically. He felt the transition of power. He had something Mr. Patterson wanted. The knowledge of Mr. Patterson's self. Mr. Patterson thought everyone loved him. He thought no one ever said anything bad about him. Sure he ran this ship like a slave one, but he gave out great Christmas gifts. He gave rewards like Scooby snacks when people met quotas. He pampered on his own time.

Pretty held on to the information like an informant did to get a better deal. What was it worth to Mr. Patterson? He watched Mr. Patterson glance at him through his bluest eye.

Mr. Patterson's voice was huge. "Well?"

"Tell me your proposition first." Pretty wasn't going to let Mr. Patterson string this proposition out for hours. He wanted to know what was going on. He needed to know the particulars.

"Enough of the bullshit, Jarvis. This proposition benefits you more than it would me." He spoke slowly, and with conviction. "What do they call me?"

Pretty laughed. "Mr. Fatterson!" He fell back into his seat and awaited his response. He figured Mr. Patterson would want to know who it was. He thought Mr. Patterson would be angry and disturbed that someone would actually call him such names. Instead, Mr. Patterson chuckled loudly.

"They've always called me that. They couldn't think of anything new? I've heard that all of my life." He patted his stomach. "Well, since I've grown this. A stomach doesn't make a man, Jarvis."

Pretty laughed with him. This was the first thing they'd ever shared. And it happened to come at Mr. Patterson's expense.

"Come back to my office at exactly one-thirty if you want to hear the proposition," he said plainly. He offered Pretty the door. He knew that he'd put enough in Pretty's head to stimulate it. He never said what it was, and he knew that would get Pretty interested. He couldn't run a ship so tight without being smart.

*   *   *

At one-thirty Pretty knocked twice.

"Come in, Jarvis."

Pretty walked in and found Mr. Patterson standing by a makeshift bar, with a drink in hand. The shabby silver cart housed two big bottles of liquor, a long slender bottle of red wine, and three glasses: one shot glass, a wineglass, and a wide glass people used when they swirled around expensive scotch.

Mr. Patterson held his glass in the air. "Scotch, Jarvis?"

Pretty stopped in his tracks. He looked up toward the ceiling and searched for hidden cameras. "No, thank you. I'm good."

Mr. Patterson noticed the apprehension and walked near. "Who runs this establishment, Jarvis?" He took great pleasure in saying the name "Jarvis." He knew he wanted to be called Pretty, but it wouldn't be by him. Every chance he got, he would let Pretty's government name put him in his place.

Pretty found the antique mirror again and tightened his tie. He pounded his braids. "Of course you run this. I don't doubt that."

"Well, have a drink, Jarvis." He walked back toward the bar. He held up an empty glass. "What do you drink?"

"Henny."

Mr. Patterson's laugh was full of pity. He not only looked down on Pretty's apprehension to drink, he looked down on his choice of beverage. He needed a go-getter, but Pretty wasn't biting. He needed to get to the crux of this black man.

"Who drinks Henny, Jarvis?"

Pretty's tone was defensive. "The brothers I hang with."

"The *brothers* you hang with?" He poured Pretty a drink. "Do the brothers you hang with drink the good stuff?"

Pretty accepted the beverage and put it to his nose. "Is this the good stuff?"

"Taste it."

Pretty put it to his mouth and before he took a sip, Mr. Patterson interrupted, "Toast first, Jarvis." He held his glass in the air. Pretty's glass made contact with Mr. Patterson's. Mr. Patterson continued, "Let's toast to a proposition you cannot turn down, Jarvis."

Pretty remained silent and took a huge gulp. He gagged, choked, and spit out the remains that didn't go down. "Damn! What is this shit?"

Mr. Patterson laughed and handed him a napkin. "Wipe up your mess, Jarvis." He took a sip of his own and uttered, "You gotta crawl before you can walk, son."

Pretty wiped his mouth with the back of his hand. "What is this?"

Mr. Patterson held his glass in the air. "This, my friend, is the good stuff." He took another sip. "This is Johnny Walker Black. Thirty dollars a shot at the bar."

"Well it tastes like crap."

"Everything tastes like crap until you get used to it. This warms the throat and soothes the soul, Jarvis." He put his glass down and offered Pretty a seat. "You ready?"

Pretty took his seat.

"I have a great deal for you, Jarvis." He closed his eyes and calculated with silence. He snapped himself out of his thoughts and continued, "I am willing to pay you three thousand dollars. Can you use three thousand dollars?"

This got Pretty's attention. His back stiffened. "Yes." His eyebrow shot up. He eased back and looked toward the door. "What do I have to do?"

Mr. Patterson pressed the intercom. "Can you send the party in, Ms. Randolph?"

The secretary answered politely.

Pretty readied himself for anything. He sat on edge, his weight rested on his toes. He interlocked his hands and waited.

The door opened slowly.

Pretty's hands went to his head. He twisted the ends of his braids and tapped his foot. He began to sweat.

Mr. Patterson grinned boastfully as he stood and extended his hand. His voice brimmed with pride. "This, Jarvis, is my wife. Tamanda Patterson."

Mrs. Patterson strode in as if she had just jumped off a high horse. She smelled expensive and looked rich. She appeared to own something. She walked with patient steps toward her husband. She reached her destination and gave him adequate affection. Their kiss was cursory; their hug was even worse.

Mr. Patterson switched hands and introduced Pretty. "My dear, this is Jarvis." He turned back to his wife. "Jarvis, this is my proposition." He walked around his desk and poured a glass of wine. Mrs. Patterson accepted his offering. She didn't kick her feet up as he did; instead, she folded her legs and fell into the throes of his leather. She took a sip of wine and closed her eyes. She inhaled deeply and let it out silently.

Pretty sat in disbelief. He looked behind; his eyes transfixed on Mrs. Patterson. Her skin was as creamy as whole milk, and her hair was as short as his, and blond. She had many features that were youthful. He assumed she was in her early thirties and regularly visited the gym. Her cleavage brought men near; her beauty made them fall. She opened her eyes and reached for her pocketbook. She moved her lips seductively as she painted them with an earthy tone of brown. She pushed her compact below her eyes and stole a peek at Pretty. She couldn't hide her smile.

Pretty watched Mr. Patterson as he sat on the edge of the desk watching the incident unfold. His eyes went from his wife's legs to Pretty's expression. He nodded his head, cleared his throat, and began, "Should I explain what I would like, Jarvis?"

"Let's see what the lady would like, Mr. Patterson," Pretty said.

Mr. Patterson ignored Pretty's feeble attempt at assertion. He asked his wife, "Do you like what you see, dear?"

Mrs. Patterson pressed her lips to a napkin and observed her print on it. Her lips were oversized and perfectly shaped. Her tongue glided easily against her teeth and she inhaled. She folded her legs seductively and let her fingers trail down her athletic calf. She spoke slowly, "I do like what I see, Geronimo."

Pretty snickered. Mr. Patterson shot him a quick glance. It stopped the laugh, but it wasn't potent enough to erase the information. No one knew Mr. Patterson's first name, and now Pretty had something to combat his disrespectful tone when he spat "Jarvis" like Pretty was his slave. Pretty glanced at the desk and reread the designer golden nameplate. G. TONY PATTERSON.

Pretty called his horse, laughed, and jumped high. "If I do accept this opportunity, I would prefer to be called Pretty." He paused. "Can you do that, *Geronimo*?" Pretty watched Mrs. Patterson's reaction. She was appreciative of his thriving nature.

Mr. Patterson exchanged glances with his wife. She won. He twitched and mumbled something incoherent under his breath before nodding in agreement. "Anything else, Pretty?" The word stumbled from his mouth.

Pretty felt more comfortable than earlier. He felt the change in power. He walked around the room, his pace full of questions. He wanted to be a part of three thousand dollars. He realized Mr. Patterson didn't make the decisions. He broke silence. "What do you want from *me*, Mrs. Patterson?"

She popped up and offered Mr. Patterson his seat. He begrudgingly obliged. She walked around and sat on the edge of the desk, watching Pretty shuffle in his chair as she positioned herself in front of him. She offered him a peek.

Her tone was stimulating. "I love black men," she started. Mr. Patterson coughed, and nearly hacked up a lung before settling back in his seat. She looked behind, shot him a glance of pity, and returned her stare to Pretty. "And you are a *beautiful* black man." Her eyes raped.

Pretty knew this feeling. He'd felt this power before. He unloosened his tie, and wrestled with his shirt before a few chest hairs snuck out. "I *am* beautiful, bitch!" he agreed.

Mr. Patterson waddled to the edge of his seat. "*Bitch?* What a minute!"

Mrs. Patterson held her hand up, not turning around. "*You* wait a minute, Geronimo. I can handle this."

Mr. Patterson must didn't know that she could handle it. He hesitantly relaxed and sat back.

Mrs. Patterson looked at Pretty with confusion and closed her legs. "Did you just call me a bitch?"

"Yeah!" He didn't hesitate. His look told her that he would do it again if given the opportunity.

She turned to Mr. Patterson, and then back toward Pretty. Her blank stare didn't waver.

For a second, everything went deathly still.

Mrs. Patterson broke the silence when she jumped to her feet. She asked Pretty to stand.

He lifted himself up and stood a foot taller than her, arms folded.

She inhaled his body. "Show me why they call you Pretty."

He laughed. It wasn't that easy. She called the shots, but he gave the bullets direction. He held out his hand for payment; his eyes never left hers.

She adjusted her shirt. She showed more cleavage and her lips pouted. She imposed her sexuality on her young thug.

"No disrespect, Mrs. Patterson, but I got to get paid before I release the hound." His joke had serious intent.

She immediately snapped her fingers. Her movements were mechanical, like she had done this before. Mr. Patterson reached for an envelope in his suit jacket; his movements were choppy and unsure. It appeared to be his first and last time in this arena.

Mr. Patterson retrieved the envelope and slid it across the desk. Mrs. Patterson scooped it up and banged it against the palm of her hand. She offered Pretty the envelope. "Will this do?"

He accepted it and pushed it deep into his back pocket.

"You're not going to check?" she asked.

"I don't need to check. My bitches never short me." He knew what she wanted. He used the word "bitch" like a tool to put women like her in their proper place. He figured Mr. Patterson wanted to call her quite a few "bitches," but they had their parameters set, and it was hard to move in that direction after years of having it one way.

"Now ask me again." Pretty paused. "Nicely."

Mr. Patterson watched in awe. Pretty saw the way he scrambled with the air to get eye contact with him. Pretty looked in Mr. Patterson's direction, but not directly. It pissed him off. Pretty would fuck with his head for all those times he called him Jarvis and meant it. Pretty figured that Mrs. Patterson would be careful not to let Mr. Patterson interfere with their situation. She was no different than the other white women that Pretty was around. They had dated white men all of their lives and wanted to see what the myth was all about. They thought that black men were hung like stallions. They thought that black men were unruly. They assumed that black men made love differently and fucked much differently than the rest of the world. Pretty put on his "black man" suit and gave the bitch what she wanted.

She changed her tone and spoke quietly, "Can you show me why they call you Pretty?"

They were a few feet away from each other. Pretty closed the gap. She smelled fresh, like a floral powder. Her cleavage showed freckled C's or possible D's trying to break free.

Pretty's demand was low-key, "Ask him to leave us first." Now he gave Mr. Patterson eye contact. Pretty's lips creased in victory as Mrs. Patterson spun around and ordered Mr. Patterson out. He put up no fight as he once again slowly lifted himself from his chair. He went to the bar and finished his scotch and, without uttering a word, walked out the door.

"Is that better, sir?" she asked, proud of showing her authority at a split second's notice.

"Sure." He looked toward the bar and pointed. "*Now* I'll have a drink."

"What kind of drink would you like, sir?"

"The same kind your *husband* had." Pretty slung the word around like mud.

She washed out the glass Mr. Patterson had used and filled it halfway with scotch. She brought it with her and watched him sip. He took smaller swallows. The fact that he wasn't used to the finer liquor made him more appealing. She wanted something short of the jungle.

He ushered her over with his finger. "Come here."

She followed direction. She wanted to touch his braids. She wanted to see if he had tattoos. She wanted him to rap about the hood. She wanted everything that MTV and the NBA had to offer.

"Why do you want this to happen?" he asked.

Her head dropped. Embarrassment crept in. She remained silent.

He sipped. It didn't burn as much as it had before. "Did you hear me?"

She whispered, "Yes, I did, sir."

He moved close. She smelled the liquor. "I don't want a whisper." He invaded her space. Got real personal. "I want the boardroom beast. I want the wild wife that can't get what she needs from her husband. I want the bitch that I know you can be. Can you give me that voice?"

Her voice reached a higher decibel. "Yes, you can get that woman, *sir.*"

"Well, why do you want to be a part of this?" he growled.

"Because my husband can't fuck, sir," she shouted.

Pretty lost his composure. "Huh?"

She stood proud even though she gave away part of her family's secret. "He cannot fuck, sir."

"So, why me?"

She gave no eye contact. The schoolgirl in her came out.

"I said, why me, bitch!"

Her answer was short and aggressive. "Because you're black, sir."

He pointed toward the door. "There are a few black men out there. You could have any one of them. Why did your husband call *me* into his office?"

"Because I asked him to." She paused. Irritation flared. *"Sir."*

"And how do you know me?"

"I don't."

"Well, why did you ask for me?"

"Because *you* are the one that they call Pretty, sir."

"Who are *they*?"

She stepped out of character. "Does it matter who they are?"

"I ask the questions, bitch!"

She fell back into place. "I'm sorry, sir." She warmed to his commands. She ate his voice. "The they that I refer to is my good friend Mrs. Charleston, sir."

Pretty coughed. He knew Mrs. Charleston as the lady with the unenviable task of time sheets. She was in Human Resources. She was Oriental and built like a sumo wrestler. How she knew his nickname was Pretty, he didn't know.

"I know Mrs. Charleston. And she told you what?"

"She told me that they call you Pretty, sir."

"Do you know why they call me Pretty?"

"I can guess. But I would love for you to show me why they call you Pretty, sir."

Pretty moved to her ear. He tugged it his way before words found the inside. "I'll show you why, but not here." Her body language showed hesitation. He took it as defiance. They got their signals crossed. "We fuck at my place." He checked his watch. His tone was disrespectful. "I parked in back. Tell Geronimo that you'll be back in a couple of hours." He pulled her near. "No questions. We do it my way. Understand?" His question was obviously rhetorical, because he didn't wait for an answer. He strolled out. Her horse turned into a pumpkin.

He beeped his car horn as soon as she came out. She hurried over and waited for him to open the door. His chivalrous nature never made the trip. He flung the door open from the inside. She started to speak; his hand stopped her. He drove down a couple of streets before making a quick right down Thurgood Road. She'd heard about it. She watched the crowds change before her eyes. Near the bank, people were light as the day. As he rolled closer and closer toward downtown, their shades got dark, like her fantasies. She didn't mind seeing it from a distance. She realized her fantasy was reality when his car came to a screeching halt near a bodega where three black men sat outside smoking and playing dominoes.

"Get the fuck out!"

She clutched her pocketbook. He cut the engine, grabbed his dick, and slid his seat back. He reached overhead and flipped his visor down. A tightly rolled cigar fell into his lap. He pushed his car lighter in and waited. He pressed his cigar into the cave of the lighter. He blew a steady stream her way. She choked and remembered the smell. Her ex-boyfriend used to smoke weed every day after class and before sex. She likened Pretty to him.

"Get the fuck out!"

She looked toward the men who continued to play games. "I'm not getting out here."

Pretty placed his smoke inside the ashtray and started his car up again. He never looked her way. "I'll take you back."

She watched him reach for the gears. She grabbed his hand. "Wait. Just tell me why I have to get out here?"

Pretty finally blessed her with eye contact. She felt his connection again. She watched him put his cigar back to his mouth. She dreamed about the places his full lips could kiss. His eyebrows were thick and tamed. His jaw was square and his goatee rode it from ear to ear. She wanted to ride him from here to there. His interest wasn't the same as before. She wanted to get him back to that level and she knew she had to eat a few slices of humble pie. Resistance always made her come quicker.

He took a slow drag. His car filled with chocolate flavor. He rubbed his moustache and watched her squirm. He played his part. He would ask for his Oscar later. "You want the hood, right?"

Her banter was awkward. "I don't know." Her fingers trailed his thigh.

He slapped them away. "No touching. I want you to walk down the block, go to number 114, ring the third bell from the bottom, and walk upstairs to apartment 3." She looked up and down the street. He figured she had more questions. He jumped in and pointed behind her. "Walk down that way. Don't talk to anyone. When you're in the crib, I want you to strip in the middle of the floor. You got it?"

She nodded. He reached over and opened her door. She got out with hesitancy. He watched her look around before pulling her coat shut. She hurried past the old men and began her journey down the darkest street in the neighborhood. He spun his car around and drove to his house, never once checking on her. He jogged up the few flights of stairs and rushed inside. He put a few things away before settling in his favorite chair. He lit his smoke again, and waited. He listened to the hustle and bustle of the street and wondered where she was. She would probably jump out of her skin when she passed the Rodriguezes'. They kept their vicious pit bulls outside on a leash that was long enough for them to munch on those who were too scared to walk near the street. Dallas and his boys would dcfinitcly harass that fresh white meat when she strolled by. No telling who would jump out of the alley a few houses up and ask to shine her shoes for a buck. He knew she needed the whole experience of the hood, not just the dick. Years ago Pretty would have done her right in the office and took her money right then and there. Now she would get it where and when he wanted to give it. He would show her what separated him from the rest of the pigeons she was used to dealing with. He turned off all of the lights and left a blue track light on. He positioned it in the middle of the floor. He impressed himself with his ability to make women perform at a higher level. He lit his cigar again and blew smoke up his own ass.

He heard noises, and then the steady patter of feet approaching. He pulled his chair behind the light. He watched the door swing open slowly. Her movements showed hesitancy, perhaps unsure that she was in the right spot. He gave assurance with a "Hello." She heard his voice, relaxed, but still stood motionless by the door. She looked out of place with her expensive clothes, her timid smile, and her unsteady stance. She wobbled. He barked out orders. She followed his directions and walked toward the spotlight. She looked better under the blue light. It gave her color and presence. It made her shape glisten. Made her feel like she was onstage. She would transform into his bitch on command. She wished her husband *made* her do what he wanted to do. He always asked.

She heard shuffling and then soft music played. "Strip!"

She whispered something to herself, lowered her head, and raised it with renewed vigor. Her top fell. He couldn't tell what color mixed with blue made red, so he concentrated on the bra's design. It was silky, half-cut, and her nipples made a strong attempt to burst through. They were the size of nickels, her breasts like cantaloupes. He loved his fruits and vegetables. He watched her undo her pants and ease them off. Her thighs were well trained and her skin was a smooth tan all the way through. He thought about Mr. Patterson. Thought about what he was going to do with his wife. Wondered what he would do when he got done and went back to work tomorrow. His hand went to his pocket and traced the swell of the envelope. He imagined if she'd come this far, no telling how far she would go. Three thousand was great, but more was better. He decided to give her that "string you out" dick. He knew if she was willing to pay for a stranger, she would pay dearly for "That Nigga!"

He filled his space with gray smoke and pushed it into her blue sphere. She acted like it was Febreze, the way she inhaled and closed her eyes, swaying to the music. He walked over, grabbed her attention and seized the moment. His grip was demanding; his scowl spoke volumes of what was about to transpire. She let her arm go limp inside his hand. She gave in to her money.

With a flick of the wrist, he flung her around and checked

out her goods. He rubbed his chin. He was going to enjoy laying pipe to her dreams. She wanted the hood; he would give her a reason to come back. He pushed her to the ground by leading her with her shoulders. She popped back up and looked down. There was nothing to comfort her fall. Nothing to soften the blow.

"You want a pillow?" he asked. He was more affectionate than earlier.

She smiled. "Yes."

His mood went back to being distant and obtrusive. "Husbands give pillows. Niggas give direction. That's what you want, right?"

She didn't know what she wanted. She wanted to control his controlling behavior. Her mind wandered; her fantasy was interrupted.

He noticed regression and picked up the pace.

"I'll show you why they call me Pretty," he said as he reached for his belt.

Her eyes dropped to his hands. She watched him expertly pull his belt without looking. She loved introductions. Most men whipped it out, hoping it would impress. He was different.

He slid his belt from around his waist and let it hit the ground. He watched her watch him. He knew she was into the slow, tantalizing introduction. She loved his ruggedness. She was intrigued by his name and its meaning. He would play it for all it was worth. Three thousand dollars' worth.

His commands were strengthened by his deep voice. "Get on your knees."

She followed his direction.

He wanted her hands behind her back. He barked for her to lift her head and close her eyes. "And open your fucking mouth."

She opened her mouth as wide as she could.

He corrected, "Open it slightly. I want my dick to fight through a closed mouth and reach for your tonsils." He laughed. "You do have tonsils, right?"

She opened her mouth and gave a loud "Ah." She closed her eyes and her mouth, finding his request easy to accomplish.

His voice was stronger and more determined. "You love black dick, right?"

Her voice got softer and weaker. "Yes, I do, sir."

He put his hands on his hips and beckoned her to open her eyes. "Release the hound, bitch!"

She hurriedly reached for his pants. She fumbled for a second before unsnapping the buttons. She brought her nose near him. She breathed his soul and kissed his stomach.

He snatched her head back. "You kiss when I say kiss. Understood?" He threw her head back to her.

"Yes, it is, sir." She reached for his pants again, and stopped short. "Is it okay if I continue, sir?"

"Dig it out," he ordered. "Slowly."

She pulled his underwear out with one hand, and with the

other, she dug deep. Her eyes slammed shut; her groan was seductive. She immediately withdrew her hand. Her hesitancy heightened his arousal. The print that outlined his piece throbbed through his pants. She could see it pulsate, jump, and then try to break free.

He admired his tool: His weapon of choice. He knew he had her exactly where he wanted. He just couldn't fuck it up. He had to keep her on the ropes with directness and sharp lashes of his tongue. He reminded himself not to get too comfortable and complacent. "Take this dick out, bitch!"

Her hand found a home back inside his pants. Her eyes slammed shut again and her nipples hardened. He stood above her and watched her growing nubs press against her bra. His rough fingers pinched her nipple before stroking it with tiny flicks of his forefinger. She almost came.

Her fingers held his piece tighter as her orgasm neared. She thought about a burglary to bring her high down. She wouldn't dare come so soon. Three thousand dollars was nothing, but it was enough for her to want to take her time. She grabbed the sides of his pants and slowly inched his jeans to his knees. She looked up and saw his "pretty." She drew back in amazement. Her eyes bulged at the size. Semi-hard, it hung from her eyes to her chin. The thickness was not to be denied. Her tiny hands barely fit around. Her thumb and fingers struggled to meet in the middle. And it was the color of wet wood. Darker than his legs, but lighter than his knees. It was pretty. Pretty fucking big. Pretty fucking chocolate. Pretty fucking thick. And pretty fucking straight. It hung to the middle. It throbbed toward the top.

She brought it to her face. Her moan was sadistic, like she never had dick near her face.

"I want to eat it. And I want you to tell me how, sir."

He held it in his hand. It was the same color as his hand. "Eat the head," he ordered.

Her mouth raced for the tip. The contrast was stimulating to her. Her white skin near the rich darkness of his dick proved enticement. She'd fallen in love with the difference years ago on a ski trip. Pretty never fell in love with the color nor the contrast, only the results. White chicks gave him what he needed. A few tried to be bossier than normal, but without slave papers, they would get hard dick and bubble gum.

She licked his head. It blossomed and got thicker. She loved portabella mushrooms, especially chocolate ones. She kissed the head, attempting to swallow his pride. His grip remained around the top of his dick. He wouldn't allow her lips to go any further down. With one hand he grabbed her hair. He couldn't get much in his grasp, so he gripped the back of her head and turned her face to the side. "I want to see those white lips on my dark dick." He knew she wanted to hear his verbal assault.

She massaged his head with her tongue. With every light flicker, she moaned like he was her favorite flavor. Black macadamia nut. He stood above and admired her work. He marveled at her enthusiasm for pleasing him. He was sure she could hear him beating his chest.

Her eyes never left him. "Like this, sir?"

"Just like that, bitch!" He released more of his brown.

She was greedy with the access she was given. She engulfed to where his knuckle began and pressed to go deeper. He gave permission in increments. She wouldn't get more than he was willing to give right then.

She dripped below. She could feel juice creep down her lips and sink between her hairs. She couldn't get enough of his thickness. She loved the way he pumped her mouth. The way he gripped her head and yanked it to the side. She wanted to be manhandled. She needed to be disrespected in a respectful way. She eased the top half of his dick into her mouth. She remembered what it felt like to be attacked on a ski trip by two black men wearing masks. It was a planned attack. She hadn't planned on it changing her life though. Now she desired more attacks. Her appetite for sex was borderline disturbed. That's what had brought her here. On her knees. Begging for unknown dick. Loving it. Paying for it.

He pushed her away. Her mouth remained open. He left the blue for darkness. He came back with his chair and ashtray. He asked her to get out of the light. She was amongst the shadows while his skin branded a crystallized brown with a blue hue. He placed the chair in the middle and sat on his throne. She watched him strip to the barest of bare, minus his boxers, which felt of silk and hid his jewel. He moved his ashtray close and put his face near the fire. He smoked his peace pipe and ordered her back.

"Lick my balls," he directed. His voice echoed. There was a blue light, an ashtray, and no furniture. It was toasty and smelled of weed. He spread his legs, opening up his invitation.

She nestled between his legs. She put one of his balls in her mouth and hummed. It tingled and sent his piece toward the ceiling. She prided herself on making a man want nothing more than to come in her mouth. She stroked him with her hand while she continued to hum a melody. She searched deeper with her tongue. She listened to his breath. She kept her eyes open as she let her tongue trail up his thickness to where his head expanded. Her fingers looked pale in comparison to his shadowy flesh. She loved chocolate. Loved to make a black man feel what they were missing.

He loved to make a white woman bow down and accept his dick. There was no difference between when a white woman did it and a sista, but it gave him vindication. He would save his love for black women and give the white ones his anger, resentment, and bullshit. She loved the way shit tasted anyways. That's what brought her here.

"Can I ride you?" she whispered in between huge gulps of him.

She heard his laugh. She shrank. She'd paid for it and he didn't want to give her the product. She repeated the question with more determination.

His laugh was the same. "I tell you what you can do, bitch!" He waited for her to say her part.

She read from the same script. "Please tell me what can I do, sir."

He blew smoke about the room and let out a hearty laugh, exposing his desires of sex.

She was shocked by his idea of sex. She ran from it.

Thought it was comical at first, but when he didn't laugh she knew he was real. She asked him to repeat himself. He blew smoke in her face and asked her if she wanted to leave. She wagged her head. He told her to get to it.

She bit her lip and took more breaths, even asked him to blow smoke in her mouth. This sexual experience was going to be new. It didn't excite her; but then again, neither did getting smashed by two unknown black guys . . . at first. She was willing to be a full slave. She was willing to give all she had. He told her she had three seconds to move her ass.

She used all of her time. On the third she carefully placed the head inside her mouth. She eased all the way down until his hairs rest on her chin. She felt his hand on the back of her head. He held her there and told her that she would remain until she gave him what he wanted. She couldn't breathe. With every slight gag she felt his hand push down on her head. She had never done anything so outlandish in her life as she was about to do. He requested something new. Her eyes slammed shut and her body shuddered. With all the thoughts running through her head, she never realized the moistness between her legs. She thought of nothing but how to please this man. She thought about the amount of come she would receive if she did as told. It excited and scared her at the same time.

His hand was joined by another hand. Both pushed her head down to his groin. She gagged but couldn't get up. Tears streamed down her eyes and for some reason she did not want to open them. She couldn't open them. She heard him bark, "Do it right now, bitch!"

She lifted the bottom half of her body and positioned it

over his leg. Her head was locked to his dick; she gripped his legs and steadied herself. She straddled his left leg and felt him pulsate in her mouth. His grip was lethal; her jaw throbbed now like his penis. She had never experienced this, but it excited her. He fucked the back of her throat and told her it was now or never. She thought about her husband. Then the two black men. Then Pretty's dick as she squatted over his foot.

He pulled her head back, her mouth released his goods. It stood perfectly straight. She tried to catch her breath, but couldn't quite do it, even though she'd learned how to inhale and exhale at an early age. He was losing his patience with her inability to do her job. He stood up and ordered her to stand before him.

She wiped her mouth and did as she was told. She bowed her head in resignation. This was different. She would never bow before anyone unless she wanted to. She had no desire to show discontent.

His reaction was the same, he could tell she was out of place. No one would do her mentally the way he planned. Physically was imaginable, almost usual. He didn't allow her to anticipate. She wouldn't know when ketchup would hit her hamburger.

He flung his shirt to the ground and walked toward the darkness. No more melodies flowed from the distant. Now voices eased between repetitive beats and the flow was angry. They spoke about pimping and teaching lessons in the hood. She looked out the window and noticed there were bars on it. Whoever rapped in the background must've lived around here. Pretty came back into the blue and folded his arms. "You pay for what?"

She stood, humbled and unpolished. Her breasts rested on her pulled-down bra; her panties lay crumpled near her feet. "I pay for whatever you want, sir."

"I will tell you your job again. I want it done to the tee." He repeated himself and sat down in the chair.

Humiliation filled her air. She didn't care. She transformed and reached the ashtray and puffed from the same cigar. Surprisingly, she didn't choke. She smoked like a veteran.

She placed it in his mouth. Even watched him take two long pulls and blow it in her face. This time she opened her mouth and took in long gray streams of gumption. Her eyes had a different look, almost distant. He was heavily limp. She engulfed him until his piece hit the back of her throat. She placed her hand around the rest that remained. He was thicker than any. She placed her hands on both legs and waited for him to begin. When he did, it felt different. She found a rhythm.

"I need noise, bitch!"

She slurped on command. She allowed fluid to trail down the sides of her hand as she pumped feverishly. Excitement replaced displeasure. She positioned herself over his leg and gave him what he asked for.

He grabbed her shoulders and ushered her closer to the ground. Her back was damp, her shoulders tight. He sensed her desire for connection, but she would connect when he said so. He would allow her a piece of history. His story. Earlier he watched her dance around the request for "foot love." Now she appeared ready to dance at his request. He'd watched a friend do something similar before and he'd promised himself the attempt. Part of it was curiosity. The other part was, he wanted something demeaning. He forced his words, hoping they would spew like a whip.

She sucked and braced herself with one hand while the other found his foot. She steadied herself over it, letting it touch her lips. She shook violently. Lost most of her composure. Was undecided on rhythm. Above her, he laughed. He was unconcerned.

She gathered herself, found his movement and matched it. She noticed his spasm and the game was on. Her squat was determined. She slow-stroked his dick with intent to disperse. She could feel herself dripping in waves. She felt his toe again, but this time she allowed herself to completely devour it. It felt strange at first, almost like a cross between a finger and a small penis. Above she felt his body tighten. That gave her the energy to come raining down again. She quivered and bucked on cue.

He felt her mood change. It excited him. Made him want to fuck her back with his toe. He arched his foot to expose more of his flesh.

She sat on his foot and began to squeeze as she sucked him harder. For a second it felt good. She would thank him for the introduction to this kind of sex later. Her back arched and she began to grind slowly, rotating her hips.

He wasn't ready for this. He felt the transition of power. He felt every piece of her insides. They felt like something good. She was warm inside. It was a feeling he hadn't experienced, but a feeling he would want again.

She practiced as he preached. He wasn't barking any more instructions, so she took over. "Do you like this?"

"S-s-shut the fuck up . . ."

She lifted herself as he spoke. He couldn't finish. She rode his toe and mashed her face to his hairs. She saved the deep throat until last. She released his hound. "Shut the fuck up what?"

He lost his timing. He couldn't decipher between the suck and the stroke. Felt like he was having a threesome by himself. He had to finish. Had to call her bitch when he ended his sentence. It wouldn't come out while she fucked and sucked him. He grabbed her shoulders. They weren't tight. They listened. "Shut the fuck up, bitch!" It didn't sound as potent as before.

As soon as the word "bitch" dripped from his mouth she raised herself and came crashing down on his foot. She pulled him from her mouth and sucked the side of his meat. He bent over and massaged her athletic thighs. It was soothing, almost caring.

She removed his hands with a flick of her wrist. "No rubbing. Let's keep this impersonal, no feelings, you know?"

The thickness of his piece came down as his ego did. She pumped them both up with strong squats and an aggressive shake of his shaft as her lips found the tip. She made love to his head and fucked the shit out of his toe.

He readjusted. "Good, bitch."

She rode him for all she was worth. She closed her eyes

and replaced everything. His toe was the larger black man on the ski trip that fucked her until exhaustion. His dick wasn't as big as the other, but the winding of his hips and the hitting of her spot, and knowing it, did the job. With every ride of his toe, she imagined her black assailant filling her from behind. The dick she sucked remained Pretty's. It was still the prettiest she had ever seen. So straight. So thick. And it tasted of fudge.

Her pussy felt like warm weather. He tried to think the feeling away, but she fucked with precision. She bucked and snapped her pussy on his toe. His friend had told him, "Imagine what your toe would feel like." They spoke of the sensation your toe has and the feeling a great pussy would have. It was a perfect match. Her face traveled to his balls. She licked underneath. He spread his legs. He held on to what dignity he had left. Gave her permission to do what she was already doing. "Lick my balls, bitch."

She licked underneath them. She felt him jerk. She went back to his head.

"Suck my dick, bitch!" he commanded.

His commands were off by a second, like a bad Chinese movie.

She found the perfect beat. She gave him every bit of soul she didn't possess. She faked it.

He closed his eyes and it felt like he was inside his girl, Tiffany. Her box was tighter than Scrooge's wallet. She knew how to squeeze before he entered. The bitch in front of him made sharp waves come over him. Her oral was to die for. She must've taught a class. He felt like her student. "Bitch!"

He arched his toe. He wanted to fuck her but didn't want to take anything out.

She slurped. And rode.

He called her high horse. She deserved it. "Bitch!"

She never answered. She figured it was rhetorical. He grabbed her head. He wasn't concerned about her comfort. She tightened her mouth and sucked him like a vacuum. The black man in back picked up the pace. Pretty grabbed her hair and brought her closer. She felt the strength in his stroke.

She gagged. Rode his toe for all it was worth. She reached another high.

Beautiful Tiffany clenched her pussy and the white bitch gagged. He lost sight. Everything was black. Her mouth professed her love for his meat with moans. His dick tightened in its skin. It expanded and he could feel the pressure. He grabbed her ears and brought himself closer. He invaded her throat. She allowed him. "Fucking dumb bitch," he yelled.

She was a good bitch, the way she joined him. They both had threesomes. She forgot about the pain in her back, the pulling of her hair, the stubby stabbing of her pussy, and the vile names he called her.

It all meshed. His grip reached her throat and went to her shoulders.

She allowed this.

"Shit!" was screamed by both.

He pumped and released. He held her head still. She quit

stroking his digit and allowed him to coat her mouth. He tasted sweet. Almost beautiful.

When he was done, so was she. She had mastered the art of the quiet come. She lifted herself and cleaned his toe with her panties. She never looked his way. Servants weren't supposed to give eye contact. The movie wasn't over. She would get her supporting actress role later.

She stuffed her panties in her bag and walked to the door.

He sat in the middle of the blue hue like a weathered saxophone player after a long set. He never looked her way.

She opened the door. Her smile was absent. "I'll be waiting by the bodega on the corner whenever you're ready, sir."

He looked up and smiled. "Watch the Rodriguezes' dog."

He paused.

"Bitch."

HOMEY, LOVER, FRIEND
Thomas Long

"Wake ya tired ass up, girl," Chastity yelled into the phone.

"I ain't sleep, fool. I'm just sitting up in here chillin'. Waiting on nothing. What's up with you?" her friend Mikala asked.

"I'm ain't doing nothing special. What you getting into tomorrow?"

"I'm probably going out to Arundel Mills Mall to do some shopping. Why? Are you tryin' to tag along?"

"Hell, yeah! The one thing I like best—next to gettin' some dick—is spending money on new clothes!"

"Girl, you crazy like a fox. Let's hook up around one o'clock. I need to get outta this house just to clear my head, ya know what I'm sayin'?"

"Is that nigga still trippin'? You need to get rid of his ass before it's too late. Jamel ain't the only fish in the sea. You can find you another man who knows how to twirk that thing," Chastity said, putting her nose into Mikala's personal business.

"Nah, me and my boo are gonna work things out. We've been together too long to break up. All we need is more time to grow, and everything will be straight between us. Our relationship is gonna go back to the way things used to be," Mikala said, like she was trying to convince herself even more than she wanted to convince Chastity.

Her friend laughed. "If you say so, but that sure wouldn't be me. If a man can't do me right in the bedroom with some good dick, then he ain't gettin' nuthin' but a one-way ticket outta my front door. I need a nigga that knows how to work that *Magic Stick*! That is, unless he knows how to eat the pussy good enough to make me cum. Then I might let him stay for a while."

"C, you are so nasty. Let me worry about me and my man. I'm about to bounce. I'ma see you tomorrow, homey."

"Aight, have it your way. If you need me to hook you up with one of my sexperts, let me know. I'ma get up with you tomorrow, though," Chastity responded, and hung up the phone.

Mikala and Chastity had been best friends since middle school. They were both fine dark-skinned sisters, but Chastity was shorter than Mikala by about four inches, even though her long legs made her seem taller than she was. Chastity had a slim figure, but what she lacked in the ass department she more than made up for with her C-cup breasts.

She was the more outgoing and off-the-hook of the two. She was open about her sexuality and made it clear that she loved to get her freak on. Men were her primary preference, but she wasn't too shy to fool around with a woman if one came along that sparked her interest. She wasn't slutty about how she carried herself, but she was blunt enough to tell a man what she wanted up front when it came to having sex. If a man wanted to be with her then he had better bring his A game to the bedroom or she would let him know his skills were whack. She kept at least three male playthings on hand at all times, so when one of them acted up she always had some backup dick waiting on the side.

Mikala, on the other hand, was more reserved when it came to dealing with men. She believed in the one-man-for-one-woman theory, and had stuck to that since she began dating. She was all about true love and putting in hard work to maintain a relationship. Like her mother, she had that old-school thinking, believing a man and his woman should stay together through the hard times, no matter what. That's why she'd put up with Jamel's bullshit for so long. But right about now he was beginning to test her patience. Her needs weren't being met in the sheets, and she

was one sexually frustrated sista. If she didn't love her man
so much she'd be out in the street searching for his substi-
tute.

Mikala laid across the bed in the plush condominium that
she shared with Jamel. She thought about their relationship
and wondered why things had been going so wrong for the
past few months. Jamel used to fill her with so much joy, but
now she was starting to wonder if she was just putting up
with his shit just to be in a relationship. Still, she was willing to put her heart and soul into working things out with
Jamel, but the way he was fronting on her was just crazy.

Whenever she tried to talk about their problems, Jamel
pushed her away. He worked long hours on the job and when
he came home, all he wanted to do was eat and sleep. The
weekends were no better because he was either too busy
running ball or shooting pool with his boys. They used to get
their swerve going at least three times a week. Now she was
lucky if he fucked her three times in a month. And whenever
they did have sex, it was usually just a quickie, with him
bustin' off in five minutes and rollin' over to crash right afterward. This nigga wasn't even considerate enough to let
her get her thing off before he did. Shit, Mikala was so horny
and in need of some good hard dick that she was about to explode.

She'd met Jamel while they were both attending Morgan
State University. Mikala had majored in Computer Engineering, while Jamel had studied Business Management.
Chastity, who shared some of the same classes as Jamel, introduced them and they'd hit it off instantly. After gradua-

tion they'd moved in together and Mikala had managed to get a six-figure job working for SciTech, the state's largest growing computer engineering firm, while Jamel worked for the federal government as a financial consultant. In the beginning, their relationship was banging. Two young, intelligent Black professionals with well-defined life goals. But the last few months had been rough as hell, and their future plans were in jeopardy of getting deaded if that niggah didn't clean up his act.

Mikala got up from the bed and lit a few sweet papaya mango candles she'd placed throughout the room. The soft, sultry sounds of the latest mixed CD of Classic Slow Jams played outta the surround-sound speakers that were positioned in all four corners of the bedroom. She was wearing a pink thong and matching bra as she lay across the king-sized bed, smelling like just enough Black, by Kenneth Cole, to entice her man. It didn't matter what kind of attitude Jamel came home with, she was planning on having an all-night fuck fest with her man tonight. That is, until she looked at her phone and noticed the message light blinking.

"Hey, baby, it's me. I'm just calling to let you know that I'ma be home late tonight. Me and a few sons are gonna get some yak after work. Then we prolly gonna go shoot some pool. I don't know when I'ma get in, so don't wait up. I luh you, girl."

Mikala sat up, pissed. She tried to call him back to curse him out, but his phone went straight to voice mail because he always turned it off when he was having private time with his crew and didn't want to be disturbed.

Mikala stood up and looked at herself in her full-length mirror. She was ready to see herself looking ugly as hell, even though the mirror told her that was far from the truth. She was as fine as fine could be. She coulda been posing as a centerfold in somebody's hot magazine with her killa smile and full lips. Her long flowing hair, curvy legs, and D-cup breasts put people in the mind of that beautiful actress Kenya Moore. It was a damn shame for a woman with a body as off da chain as hers to have a man who dissed her in the sheets. While Jamel was out running the damn streets with his boys, Mikala was home alone and was gonna have to handle her own business if she wanted a nut tonight.

She reached under the bed and felt around for the shoe box where she kept her collection of intimate secrets. Jamel wasn't even up on her private stash. She used all kinds of sex toys to take care of that spot he neglected. She had warming massage oils, fruity-flavored whipped cream, handcuffs, and mad dildos that she's bought off of the Internet. Chastity had put her down with the website www.getyafreakon.com, and now she was a regular customer. She'd never used any of her toys with Jamel because he never wanted to try anything new with her.

Mikala's favorite sex toy was the Bullet. It was a small silver vibrator that had a cord attached to it with a control switch that allowed you to adjust the intensity of the vibration. It could go hard and fast, if you wanted to feel a throbbing motion like a man was pounding on your pussy nonstop, or it could go slow if you wanted to take your time to savor your orgasm. *That lil' gadget was the truth!* If the Bullet couldn't make a woman cum, then a bitch had something wrong with the nerves in her coochie!

Mikala held the Bullet in her hand and took a bottle of Pure Satisfaction oil outta her shoe box and then placed the box back under the bed. She slid off her thong and unhooked her bra to get a little bit more comfortable as she reclined on the silk sheets with her head resting on the fluffy pillows. She took a few drops of the oil and placed it on the tips of her fingers. She gently rubbed it on her clit and slowly the oil began to heat up. Goose bumps rose on her arms. She adjusted the level of the Bullet until it was just right and placed it up against her clit as her mind slid off into a world of ecstasy.

Within a few minutes, she could feel the juices begin to run from her warm vagina. She caressed her nipples one at a time. She lifted them toward her, then used her tongue to bring them to full attention as she licked and sucked with delight. Her ass cheeks clenched tighter as the Bullet vibrated. The sensual sounds coming from the stereo made the episode that much more erotic.

In her mind, Mikala was getting down with a masked stranger who packed a big dick. She'd had this fantasy many times before, and it got better each time she relived it. Since her man refused to address her needs, she used her imagination to create the ideal man that could do the job. At first, she felt like she was cheating on Jamel to have thoughts of sleeping with another man, but, over time, that feeling faded. She called the brothah in her fantasy Borne. He was baldheaded and had dark brown, island-tanned skin. Jailhouse tattoos were all over his chest and back. His hands were rough, like he worked construction or something, and they sent chills up and down her spine when he touched her flesh. He was muscular from head to toe and had an ass that she loved to dig her nails into. She didn't give a damn what Borne's face looked like because it was about the way he made her body feel and riding his big dick until she got hers.

As she got more aroused by the Bullet, she decided to take this fantasy to the next level. She slid it into her love cave, enjoying its magical powers as it pressed against her pussy walls. She let her fingers roam over her dripping-wet pussy, then placed them in her mouth to taste her own juices. The rush was unbelievable. She squeezed her eyes shut and pretended that the Bullet was Borne's dick going in and out of her with precision. Her fantasy seemed realer by the minute as her body played out a hot movie in which she was the star actress. Every stroke of Borne's penis made her feel like she had died and gone to heaven. She envisioned him turning her over on her back and digging himself deep inside of her as she grabbed hold of the headboard. Borne beat her pussy up just the way she liked it. Every position he put her in felt better than the previous one. *Damn, why can't Jamel make me feel like this! I need me a thug nigga in my life to do this pussy right!* she thought.

After she came for the third time, Mikala groaned as she imagined Borne pulling his dick out of her and smacking her across the face with it. In her fantasy, she was a pro at the head game, but in reality she was still learning how to do it right. Jamel didn't like head anyway. He refused to go down on her because he said oral sex was disgusting. Deep in her fantasy, Mikala got down to business and sucked Borne's dick to death before he released a tidal wave of liquid protein straight into her mouth. The sweet taste of his cum was better than Grandma's blueberry pie.

Borne returned the favor as he wrapped her legs around his neck and dug his tongue into her pussy with reckless abandon. Every time he licked her clit, her whole body jumped up off of the bed. When he sucked her pink sugar walls, she grabbed his head and screamed so loud she probably woke up her neighbors. After letting her come all over his face, Borne wiped his chin with a towel and got dressed. He walked out the front door without saying a word. Her fantasy man was gone for now, but Mikala knew he would return anytime she needed his services.

Satisfied, Mikala went into the bathroom and washed the Bullet off and put it back into the box. She changed the bedsheets, which were soaked with her juices, and got back under the covers to go to sleep. It was 1:00 A.M. Jamel still wasn't home. *That motherfucker is about to make me leave his ass if he don't give me what I need,* she thought as she drifted off to sleep.

* * *

The next few weeks were pretty much the same thing for Mikala. Every weekend Jamel was out in the streets while she was home all alone. Chastity had tried to get her to go out to the club with her on numerous occasions, but she refused. She chose to stay home and play with her best friend, the Bullet. She remained committed to trying to make things work in her relationship, even though the arguments between her and Jamel had become more intense. The whole situation came to a head one weekend when Jamel went out on a Friday night and didn't come back home until Monday morning, just in time to get ready for work.

Mikala was pissed. She'd called his cell all weekend and got no response, so she took Monday off from work just to lay in wait for him. Jamel had never stayed out all night before, let alone a whole weekend. He had crossed the line this time and totally disrespected their so-called relationship, and when Jamel put his key in the door Monday morning, she was laying across the living room sofa waiting for him.

"Where the fuck have you been, niggah?" she yelled. As he walked past her, she caught a whiff of women's perfume in a brand she didn't own.

"I was out with my boys. Don't question me. I ain't got time for this shit right now. I gotta go to work," he replied.

She couldn't believe he could be so bold and nonchalant after being out all weekend. All of her anger came flying out.

"You ain't got time? Well you better make time. You weren't out with ya boys this weekend. Chastity saw Bobby and Ju at the movies on a double date. You have the nerve to lie to me and come up in my house smelling like some other bitch? Oh, hell no, it ain't even going down like that!"

Mikala ran into the kitchen and grabbed a knife off the counter. Jamel sensed danger, ran into the bedroom, and locked the door behind him.

"Mikala, put that knife down. Are you crazy? Stop acting

like a maniac. Let's talk about this shit. It ain't what you think. I never meant for shit to happen like this!"

"You're fucking around on me and you want me to calm down? I've been sitting up in this house being faithful to your ass and this is what I get in return? You better open that fucking door. Who is the bitch?" Mikala screamed.

"Hell no, I ain't opening this door. Let's be for real, Mikala, this relationship has been headed nowhere for a minute now. I let it go on for this long because I didn't want to hurt ya feelings. Well since it's no longer a secret, her name is Shelby. She works with me. She's a secretary. I didn't plan on getting with her. We worked late together some nights and shit just happened."

"You fuckin' over me with a secretary? You know what, Jamel? You ain't even worth going to jail for. I ain't gonna stab ya ass. You could've at least cheated on me with some- body who has a better job than me. Just pack ya shit and leave, niggah. This relationship is done."

• • •

Now that Jamel was out of her life, Mikala had a new attitude. To celebrate her independence she bought herself a dark blue 2006 Lexus SC 430. She got it fully loaded with all of the finest amenities that Lexus had to offer. The new car matched her new personality. It was fast, flashy, and stood out in a crowd. That was just the vibe Mikala wanted to send off when she went out in public. She made heads turn every- where, and that gave her a sense of confidence that she'd never felt before.

It had been two and a half months since her breakup with Jamel. He had tried to call her numerous times to try and get back together, but she shut him down every time. He had nothing coming from her. She ran into him and Shelby in the mall one day and it only reinforced her confidence. Shelby wasn't in her league. She was short, a little over five feet tall, and round-shaped. She had on a midriff shirt, with her belly hanging out. Her face was chubby and she had some big-ass lips. Jamal could have his little chickenhead if that was what he wanted to settle for, she reasoned.

It was Saturday night and Mikala and Chastity planned to party at the Eden's Lounge. Mikala hadn't really dated too much since the breakup and tonight she felt her jones kicking in. If she didn't get some good lovin' soon, she was gonna erupt like a volcano. She wasn't looking for a man to run her damn life. All she wanted was somebody who could take care of her physical needs. A homey-lover-friend would be great right about now.

Mikala pulled up to Chastity's apartment ready to get the party started. She had on a pair of skintight Apple Bottom jeans that hugged her ass just right, and a T-shirt that had the word "Devilish" scrawled across her ample chest. Her open sandals showed off her freshly manicured toes.

But Chastity came out of her apartment looking a mess. Her hair was still wrapped up in a scarf, and she had on a wrinkled sweatshirt and her house slippers. She wasn't dressed to go out and Mikala wondered why.

"Come inside, Mikala!" Chastity yelled. Mikala did as she

was instructed, parking her car and making her way into Chastity's apartment.

"C, why are you not dressed yet? You know the half-priced apple martini special ends at ten. It's nine o'clock now," Mikala said.

"We're not going to the club tonight. I had something different in mind," Chastity said.

"And what is that?"

"You remember my friend Pierre who drives the silver Escalade?"

"Yeah, the dude you met at the gym. What about him?" Mikala asked.

"Well, I invited him and his friend Kareem over to play spades with us tonight. We can play a couple of hands, eat some good food, and get our drink on. I don't feel like doing the club thing tonight. You're not mad at me are you?" Chastity asked.

"Nah, that's cool. You should've at least warned a sista first though. Tell me about this Kareem character. What do you know about him?" Mikala asked.

"I know Kareem has money, for one thing. He was locked up for four years and came home like a year ago. Since then, he's been outta the hustling game. I also know that he runs his own office-cleaning business. Trust me, when you see him you will definitely be pleased. The brother is fine," Chastity said.

"You hooked me up with a jailbird? Chastity, what the hell were you thinking?"

"Don't be so damn judgmental. Just because he was locked up doesn't mean he's not a good brother. Remember, that bum Jamel was a college boy and you see how he treated you. Give this dude a chance," Chastity said.

"Your point is well taken. You're right, girl. I'll see what's up with him. I guess it couldn't hurt. What time will they be here?" Mikala asked.

"I told them to be here around ten thirty. I gotta go take a shower real quick. Order us some pizza and buffalo wings. The menus are in the kitchen in the drawer underneath the cabinet where the glasses are," Chastity said.

Mikala went into the kitchen to get the menu. When she found it, she called the carryout spot and ordered the food. She took the strawberry daiquiri and rum runner Bacardi Mixers outta the freezer to hook up some drinks for the night. Ten minutes later she had two pitchers full of alcoholic beverages chilling in the refrigerator. She sipped on a strawberry daiquiri and watched *Two Can Play That Game* on Showtime. Seeing Morris Chestnut on the TV screen and the effects of the drink had her feeling a little horny. She could use a sexy Dark Gable up in her life right about now. While she watched the movie, Chastity walked into the room.

"So, how do I look?" Chastity asked. She was dressed in a lime green South Pole sweat suit and had curled her hair.

"Like a ghetto princess," Mikala said jokingly.

"Forget you, hooker. You know I look good," Chastity said.

"I know you do. I was just playing. Go get one of those daiquiris out the fridge. I want you to taste it. I think I made them kinda strong."

Chastity went into the kitchen to get a drink then called out, "Nah, girl, this drink ain't hardly too strong. It's just right. I'm trying to get a little tipsy tonight. Turn on the stereo. I wanna hear some music."

Mikala went over to the CD player and popped in a DJ Whoo Kid mix tape to get the party started. She threw in two other rap mix CDs that were put out by a couple of local DJs. She planned to end the night off with the soulful sounds of a Slow Jams mix tape that included songs from R. Kelly, Ginuwine, and Gerald Levert, amongst a host of others.

Relaxing on the couch Mikala heard the doorbell ring. It was the delivery man and as she paid him for their food she glanced behind him and laid her eyes on the finest Black man she had ever seen in her life. There was a tall light-skinned brother standing right next to him. She dropped every dime of her money as she tried to hand it to the delivery guy.

"Damn, Ma, are you okay? My name is Kareem. This is my friend, Pierre. You must be Mikala. Am I correct?" he asked.

"That's right. I'm Mikala. It's nice to meet both of you. Come on in," she said.

Mikala's heart raced as she looked at Kareem's pretty white teeth. He had on a pair of baggy jean shorts and a G-Unit wife-beater. His head was bald, and his lips looked so tasty she wanted to take him in the bedroom and have her way with him right then and there. Pierre and Kareem walked into the apartment and she followed behind them. Her nose was blessed by a whiff of the Onyx cologne by Azzaro. *Damn, he's a fine specimen,* she thought.

Chastity zeroed in on Pierre. "What's up, sexy? I see everybody has met. Pierre, come help me out with something in the bedroom for a minute while these two get acquainted,"

"So, Mikala," Kareem said after they left. "My man Pierre tells me you're an engineer—is that right?" Kareem asked.

"Yes, I am. I like what I do and my job pays me well," she replied.

"I can feel you on that. I got several contracts across the city to clean up a few big office buildings. The money is good and the work ain't that hard," he said.

"Do you want something to drink?" Mikala asked quickly. She had a low tolerance for alcohol, so the one drink she had downed had her buzzing.

"Yeah, I'll have a glass of whatever you're drinking," he replied. She went into the kitchen to get him a daiquiri and fixed another one for herself.

"Here you go," Mikala said when she returned. "I hope you can handle ya liquor because it's kinda strong. My girl tells me you were locked up for a few years. So are you still a thug, or have you left that part of your life behind you?"

"Yeah, they locked a brother down for a minute. It's true that I sold drugs. I'm not ashamed of what I did. However, I've grown and moved on to better things in my life now. So do you think that a good girl like ya'self can handle a nigga from the streets like me?" he asked.

"We'll just have to wait and see. All good girls have a bad side to them. You just remember that," Mikala responded.

They talked shit back and forth to each other for a few minutes. Mikala became more and more attracted to Kareem as the alcohol started to filter through her system. She told him about her relationship with Jamel, and he shared a few details about his personal life too.

The conversation was getting even more heated when they were interrupted. Pierre and Chastity had returned from the bedroom and both of them had silly grins on their faces as they tried to fix their disheveled clothes.

"So are we gonna get this card game started or what? I'm tryin' to whip y'all butts in some spades tonight," Pierre said.

"Don't talk shit, nigga. Me and my girl are ready to do our thing. But let's eat first. We wouldn't want y'all to get this ass whoopin' on an empty stomach," Chastity said.

They devoured pizza and buffalo wings while talking trash for the next hour. The first two pitchers of mixed drinks were already history and they were on the second round. Everybody felt loose and you could see the chemistry developing between Mikala and Kareem throughout the night.

They couldn't keep their eyes off of each other. He fondled her thighs under the table and she didn't resist. In fact, she returned the favor by grabbing hold of his dick and squeezing his thick erection. Chastity and Pierre were feeling the heat too. She leaned over and nibbled his ears while he massaged her full breasts.

Chastity and Mikala won the first two games of spades,

but lost the next two. Pierre was determined to take this night to another level. He pulled out a sandwich bag full of some of the finest herb that B-More City had to offer.

"Y'all trying to smoke?" he asked.

"I am, but my girl here doesn't indulge," Chastity said.

"I don't need you to speak for me. Yeah, let me hit that shit," Mikala said.

Kareem rolled up a phat Philly and they all took turns taking it straight to the dome. Mikala choked on her first toke, but it took her no time to get the hang of how to properly partake of the cannabis sativa. They shared several more blunts as the night went on.

"Aiight, it's two games apiece. This last game right here is for whoever wants it the most. The winner takes all. Let's put some money on the table. Are y'all scared?" Kareem asked.

"Fuck money, niggah! We want something hotter than that. If we win, we get to have our way with y'all. If y'all win, then y'all get to do whatever y'all want with us. How does that sound?" Chastity asked.

"Are you sure that your girl is game for that?" Kareem asked, staring into Mikala's eyes.

"Hell yeah, I'm game. Now stop talking shit and let's play cards," Mikala said.

Pierre dealt the first hand and from the start it was no contest. They set Mikala and Chastity three straight times to win the bet. It was almost as though the girls lost those hands on purpose, which wasn't a problem because Kareem and Pierre were only too eager to collect on their debt.

Without a word Chastity followed Pierre into her bedroom. Kareem was left alone with Mikala in the living room.

"So, I finally got you to myself. Don't get scared on me now," Kareem joked.

"I ain't never scared, niggah. You lead the way and I'm right behind you," Mikala boasted. The liquor and the weed had deadened all of her inhibitions and she was one hundred percent down to get freaked tonight.

Kareem lifted her off the couch and carried her into Chastity's spare bedroom. He placed her gently down on the bed and began to unzip her jeans. He pulled them down to her ankles and took off her sandals one at a time. Mikala pulled off her shirt and removed her bra, exposing her breasts for him to see. He took her left foot and ran it across his muscular, smooth chest. Her foot took a southbound journey down his stomach until it reached his rock solid penis. She playfully teased it with her toes. Kareem got down on his knees and kissed her thighs passionately while his hands held a tight grip around her waist. He pulled off her thong and threw it to the floor. Mikala sighed in ecstasy when his kisses reached her secret place and his tongue corralled her clitoris into his mouth. He licked it like a lollipop and sucked it until she begged him to stop. Kareem lifted his head from between her thighs as her juices dripped from his chin.

"I want you to taste me too, baby," Kareem said. He took off his pants and lay on the bed next to her. He guided Mikala between his legs and down to his stiff member.

Mikala squealed out loud. He was a good eight inches of prime certified beef. The tip was a perfect mushroom shape and his skin was nice and smooth.

"I want you to grab my dick on both sides at the base with your hands and gently run them up and down my shaft, nice and slow. Aaah, yeah just like that," Kareem sighed in approval. She continued to stimulate his penis with her hands until he told her to stop.

"Open ya mouth wide and take me into it slowly. Make sure that your mouth is nice and wet. Don't swallow the whole thing at once. I want you to gradually put it in and go up and down as it hits up against your jaws. Put your tongue into it while you're sucking it. Ooooh, baby. Mikala, that's it right there. Keep doing that shit! I want you to go faster!" he yelled. She did as instructed and increased the pace of her sucking motion. Kareem's sighs of approval increased her arousal.

"Now take your hand and rub it up and down my shaft while you suck on the head. I wanna feel ya lips on me, baby! Swirl your tongue around on the head real fast. Yeah, yeah, that's it. Now go down further and lick my balls!" he instructed her.

She did as she was told. Mikala put her thing down like she was a wily veteran at the trade. After she teased his balls with her tongue for a spell, she worked her mouth back up to his dick and took the whole thing in her mouth at once, without gagging on it. Her head game was on point. Pleasing Kareem made her hornier and hornier.

"Don't stop, baby! I'm about to cum! Let me shoot this

shit in ya mouth! Don't pull away! Take it like a soldier!" Kareem yelled as he released all of his little soldiers into Mikala's mouth. She swallowed every drop of his semen and loved the taste. *It tastes just as good as it did in my dreams,* she thought.

The night wasn't over yet. Mikala allowed Kareem to recuperate for a while, then sucked his penis gently until it was hard again. Kareem got on top of her and proceeded to take a voyage into her precious garden with his love tool. Her pussy felt like an ocean as he did a freaky slip 'n slide in and out of her without losing a beat in his stroke. They went at it so hard that the top mattress slid off of the box spring and hung halfway onto the floor. Mikala held on to the headboard with both hands to maintain her balance.

Kareem took the game up a notch when he lifted her off of the bed while he was still inside of her. He pounded her insides relentlessly as he leaned her up against the bedroom door. Next, he carried her across the room and sat her down on the dresser as they continued fucking. The heat coming off Mikala's back steamed up the mirror on the back of the dresser.

"Hit this ass, baby. Damn, my pussy ain't never felt this good before!" Mikala screamed. Her legs began to tremble from the good vibrations Kareem was giving her. Each orgasm released miles of pent-up sexual frustration that had built up in her. Kareem knew how to hit all the right spots on her body to get a response from her. Jamel had never made her cum this many times in one night!

Kareem turned her around and tapped that thing from

behind as he watched himself in the mirror. He grabbed her hips with both hands. Watching her ass jiggle with every stroke made him more and more excited. He took his finger and stuck it in her asshole. Mikala lost any composure that she had left as she screamed at the top of her lungs for him to keep doing what he was doing. The double penetration sent her into convulsions as her body shook uncontrollably. Kareem couldn't contain himself any longer. He pulled his penis outta her and instructed her to turn around. Mikala lay on her back on the bed and eagerly awaited his eruption as he stroked his member. Kareem took his enlarged penis and placed it between Mikala's breasts. The friction between her twins left him invigorated and craving more. When he couldn't control his dick any longer, he ejaculated all over her mouth and face. She eagerly received his semen until there wasn't a drop left.

Drained, the tired lovers pushed the top mattress back onto the box spring and passed out from exhaustion. They awoke the next morning in each other's arms.

"So did you enjoy yourself?" Kareem asked her.

"No, you were a lousy lover! Sike, Kareem, I was just playing. If you ask me a stupid question, then expect to get a stupid answer," she laughed.

"Oh, I thought so. I know I can handle my business," Kareem said cockily.

"Yeah, I can't even front, you're a stud. You had my body tingling in ways I have never felt before."

"So where do we go from here?" Kareem asked.

"I'm not sure. I'm not really looking for a man right now.

You know I just got out of a bad situation. I'm just trying to do me for a while. I say we just enjoy the moment and let tomorrow take care of itself when it comes," Mikala replied.

"I'm cool with that," Kareem said. "But I'm digging you already, boo, and I would really like something more."

Mikala just looked at him. She'd never been anybody's freak the way she had freaked for Kareem. He'd touched her heart and given her the best sex she'd ever had, and she damn sure didn't regret the experience.

"Me too," she finally said, refusing to front. She had a real good feeling about Kareem, and wanted to see what the future held. Borne didn't have to be her fantasy anymore, and she could leave that Bullet under the bed and let it gather dust. Who needed fantasies anyway? Mikala had a feeling she'd found herself a real live homey-lover-friend, and his name was Kareem.

CHARGE IT TO THE GAME
Jamise L. Dames

Flame's body pulsed. Tensing and relaxing her muscles, she made her succulent booty clap in the mark's face as she bent down to touch her pedicured toes, then got low with it, butterflying her legs. Bringing her knees together, then apart, she allowed him brief glimpses of her perfectly waxed, milk-chocolate-covered cherry, then flowed her deliciousness into a bobble.

Gyrating her firm, round onion, she backed that thang up until her ass jiggled a few centimeters in front of Robert's nose, then swung it like a pendulum, hypnotizing him with her rhythm. Far away enough to make him beg for more, she closed in on him to tempt him with her juicy slit and iced-out clit ring. Magically, she worked her sweetness clockwise, then rolled her jelly counterclockwise while hooking her arms through the inside of her thighs, spreading herself further. Looking back at him, she knew it was only a matter of time before she'd get what she wanted: him to sign on the dotted line so she could make enough change to take care of her fifteen-year-old sister, Mercedes, and hopefully get Enrique off her back for good.

Shaking *papi chulo* was going to be the hardest. He wasn't the kind of brotha you could just blow off. He was a crazy-ass kingpin from Spanish Harlem who'd put more bodies in the ground than a cemetery.

Fuckin' Power.

Snaking her body, she rolled in a deep grind, winding her hips and popping her coochie. Rubbing her perfectly rounded, toffee titties under the black light, she thought about her man. Power had fucked up royally, sticking Enrique for the couple of kilos he'd fronted him. Now Flame would have to dance *and* fuck their way out of it until Power surfaced from a major lick he was putting down somewhere in the Carolinas. Either that, or Flame hoped his gangsta-azz homeboy Whiz came through with half of the bricks in exchange for her freedom, which was unlikely because he hadn't touched base with her in a week. In the meantime, Enrique held Flame responsible for Power's sins. A down-ass bitch always held her nigga down.

On her knees, she stopped, dropped, and humped the floor as Robert sprinkled her with oil. Rubbing her skin, she slathered her body, ran her hand down to her triangle, and squeezed her phatness through her now oily G-string. Her eyes never left the vic. Although Power was on her mind, her focus was on Robert. He was her one and only way out.

The hidden camera, tucked in a far-off corner, had been capturing their images for weeks. Her, pole dancing on the bar he'd had installed in the apartment. Robert, thirstily lapping her parted coochie lips for one more drop of her nectar. Her, riding his white stallion backwards like an untamed bull.

She had just about everything she needed on tape. Almost every blackmailing detail that would make his wife run to the divorce lawyer demanding half her husband's shit, Flame had recorded live and in living color. Now all she needed to do was wait for Power's call that would confirm that the game was over, and make Robert tell her he loved her. She knew from experience that many women could forgive their husband's sexual infidelities, but she'd never met one who could overlook their man falling in love with another woman. She grinned, her iced-out gold crown gleaming in the light. Either Robert would get served by his Mrs. or he'd dish out Flame's demands.

Tsking, she found herself almost feeling sorry for him as he jacked away at his erect, pink dick, but she quickly recovered. Robert had had no remorse when he'd rented an on-the-low fuck spot for them to get their mash on, and his wife wasn't even a fleeting thought when he was pounding and stirring in Flame's sweetness. No, he was just another dick who was trickin' for her treat. An attorney who broke the laws of his marriage when he left the office. Robert had played for almost a month, but now he'd either come up short a grip because he'd fallen for the slip, or he'd have to cut his wife a check for a lifetime. It was his call. Either way, Flame was going to get hers, or she'd sell his bitch the video-tape to play in front of the judge.

Moving back an inch more, Flame squeezed her muscles until her pussy sucked the breath out of his nostrils, forcing him to breathe through his mouth. She shivered as he exhaled hot air against her entrance, blasts of excited, warm breath climbing her walls.

"Breathe for me, baby. Now blow in my booty," she said, closing her eyes. If she imagined hard enough, her mind could transform Robert into Power so she could really enjoy fucking.

"Yes, honey," Robert panted. "I'll blow wherever you want me to. Even your cunt. Tell me that you want me to blow in your cunt. Say it, my chocolate whore."

Flame tensed. "Cunt" irked the hell out of her. Got on her last damn nerve along with having a white man call her any kind of ho. Rolling her eyes, she went along with his game. Had no choice because she needed the paper, but she swore it would be the last time. She was a Harlem girl and hustla by nature, had worked many a brotha over for his cream. But she wasn't a ho—'til life gave her no wins.

"Give me that sweet chocolate," Robert urged.

Flame rolled over onto her back, widely parted her legs,

then made her lower lips smack like they were kissing at him. Inching away as he crawled toward her, she slowly slipped her finger inside her heated tunnel, grinded against it until she became moist enough for him to hear it, then carefully removed it and sucked her juices until her hand was bone dry. Scissoring her thighs closed, then open, her pussy played peekaboo, teasing him. If she was putting on a show, Robert had to put on one too. He had to beg for it. She couldn't settle for him just wanting the pussy, she had to make him foam at the mouth for a taste.

Without words, she talked to him. Wrapping her ankles around his head, she thrust her hips upward, making her clit ring brush his nose, then released herself back onto the floor when he attempted to lick her. Five separate times she seesawed her midsection to his mouth, causing his patience to weaken and her wetness to overflow. She didn't give a damn that Robert was just a vic or how pink he was, with the blaze that was burning between her legs and no Power around to satisfy her fire, Robert was getting fucked today. And so was she. Getting *herself* off was the only way she could live with fucking for a dollar, because when it came down to it, that's exactly what her hustle had become. Selling dreams and ass for cash—and her life. So she saw no reason not to get her nut off too especially because it could be her last one. Just the thought of her breath being snatched away twisted her up, made her work her middle even though Robert's dick was little. Flame wasn't gonna half-ass nothing, she was goin' hard to make the scam phatten her *and* Enrique's pockets.

"Come here." Robert gripped her dancer's waist and slid her toward him. "Why are you running away from me? You know I want you," he whispered, on the verge of exploding thick in his voice.

Flame ran her fingers through her fire-engine-red hair. "I know, baby. I know," she cooed. "But you've got to give me more than that if you want some more of this puddin'. Don't you want . . ." she dipped two fingers inside her twat, rubbed her milk on his lips ". . . this?"

Robert nodded, hungrily taking her fingers into his mouth and sucking them.

"Well get down and show me. Prove it," she said, standing.

Robert lay down and she climbed over him, squatting and aligning her pussy with his mouth.

"Open up for Mommy," she demanded, then began to stroke between her split and toy with her clit. Moaning, she gave in to the throb of her pussy, removed her fingers, then bounced her ass on Robert's neck as she covered his face with her wetness. Playing with her clit ring, she began a slow grind on his jutted-out tongue. In seconds she was ready. Lifting up a couple of inches, she massaged her hooded pink pearl until it swelled and hardened. "Now, baby," she forewarned him as she contracted her pelvic muscles, milking her sweet juice into his opened mouth. "Tell me you love it."

Swallowing her creamy sap, Robert reacted quickly. "You know I love it," he answered, pulling her body to his, then rolling over on top of her.

"Is that all you love?" Flame asked, spreading her legs and opening her caramelized coochie lips.

Robert stroked his dick until his veins bulged. Heavily, he breathed into her ear, and slapped her thigh with his hardness. "You know I love you, Flame," he said, finally thrusting inside her, and pumping away as if he were really doing some damage.

I ain't doin' this shit no more. Fuckin' Power. See what you made me do?

"Jeez-us, Mary, and Jos—umpf! This is the best cunt I've ever had," he roared and panted.

"Yeah, baby. Work this shit out!" *And hurry the fuck up and raise up off me.*

"For the love of—oh, Flame." Roberts's body shook, a forewarning of his squirting off.

Nah, for the love of my man, my family, and my money, mu'-fucka. I'm only doin' this cuz I gotta.

*   *   *

Power sat at the bar sipping on Henny and Coke. He'd been fuckin' with Kirsten all day, and knew he was driving her crazy. Bourgeoisie bitches like her had always fallen for him. He didn't know if it was his swagger or his game that had attracted them, but he'd bet long dough that his big, black dick had everything to do with it. The white women he'd known had always swooned for the stereotype, and she was no exception. Especially because he'd fit the "blackman-is-packin'" bill like a mutha.

Running his thumb over the scar on his right cheek where a nigga on Riker's had blew him with a razor, he licked his Cool J lips and checked the time on the Presidential she'd blessed him with. He gritted his teeth. His boy Whiz was late coming through. And now was not the time for him to be rolling on CP time. He was already a day late, he'd be damned if he came up a dollar short too. If he did, it'd be his boy's ass. Everything he had was riding on Whiz's call, and he was tired of waiting.

"Ay, when your boy gettin' home?" Power asked gruffly, swishing his drink.

Kirsten smiled. "I told you, not for hours. He'll be in meetings all day, like always. Why?" she asked, tossing her long, strawberry-blond hair. "You feel like playing?"

Power shook his head. "Nah, I look like a mu'fuckin' child to you? I don't *play* shit." He licked his lips again, then winked. "But I wanna watch you play."

Kirsten stepped out of her Blahniks, began tugging at her skirt as she walked toward him with a sinister grin plastered on her freckled face.

Power chuckled. Before he could say jump, Kirsten's feet were off the ground. It'd been less than a month, and she thought she knew him. Her assuming he'd wanted to bang her irked him because it was true, but he had to switch gears. Surprise the ho when she wasn't looking. "Put yo shit on, baby. We gettin' ready to roll out."

"Where are we—"

Power held up his hand, freezing her grill. "Kirsten, what I tell you 'bout that whiny white-girl shit? If ya wanna hang with a nigga, you gots to blacken up, Ma. Learn to stop askin' so many questions. In the hood it's all good. When we roll, we mu'fuckin' roll, baby. No questions asked. Now let's go see how much you really love a nigga," he said, putting his pimp game down and snatching her car keys.

Power smiled when he saw discomfort sprawl across Kirsten's face as he whipped her candy-apple Benz through Park Slope and crossed over Flatbush Avenue, zigged to Lafayette, through Carlton, and finally hung a turn on Dekalb, headed toward Marcy Projects. Bustin' a U, he sped into a parking lot, and jumped out, then snatched up Kirsten and ushered her into Slim Goodies's Pawn Shop.

Getting buzzed into the secured door, Power nodded what's up to the man working the shop behind bulletproof glass, then stopped in front of another door. A secret knock later, and he was guiding Kirsten past an armed guard and into Slim's Pussy Palace, a whorehouse and gentlemen's club tucked in the basement of the pawnshop. Music blared, and body heat filled the air as they walked past the bar, the stage where an entourage of naked hoes flung coochie and participated in orgies, then took their seats at a table in the rear.

"What's good, man? I ain't seent you in a good minute." Slim carried his four-hundred-plus rolls of heft Power's way and gave him a pound.

"Can't call it. You tell me what's really, *really* good, man," Power said, already knowing the answer.

"Long as sugar is sweet, Goody is good," Slim answered his usual. All his top-notch hoes were named Goody. "Delicious as a mu'fucka, bring in twice mo' change than the rest of these broads. Wanna sample?"

"Come on, Slim. Ya know a nigga don't turn down nothin' free 'cept his collar."

Kirsten looked from one man to the other, confusion etched on her face. A telltale sign that she was at a loss on the lingo.

"It's good, Ma," Power assured her, patting her leg.

"Are you sure?" she asked with a shaky voice.

"Am I *black*?" Power laughed, then cut it short when a thick sista sporting a phat-ass booty, firm ta-tas, blue scarf that he was sure she rode while performing onstage, and a dental floss G-string sauntered their way.

"Heard y'all wanna sample my goodies," Goody purred, straddling Power without waiting on an answer.

"Wait a minute," Kirsten began to protest.

Power smacked Goody on the ass, then pointed at Kirsten. "Give her a taste."

Goody hopped from his lap to Kirsten's, ignoring Kirsten's apparent discomfort.

"You said you loved a nigga," Power reminded, rubbing Kirsten's shoulders, then working his way down to her titties, fondling them and pinching her almost hard nipples through her flimsy white blouse. "Show me how much."

He knew he had her when she closed her eyes, melting to his touch and Goody grinding on her lap. Taking Goody's scarf from around her shoulders, he blindfolded Kirsten, then pulled her to her feet. "Follow me, Ma. I forgot to thank you for the Rolie."

Goody's room was as pink and sweet as the sugar walls that would be bumping in it, Power thought as he handed Kirsten over to Goody. With fluid motions, Goody slowly undressed the snow bunny, revealing erect pink nipples and a blond snatch.

"Mmm," Goody moaned, stripping out of her G-string, then gently pushing Kirsten onto the bed and pinching her nipples until she squirmed and groaned.

"Like that?" Goody asked, taking one of the pink peaks into her mouth, flicking her tongue over it, then licking her way down between Kirsten's legs.

"Yes," Kirsten admitted while Power released himself from his pants, strapped up, and positioned Goody's ass up in the air.

Spreading her booty cheeks, he tickled her clit with one finger, stuck two others in her pussy. Like a pro, Goody lap-danced on his hand, swishing her loaned-out liquid in circles as she dipped down and up, making herself warmer and wetter with each bounce of her hips. Getting into Power's groove, she arched her back in anticipation of his dick, ignoring the snow bunny's naked flesh.

Pushing Goody's head back down, Power instructed her to keep licking as he positioned himself between her lower lips, and pushed his hugeness inside her with one single plunge. Goody hollered out in shock, pain, pleasure, then got back down with the get-down as he worked her middle until it spilled over.

The cell phone buzzed on his hip just as he was about to bust. "*Fuck!*" he complained, but didn't hesitate to answer the call. Pulling out, he decided he could get his rocks off anytime. Pussy waited on him 24/7. But come-ups like the one he'd planned came through only once in a lifetime, if a nigga was lucky.

"Gimme what'chu got," Power answered.

"Enrique's real stash is near 115th and Lexington. My boy's got a spot on 112th right off Lex, so watchin' him ain't a problem. I already know how many men he got workin' days."

"Cool. Hit me lata—"

Whiz laughed. "Ya forgettin' somethin'."

Power rubbed his stubbled chin. "What's that?"

"Ya girl Flame, nigga! You want me to go get her or what? You know Enrique's still holding her. He'll let her go for a brick—from me anyway. But he's out for ya whole ass!" Whiz laughed.

Power looked back, saw his snow bunny's face buried between Goody's legs, and grinned. "Let 'im keep her, it's too risky," he said, slapping Kirsten on the ass. "If she slipped and got caught once, she'll do it again. I can't let no broad bring death to my door. Plus, how ya know that nigga won't bank you soon as you hand the bird over?"

Whiz choked on the other end of the line, then exhaled smoke as he spoke. "You a cold mu'fucka, Power. You just gonna leave Flame to the wolves like dat? After her being down wit'chu for a nickel?"

Power shook his head. Whiz had all the connects and could find a grain of red dirt in a sandstorm, but he was slow when it came down to broads. "Let me do me. Flame knew what kinda nigga I was from the door. Let her charge it to the game!"

●   ●   ●

Flame sat as still as she possibly could and tried to disappear into her chair as Enrique hemmed up one of his workers, slapping him around and pulverizing his face until he was barely recognizable. She winced every time the man cried out and pleaded for his life. She empathized with him because she too was bargaining for hers.

"What up, *mami*," Carlos, one of Enrique's soldiers asked.

"Que? Did I hear you speak to Flame, *cabron*?" Enrique turned his rage on his worker. "You don't fuck wit my money, right? So don't fuck wit her." He looked at Flame. "Mami's got dineros in her cho-cha. Dat's right, right? There's money in your pussy? At least thirty-four grand."

Flame froze. She didn't know if she should answer him.

Enrique snatched her by her red hair and pulled her to her feet. "Show me some fuckin' respect when I talkin' to you. I show you some just by lettin' you live." He spat in her face and mushed her back down onto the chair.

Flame balled up and cried like a baby, hoping Enrique would ease up off of her. Grabbing her temples, she screamed. She was doing the best she could to pay back Power's debt, selling her ass and soul, and hadn't a thing to show for it. But tomorrow that would all change.

"*Mira*, that way." Enrique pointed toward the bedroom door, and Flame dropped her stare at the floor. "Don't act like you don't know what the fuck I saying. All *morenos* know 'mira' means 'look.' Take ya ass in the back 'til I finish here. *Comprende*?"

Fuckin' Power.

The room was hot and stuffy, with barred and boarded-up windows. Flame sat on the edge of the bed, tears streaking her pressed powder, and wondered what her sister, Mercedes, was doing to survive without her. Flame had been the one to feed, clothe, and make sure Mercedes had had a proper education ever since their momma decided to trade them in for a heroin kick almost seven years ago. She'd given up her dreams of going to college, learning a trade, having a workingman who pulled a 9-to-5, to make sure her sister didn't have to live the life that she did. No one deserved the shit she was putting herself through for Power. She exhaled and sighed, wiped the tears from her face and assured herself *I ain't doin' nothin' for Power that he wouldn't do for me. He's gonna come through. Got to.*

Enrique stood in the doorway eating out of a bowl. "You hungry, *mami,*" he asked as if he hadn't just spit on Flame. "There's *arroz con pollo* and sweet *plantanos* in the kitchen."

Flame just shook her head. Her stomach was growling, but she didn't feel hungry. Stress had fucked up her blood sugar levels. "No thanks," she answered, remembering Enrique's *talk* on respect.

Enrique dragged his slippered feet into the room and sat next to her on the bed. Softly, he touched her shoulder, and she flinched and trembled. Setting the bowl down on the white sheets, he rubbed her face with the back of his hand. Instantly, her tears came to life again, running down her face like she wished she could haul ass up out of there.

"Listen to me, Flame. I don't like hurting you, *mami*. I a business man, not a bully. And I know this ain't your fault, but you bait—the only thing Power'll come back for." He held up his hands, then let them fall to his lap. "Then again, maybe not. He not show up yet. Why you stayed with this nigga?" he asked, shrugging his shoulders. "I don't know. He ain't hard, all that tough shit he be slangin' ain't nothin' but window dressing—a front. If you was mine, Harlem would've been raining with my bullets the minute I found out you was snatched."

All Flame could do was nod. Enrique had made his point, but she knew her man better. And he was gonna come through. She'd put her life on it.

"So, what up with that vic? You ready to move? 'Cause I can't let you hit 'im with the bad news by yo'self. Carlos or Crazy Lucky will go wit'chu."

Flame relaxed a little, knowing that she had just the right thing to say. "I'm good to go. You just say when."

Enrique patted her knee, and a seldom surfacing smile crept across his face. "That's what I wanna hear, *mami*! Matter fact, I going to be there to hold you down myself. As much work as you had to put in to keep me happy, I wanna see the smile you have for me when you get to walk away. Tomorrow," he said, confirming when their lick was going down.

* * *

Power sat in Slim's Pussy Palace for the fourth day in a row, drinking and slangin'. Posted up at the bar, he sloshed his Henny and Coke in his glass, then threw back his head, downing what was left. Rapping his knuckles on the bar to take Slim's attention away from a knucklehead, he held a finger in the air, signaling he wanted a refill.

"Come the fuck on, Slim. How long I done known you, and you got a nigga waiting?" he slurred.

"Got-dammit, boy," Slim said, moving his heft slowly. "I'm tryin' to help yo black ass make a dime." He slammed an empty glass in front of Power and started pouring Hennessy. "But if you don't wanna get paid . . ." He finished making the drink, splashing a little bit of soda in the tumbler, just barely coloring the cognac.

Power perked up. "Talk to me, then."

"Money over there," Slim tilted his head toward the other side of the bar. "That's my boy Low. Been knowing him for years, and he's good. Well he lookin' for a lil sumptin' sumptin'. Looks like his supplier got knocked, and I don't mean by the po-lice."

Power nodded. "What's a lil somethin'?"

"Few eights."

"Ya sure that nigga straight?"

Slim frowned up. "Nigga, if you can't trust me, *shiiit,* that mean I can't trust you neither. And I let you do your dirty in my spot."

Power stood. Gave Slim a pound. "Tell him I said he has to use the bathroom. Real bad."

•   •   •

Flame arrived at her and Richard's fuck spot two hours before their lunchtime date and played maid. Searching dresser drawers, under the bed, behind furniture, she packed everything that could prove she'd ever been there, dumped it in the incinerator, then called the super and pretended like she'd lost something to make sure the trash was already burning. With bucket after bucket of bleach and water, she scrubbed down everything, practically Cloroxing the place to death.

At noon, Richard's key clicked in the lock. Flame posted up on the sofa wearing nothing but a smile and the little black nightie he'd bought her from Vickie's Secret that said everything but "Hush."

"Hello, my chocolate kitten," he said, dropping his briefcase.

Flame's nerves were rattled again, but she pushed them aside knowing this would be the last day she'd be his "chocolate" anything.

"What up, Rich," she replied, emotionless. No longer did she have to coo and pretend, roll over and fuck. The game was over, and Enrique and his crew were hiding in the back room.

Richard walked over to her, confusion etched on his face. "Bad day?"

"Could be worse," she said, then stood and switched up her mood a little. "I just need to take a shower, relax a little." She ran her fingers through her wild hair. "Can you meet me in the room when you get settled and help me undress? Please, Daddy?"

"Sure, I'll be there as soon as I leave my client a message."

Flame closed the door behind her, nodded okay to Enrique when he pointed toward the closet, tossing her clothes to her. Huddling, her body began to tremble as she thought about the fear Richard would soon face. She hated to do it to him, but when it came down to it, it was either him or her. Reflecting on all the "chocolate whores" he'd called her, she shook the feeling and decided that he deserved what was coming to him.

She heard the door open, a short scuffle, then a burner cocked. Enrique called her name, and she knew the game was over. Quietly, she opened the door as if creeping would make her less accountable. Keeping her eyes on Enrique, she stood there waiting for instructions.

"Tell 'im what'chu want, *mami.*"

Flame looked at Richard, forced a scowl on her face. "I want the deed to your house. Not the place you and your family live in, your vacation house. The deed."

Richard laughed nervously. "You can't be—"

Enrique's henchman, Crazy Lucky, gun-butted him. "Shut da fuck up. Let'er finish."

"Oh, but I *am* serious. Let me show you how serious," she said, gulping back the embarrassment she knew she was going to face once she played the DVD. Inhaling deeply, she pressed PLAY on the VCR. When she saw her lips wrapped around Richard's dick she gagged. When he fucked her from behind, her stomach turned and its juices pushed up through her lips, thick and dripping. But when she heard Richard's voice tell her he loved her, she wiped that nastiness away and smiled at three words that would seal the deal.

Enrique watched her, concern masking the usual "I'm hard and I takes no shit expression. "You a'ight, *mami*?"

Flame nodded.

"Can I speak now?" Richard asked.

"You got the floor." Flame gave him permission.

"But why? How?"

Enrique stepped in. "Easy, give her the deed, you get the tape back. Otherwise . . ."

"I sell it to your wife," Flame finished for Enrique. "I already know what kind of prenup you have—some info ain't too hard to come by if you know the right people—and if she gets her hands on this, you fucked kid." She winked, knowing she was lying about the prenup, but didn't care. Richard and his wife had been together fifteen years, she'd helped him build his law practice from the ground up, so justice pretty much guaranteed that the Mrs. was entitled to half. It didn't take a genius to add two and two.

"But I don't have my deed on me. This'll take lawyers and time."

Enrique laughed, deep and hard while dialing a number on his celly. "You can't be serious, bro. You a fuckin' lawyer, all you need is to sign here," he said, handing a batch of papers to Richard, pointing to a signature line. "And our friend here . . ." he patted one of his boys on the back ". . . is a notary public, and this person on the phone, this my attorney. He's just gone hold a lil somethin' of yours for collateral." Enrique paused, turned his attention to his cell and said a couple of words. "Looks like yo collateral can talk." Enrique handed his phone to Richard.

Flame watched agony twist Richard's red, defeated face as he listened to what was being said on the opposite end of the line. He winced when Enrique snatched the cell and closed it. Tears gathered in his eyes. "My *sister*? You've taken my sister for collateral? I wouldn't have stiffed you guys."

Flame rubbed Richard's face, then kissed his cheek. "Don't worry, ain't nobody gonna hurt Becky." She smiled, noticing him flinch when she mentioned his sister by name. "She just met a wonderful man who she couldn't resist and decided to hang out with him. It was all on her—we just planted the bait, she went for it," she continued to assure him, finding a sense of relief in knowing she was telling the truth. "Just hand over the deed, Richard. You got five hours left. Work it out by the end of the day, and you'll get Becky back." *And Enrique will let me go too.*

"You good, *mami*. Real good, and I ain't talkin' 'bout what I seen on tape," Enrique said, then whistled loudly. "But that was some hot shit too. So tell me, what'chu plan to do wit your life after tonight?"

Flame put on her shoes. "I don't know."

A knock on the bedroom door halted the conversation. A man came in.

"What up, Low!" Enrique greeted the man, gave him a brotherly hug.

Low nodded what up to Flame, then whispered in Enrique's ear.

Flame looked on as Enrique scratched his head, went from being cool and laid back to deadly cold. "That right, bro?" he said to his friend, then turned to Flame. "Ya job is finished."

"What?"

"You can go now. Power is already in my hands, only he don't know it yet. Seems he's been poppin' my shit off in BK the whole time. He's been in arm's reach and lettin' you suffer his consequences for him. What'chu think about that?" He let his words marinate for a minute.

Flame thought about everything she'd been through for Power. She couldn't believe he'd planned to leave her there. Had shit on her loyalty like that.

She shook her head and stared at Enrique.

"I think I'm rolling with you. My job ain't over yet."

* * *

Kirsten's legs were spread farther apart than the North and South Poles while Power and Goody pleased her at the same time. With her ass almost hanging off the bed, Power gripped Kirsten's ankle tight as he fingered her backdoor to loosen her up while Goody contributed her half to the 69 the women were deep into. *Damn, I love fuckin' with snow bunnies, they give up the ass fo'real.* He tipped his head in her rim, gave her just an inch of his dick to get her ready, then eased in and out a little at a time, working her in slow circles. High off of Power's supply, Kirsten moaned, then bucked up on his hardness, trying to get as much of him into her as possible.

"Yo, Power!" Slim busted through the door.

"Fuck ya tryin' to do, Slim? Can't you see a nigga gettin' him some serious ass?"

"Ya better put that ass on pause, nigga. It's some shit goin down you wanna see!" Slim slammed the door closed behind him.

Power followed behind Slim, pulling up and adjusting his pants. *This shit betta be damn good, or I'ma put my foot dead in Slim's big ass, then—* Before he could finish his thought, he choked on the spit pooled in the back of his mouth because no matter how hard he tried, he couldn't breathe. Move either. Happiness and anger twisted a knot in his stomach like swirled ice cream, one flavor blending smoothly with its opposite. *Flame?* He questioned his eyes, then accepted the truth about the fire-engine hair he saw swaying back and forth over the gang of men in front of the stage. He'd been away from her for a good minute, but he'd know his woman anywhere—even by the back of her head.

"Get the fuck out the way," Power said, parting the sea of hard-ups. Freezing in his tracks, he watched in fascination as his woman twirled her damn-near-naked ass onstage like she'd been doing that shit for years. *Flame?* He couldn't believe it. He had no idea how she'd made her way onto the Pussy Palace's stage; he'd made certain she didn't know about him and his Brooklyn ties, but he had to question how she'd gotten away from Enrique. *She must've fucked him, just like she came here to get her swerve on.* Raging like a slapped bull, he bum-rushed his way forward, intent on snatching Flame from her pedestal.

Slim's heavy hand landed on Power's shoulder. "Cool or

not, Power, you can't fuck up the show, man. I runs a 'spectable joint, and my guards keep it that way. Got me? Check yo broad on yo own time."

• • •

Flame watched Power through her peripheral, his eyes digging into her flesh like the symbolic knife he'd stabbed her in the back with when he'd boned out on her. Just to fuck with him, she stepped out of her thong and worked her naked-ass magic for him just like she had for Richard. After all, Power was her mark now too. Serving up vics somethin' nice had become her specialty when she'd had to fuck, suck, and shake to save their behinds.

Problem is, your nasty black ass didn't need saving.

Flame's hypnotics had Power so mesmerized he seemed lost when she looked him in his eyes and sucked her index finger like she was giving head. Like fluid, she melted to the floor, raised up on her knees and popped that pussy for him one last time. Holding him with her seductive look, she didn't flinch when she saw a burned-out white girl pull on his arm, then try to kiss him on his cheek. A move he would've never allowed unless . . .

So you been fuckin' around on me while I was sellin' my ass for you? And a white girl, Power? You done straight bumped your damn head.

Vic or no damn vic, she decided to play her trump card, show Ms. Crossover who was really in charge. Hopping from Slim's stage, Flame strutted her jiggling jelly over to Power and snatched him up.

"Miss me, Daddy?" was all she said as he snatched her up by her arm and practically dragged her to one of Slim's back rooms.

Flame tried to contain her smile when Power cursed, but she couldn't. He was a joke to her now, and she'd risk a beatdown, knowing it'd only be a short one with Enrique lurking around somewhere in the Palace. Nothing Power had to say moved her; he was full of shit. Window dressing, like Enrique had said.

"So you were comin' back for me?" she asked, deaf to anything that had fallen from his lips.

"Come on now, Ma. You just caught a nigga where he re-up at. Y'know I sold Enrique's shit, right? Only got a quarter left. I just got here right before you came. Matter fact, what the fuck you doin' up in here?"

She shook her head. "No you didn't, lying bastard. You been laying your head here in Brooklyn the whole time. Wanna know what I'm doin' in here? What I did while you was gone?"

"*What?*" Power snapped. "What the fuck you say, Flame? What the fuck did you do that was so got-damn important?"

"She freed herself and got her a house," Enrique said from the doorway, AK in hand. "*And* handed me the mu'-fucka I been looking for."

The widest grin spread across Flame's face. She'd been so consumed with catching Power, finding out that he'd left her to Enrique's fate, she hadn't thought about being free to walk.

"Go 'head, *mami.* You earned everything you got—including cuttin' loose from him. A woman like you," he said, nodding his head, "could be on my team anytime." He reached in his pocket, pulled out an envelope, and handed it to her. "Good ol' Richard moves fast. This was just delivered to me. I don't need another house, I got what I want right here." He kicked Power in the gut, started pulverizing him with the AK.

Flame nodded and thanked Enrique, then started to haul ass before he changed his mind, then a thought occurred to her: *Power has to pay, beg just like Richard.* "May I?" Flame interrupted Power's ass-whooping.

Enrique grinned, handed Flame a burner. "See, Lucky," he said to his worker, "this is what I talking about! Mami here, she nut'ing to play with."

Crazy Lucky laughed, took a hit of cocaine he had in a baggie.

Flame held the gun with shaky hands and watched Lucky. "Enrique, is it true that shit numbs you?"

"Yeah, *mami.* Why? You need a little?"

Flame nodded. "Yeah, I need a lot."

"Give 'er your stash, Lucky."

Lucky tossed his bag to Flame. With one had she caught it, kept the gun aimed at Power with the other. "Pull your pants down, nigga!" she demanded. "And shove this powder up yo ass."

"What?" Power answered through bloody lips.

"Put it up yo ass and then thank me for numbing you first." She turned to Enrique. "You got a man that swings both ways?"

"Aw, hell no," Power gurgled.

Enrique laughed. "No, *mami*. But'chu know I can make any mu'fucka in here do what I want, right?" he said, signaling to Crazy Lucky. "Go find me someone."

Power broke down pleading. "C'mon, Flame. You ain't gots to—"

Flame kicked him in his grill, kept the burner to his dome while she pulled his pants down.

Crazy Lucky pushed a tall, butterscotch-complected ho through the door. With low lids, her glazed eyes fluttered. Chick was as high as Mount Everest, and her flawless skin, perfect teeth, and tits and ass for days couldn't mask the heroin fix Flame knew she'd had. *Crazy Lucky must be loony and deaf.*

"What the fuck you doing? I said bring me a man, bro!" Enrique yelled, spit flying from his mouth.

Crazy Lucky smiled. "Transsexual, Enrique. A chick with a dick? You know, still a man."

Flame took pity on the boy-girl despite her highness reminding her of her own heroin-addicted mother. "You ain't fuckin' for free. I can promise you that."

Power squirmed on the floor, enlarging his own bloodstain below him. "Don't do this—"

A kick to his groin shut him up.

"Handle it," Flame said, handing the baggie of powder to the girl and deciding to let Power ride it out raw dog.

The chick inhaled almost the whole bag of cocaine like it was just a pinch. Wobbling, she stepped out of her dress and her panties, carefully removed the tape that had kept her dick tucked back. Licking her hand, she wet her soft penis and rubbed some of the potent powder on it. It stiffened, growing into a long pole. She spoke for the first time, her voice a hint of a baritone hidden under softness. "Can you hold him? I don't wanna get kicked."

Enrique nodded. Crazy Lucky and one of his workers spread Power's legs in a V while Enrique and Flame held guns to his dome.

Flame watched intently as the he-she mounted Power from behind, spit between his cheeks, then went in for the kill.

Power screamed out like a bitch, causing every man in the room to flinch and Flame to giggle.

"Flame, I can't believe . . ." he grunted, tears plummeting from his eyes ". . . you did me dirty."

"You fucked me in my ass with no Vaseline. You bounced on a bitch, leaving me for dead. So don't blame me, baby. Charge *that shit* to the game!"

ME, HE, AND SHE
Aretha Temple

Somebody had brushed up against my ass. I turned, saw a nigga so fine my lips *and* pussy watered. Around six-three, he wore a low haircut, and his skin was the same Hershey's Kiss chocolate color as mine. From my brief encounter with the hardness of his body, I could tell he was built. He smiled, showing off his platinum fangs. My pussy said, "Get him, girl!" but I satisfied myself with a hot wink and a smile of my own.

"Is your name Tia?" a high-yellow female with red hair asked me, covering the mouthpiece of her cell phone.

"No, my name's Star," I said, stopping in front of Kroger's exit. I opened up the pack of gum I'd stopped at the store to get before I went to the club.

"I'm so sorry. You look like my cousin's friend Tia."

"That's all right. I'm always mistaken for someone else."

Redbone smiled, still on her phone. "Your hair is pretty. Who does it?"

"My girl, Lil Shit."

"It's pretty."

"Thanks!" I peeped redbone. She was a lot taller than me, and her hair fell to her shoulders. She was fly, dipped in all pink.

The fine chocolate dude walked by with his celly to his ear as redbone and I continued to talk.

"I'm Brooklyn," she introduced herself. "You should come check me out. I have a shop on Nineteenth Street."

"Top Notch?"

"Yeah, that's my shop." She reached into her Baby Phat purse, and handed me a card. "Come check me out."

•   •   •

The DJ was playing my theme song, "Conceited" by Remy Ma when I walked into the club, and headed straight for the bar.

"What's good, Star?" Paula was the bartender and she already knew I wanted a muthafuckin' chocolate martini.

"Shit, on this paper chase."

"You always on a paper chase."

"And we both know this!" We laughed as she handed me my drink. Before I took a sip, a deep voice grabbed my attention.

"Let me get another double P." I turned and saw the fine-ass nigga that had brushed up against my ass in Kroger. My heart skipped a beat as he turned and walked away while Paula made his drink.

"Who is that, Paula?"

"Girl, that's Telly," Paula said as if I knew who he was. "He's from Jersey, and got cheddar for yo rat ass too!"

"Call me what you want, but don't hate 'cause I like cheese."

Paula laughed.

Telly brought his fine ass back over to get his drink. "What up, ma?"

"Hey, what's up?" I answered.

"Didn't I just see you?"

Felt me too. "Yeah at Kroger's."

"I knew that was yo sexy ass. What you drinking on?" he asked, looking at my glass.

"A chocolate martini."

Telly smiled, showing his fanged-out grill. "What you know about martinis?"

"I know I love them."

"I see you got a little class."

Got a lot of ass too, I thought.

198 | From the Streets to the Sheets

Telly was looking good in his green, fur-hooded G-Unit coat and matching broccoli-colored Tims. I'd been so busy lusting him in Kroger's, I hadn't noticed his 'fit.

"Paula, give her another one."

Paula did as she was told.

Telly sized me up, then sat down next to me. For hours he filled my head with compliments and my body with drinks. We were tipsy, but knew what we were doing, what we wanted, and wasn't scared to admit we was gonna fuck.

"Anything you wanna tell me?" I asked, noticing for the first time he wore a ring on his wedding finger.

"I'm married," Telly stated, looking me dead in the eyes. "That a problem?"

His honesty turned me on. "If it is, it ain't mine."

"What about you? You gots sumthing you need to come clean with?"

"I used to be a stripper. And I don't fuck for free." I hit him with my honesty, and it didn't daze him.

He smiled, then squeezed my thigh. Moving his hand up toward my pussy, he licked his lips. Baby was craving me. "I feel you on that, ma. I love a bitch that's 'bout her business."

Before I knew it, I was sitting in his blue Cadillac truck. "You need me to take you home, ma?"

"No," I said, shaking my head.

"You wasn't going home anyways," he said, then drove off.

My pussy instantly became wet, and I couldn't resist scooting over next to him and kissing on his neck. Couldn't help rubbing his dick through his jeans.

"Don't start nothing you can't finish."

"Oh baby, I can finish," I whispered in his ear.

"Well do you, baby." He tried focusing on the road.

At that I unbuckled his belt, then unzipped his pants. "Raise up," I told him. He did as he was told, and I pulled out his pretty chocolate dick. "Umm, I bet it taste like candy." Telly laughed.

I dove in to see for myself. "Umm," I moaned, licking the tip of it, then started deep-throating him real slow. It tasted so good I started slurping.

"Yo ass gone make me crash something."

I didn't pay him any attention; I just kept giving him my head pussy. I knew my shit was tight, and from the sounds he was making, he knew it too. Telly bust a left, then a right, then parked and killed the engine.

"Damn, ma!" he said, reclining his seat, giving me more room to do my thang.

I looked up and saw it was light as fuck outside, but I didn't care. I moved away from him long enough to strip down to my black lace bra and panties. I then pulled down my thong, and lay back in my seat. I started fingering my wetness, then put my fingers in my mouth. Tasted my own sweet juices. Drove Telly crazy.

He grabbed me, started kissing and fingering me. "This pussy wet."

"Mmm-hmm," I moaned. He just didn't know there was more where that came from. Rubbing my titties, he took them out and squeezed them together, then suckled on them like a baby.

I rose up, kicked my thong off my ankle, and swiftly

straddled him. Taking his dick in my hand, I rubbed it on my pussy. You could hear the wetness as I slid down on his big, hard dummy. It hurt like hell, but then it started feeling good when Telly opened up my ass cheeks for better entry.

I felt myself about to make his juicy dick even juicier when he pinched my nipples. "Shit!" I yelled out. "I'm about to cum!"

Telly took me by my neck. "Cum on this dick then!" he moaned as I bounced on his hardness.

"Oh shit! Oh shit!" I yelled as I came all over his dick.

"What the fuck? You a *squirter*?" he asked.

I was too out of breath to answer.

He pulled his seat back up. "Yo ass gone fuck around and make me kidnap you."

"You don't have to kidnap me, baby. I'm willing to go without a fight."

Telly pulled up his pants, then started the car. "I gotta hurry up and get yo ass to a hotel. I gots to get some more of that!"

A week later there was no more mention of a wife. A month after that, it had become all about me. I'd begun to really like Telly, and he was feeling me too. He'd showed me off from Detroit to cold-as-hell Canada, taking care of me like I was his Mrs. And fucking and sucking me like I carried his last name.

"Damn, ma. You fuck a nigga so hard you be sweatin out your 'do," he teased, playing in my damp hair after one of our sessions. "Why don't you go get it tightened up?"

I just looked at him. My girl, Lil Shit, was big and pregnant and didn't feel like doing hair anymore. "My girl is outta commission until she drops that load."

"What about that spot down on Nineteenth Street? My homeboy's girl goes there," Telly suggested, giving me a hand full of money.

I had forgot about Brooklyn's spot, but it didn't take me long to remember once I saw myself in the mirror. My 'do needed more than just tightening up, it needed an overhaul.

●　●　●

I discovered Top Notch definitely had the right name when I stepped through the door. "Dang Brooklyn, this is *your* shop?" I asked.

"Sure is. I worked my ass off to get this ma'fucka too," Brooklyn answered, walking over to give me a hug. "How you been?" she greeted me like she'd known me for years.

"Other than this," I said, pointing to my hair. "I'm good."

"Well, you came to the right spot."

"I see. You got this place on your own?"

"Nah, my husband helped me out."

"Your husband? How old are you?"

"Twenty-nine," she answered, escorting me to the back.

She was just a year older than me and had her own business. I was impressed. "How long have you been married?"

"Two years."

I was lying back while Brooklyn shampooed my hair. Her gently scratching and massaging my scalp made a tingle shoot up my pussy. As she kept making love to my scalp, I thought about Telly and his hurricane tongue. How he'd made me bend over and touch my toes while he fucked me from behind, his balls slapping my ass until he made me milk everywhere. He was a nasty mutha'fucka, and I loved it.

Brooklyn sat me under the dryer, and stood with her ass toward me while talking to one of her clients. Now trust me when I say this, I am not gay! But Brooklyn was sexy as hell. An Apple Bottom blue jean bodysuit hugged her tiny waist and onion-shaped ass. I'm not sure what I was feeling, but it wasn't right.

After hours of chatting with Brooklyn and a tight little roller set, I was done.

"What you doing tonight, Star?"

"Nothing. Why?"

"I thought maybe you'd like to stop by my house for drinks. My husband's gone to D.C. for a couple of days, and I'm tired of being alone and bored in that big house all by myself. Well, I do have Lil Kim, but she's no company."

"Lil Kim?"

"Yeah," Brooklyn laughed. "My husband's puppy pit."

"Maybe I can swing through for a minute. What's your address?" I asked, handing over her payment.

"Girl, put it in your pocket. Swing by tonight, and we'll just say you owe me one."

• • •

"Damn, baby!" Telly said when I walked in. "That's what I'm talking about," he complimented my hairdo.

I walked over to him and tongued him down, causing sparks to shoot through my pussy.

"Umm," he moaned between kisses and him rubbing my titties. "Daddy wants some pussy."

"Well Daddy can't have none," I said, joking. "I'm meeting the chick who owns the salon later for drinks."

"What?" he said, pulling me on the couch and stripping me out of my coat. Lifting my shirt, Telly kissed my flat stomach, then dropped to his knees and stripped me from my waist down, revealing my goodies. With a hot tongue, he licked my clit, then started sucking on it.

"Shit!" I yelled. "Put yo fingers in me, baby."

In seconds, Telly's thick fingers were working my pussy like he worked it with his dick.

I wrapped my legs around that nigga's neck. "Don't stop, baby!"

Telly slurped on my pussy until I bust a big nut on his face. I sat there with opened legs, playing with myself as he took his pants off, then pulled me toward him. My ass was hanging off the couch when he stuck his dick so far in me that I dug my nails in his back.

"Take this dick," he demanded.

I was trying to. Telly and I did a lot of fucking, but taking all of him was impossible. But I did fuck him until he passed out. I had to make him go to sleep if I wanted to go somewhere.

• • •

Brooklyn greeted me with the same embrace and smile. She looked comfortable in her black Rocawear jogging suit. Her booty jiggled in my view as she walked through the nice and cozy house, furnished with a pink leather pit and candles. India. Arie sung in the background.

"What you drink?" Brooklyn asked, standing behind the bar.

"I like chocolate martinis, but I'll take whatever you have."

She handed me a glass. "Remy," she said.

"Oh, my man drinks Remy."

"Mine too." Brooklyn laughed.

I heard something running toward me. I looked down, and the cutest puppy stared back at me with an iced-out collar with LIL KIM hanging from it. "She is so cute, Brooklyn."

"Girl that bitch is bad. Kim, go!" Brooklyn ordered her out. The dog looked at Brooklyn with her tongue hanging out, then left the room. "So Miss Star, how are you?"

"I'm good."

"And I'm bored. My husband is always out of town."

"Shit, that was me a little while ago."

"What, bored?"

"Girl, nah. I use to run around like crazy chasing money and shit."

"Ain't shit wrong with that," Brooklyn stated, putting her little lips on her glass.

Brooklyn and me chatted for a while, both getting tipsy as hell. My head was straight spinning, giving me a headache.

"You got some aspirin or something?" I asked, pressing down on my temples.

"I got just what you need," Brooklyn said, disappearing into another room.

I set down my glass, and closed my eyes, then felt warm hands on the sides of my head. I turned my head, saw Brooklyn standing behind me.

"My husband rubs my temples when I get headaches. It helps a lot. You mind?" she asked, continuing to massage.

Normally I would have, but her hands felt so good taking the pain away that I closed my eyes again, almost falling asleep. But I couldn't drift off, not after her rubs traveled south to my titties. I don't know if it was all the drinking I had done or what, but it felt good. Too good.

"Stop!" I said, getting up.

"I'm sorry. It's just that you're so sexy with your smooth, chocolate skin. I couldn't resist touching you."

I wanted to tell her she was sexy too, but I didn't. Instead, I reached for my coat.

"Don't leave, Star. I'm sorry."

"It's okay," I lied. "I have to go anyway. My dude's probably wondering where I'm at," I said, looking at my watch and walking to the door.

Brooklyn followed. "I hope we can still be friends, Star."

"Yeah, we still friends. I'll call you."

Brooklyn hugged me, putting her soft breasts on mine. She smelled so damn delicious.

"Sure you can't stay?" she whispered in my ear, then licked the lobe.

I bit my bottom lip. I was curious as hell, but I refused to go there. She'd made my pussy wet, and I wanted to show her how moist she had me, but I didn't. I just got the hell out of there, hopped into my car and sat for a minute, wondering what had happened. Finally, I cranked my engine, deciding to forget about what had occurred behind Brooklyn's front door. I'd slipped, not fallen. But I wanted to jump in bed.

* * *

Horniness rode me all the way home, and I hoped like hell that Telly was there to help me release my heat. But all there was was an empty space where his whip had been. *Damn.*

"What up?" he answered when I hit him on his celly.

"Where you at, baby? I need you," I said, entering my place, tossing my purse on the couch, and hightailing it to my bedroom.

"I'll be there in a few. How was your drinking date?"

"It was cool. I'll fill you in when you get here. But you gotta hurry, baby. I'm horny!" I rushed, searching my DVD collection for a temporary fix.

"All right, get it ready for daddy," he said, then hung up.

I got it ready for him, all right. I took off my clothes and got into bed, turned on my *Phatty Girl* DVD, starring sexy ass Justin Slayer who fucked in Timbos and sunglasses. As Justin slurped on some chick's pussy, I played with mine. I was so hot it was stupid. I got dicked down all the time, but right then it felt like I didn't get fucked at all. *What the fuck did Brooklyn do to me?* I knew one thing, I wasn't talking to her anymore.

I was so wrapped up watching Justin slay fat-assed bitches that I didn't hear Telly slide into my bedroom.

"Hey, ma," he said, stripping out of his clothes. "I was right about your friend, wasn't I?"

I didn't say shit. I just opened my legs for him as he climbed on top of me, and began fucking me hard. He knew what I needed, and I loved that rough shit.

"She tried to take my waterfalls, didn't she?"

"Yeah," I moaned.

"Did you let her?"

"No!"

"Why?"

"'Cause I want dick!"

"You want this dick?"

"Yeah. Yo dick, daddy!"

"How you want it?" He stroked me slow and hard.

"Just like that," I said as I moved my hips up under him.

"Shit, get that dick, ma. Work that pussy!"

Telly and me fucked 'til the birds started chirping outside. The next day Telly and I lay around tired from all the fucking we'd done. I told him what went on at Brooklyn's. He didn't understand why I didn't let her suck my pussy.

"Why don't you call her up, and we can have a threesome," he said, dead-ass serious.

I told him he was crazy.

Telly wasn't playing, though. "You don't want the best of both worlds? Hard to believe you haven't explored the other side; your sex drive is so high."

"My sex drive don't mean shit. Maybe one day I'll try it, but not now."

"Are you feeling this girl?"

"She's cool. Pretty and thick. I'm not gone lie, she turns me on. I have never looked at a bitch like I looked at her."

Telly sat back and stared at me, but didn't say shit. He just listened as I went on about how Brooklyn had made my pussy jump.

* * *

Summer had finally hit, and it was hot as hell outside as Telly and I made our way through his boy's crowded backyard where the bar-b-que party of the summer was being held. The music was blasting, and ma'fuckas was walking around half-ass naked by the pool. A couple of girls hawked Telly, then looked me up and down, turning up their noses. Not giving two fucks about their jealousy, I grabbed Telly's hand to let them know he was taken. Yeah, he still rocked that wedding band on his finger, but it was me he wore on his arm. As far as I could tell, I was his wife.

We were there about a good twenty minutes when I spotted Dino, a nigga I'd met when I was stripping, coming our way. I turned my head, hoping he'd keep it moving, but no such luck. He had sweated me back in the day, and it seemed things hadn't changed. I'd given him the pussy once, and he had fucked like a jackrabbit. A straight turnoff that caused me to cut him off.

Dino walked up to Telly and gave him dap. He looked at me and nodded.

"Let me holla at you for a sec," Dino said to Telly.

They stepped away from me and started talking. I knew Dino's hating ass was going to tell him he knew me, but I didn't care. Telly knew what I was all about from the beginning. Telly nodded, kept shooting me looks. I rolled my eyes, then made my way to the bathroom.

I was washing my hands when Telly's crazy ass bust through the door.

"Did you fuck that nigga?" The look in his eyes told me he was serious.

I didn't want to lie to him so I stayed quiet.

Telly pushed me against the wall, and tugged on my shorts. Putting his hands down them, he found my pussy. Fingered my clit. "Did he make you feel like I do?"

I'd never seen Telly act like this, and it turned me on. He grabbed my face, started kissing me. I didn't try to fight him. There was no use. He was gonna do him regardless, so I let him. Stopping abruptly, he sat on the closed toilet lid, pulled down his jogging shorts. His dick stood tall and proud, calling me. Walking over to him, I got down on my knees, and let him fuck me in the mouth. I bobbed and weaved on his dick like the pro I was.

"Stop! Sit on this dick!"

I stood. Took off my shorts and panties. Sat on his dick. Bounced my ass, taking in every inch.

"Yeah, ride this dick!"

I buried my face in his chest while I worked his dick.

"Look at me!"

I looked in his eyes while I fucked him, biting my bottom lip.

"You so damn sexy," he said, rising up, lifting my body weight with his. He set me on the sink.

"Shit, T!"

"Shut up!" Telly commanded, sliding his pole in me, fucking me hard. He didn't give a fuck about my pussy right then. "When I cum, I want you to suck my dick!" I couldn't believe he was acting like this. "I'm about to cum. You want it in your mouth or pussy?"

It didn't matter where I wanted his cum because he exploded inside me, then pulled up his shorts. "Let's go!" he ordered.

Like his good little bitch, I put on my shorts and followed him.

• • •

Without words, he had mind-fucked me all night. I knew I hadn't done a damn thing to him. Who I'd slept with before him wasn't his business, but he'd acted like it was. Treated me like I'd cheated on him, and wouldn't break me off no matter how much I'd begged for it. It was his show, he'd said, and he'd give it to me when he was ready. And the next morning he was, sliding up in me from behind. Waking me up with the hardness of his dick and the roughness of his attitude.

"I'm gonna have to stay away from you for a while. My wife's been tripping," he said, avoiding my stare.

Wife? Since when did he care about her?

"I don't want you out here fucking nobody else, Star."

"Boy, I ain't thinking about nobody else."

"You bet not be. 'Cause you don't see me don't mean I won't be watching."

• • •

A week had passed, and no Telly. I didn't know what to do with myself. I really didn't have any friends. Didn't fuck with bitches. I wanted to go out, but going out would only lead to something else—fucking—and I had promised Telly I wouldn't do that to him, even though he was laid up somewhere with his wife. I threw myself on the bed, depressed as hell. This nigga had really gotten to me. Star Hamilton, sprung? Who would have thought such a thing?

Another week passed, and still no word from Telly. I decided enough was enough. I didn't give a damn about his wife. It was my turn, I thought as I dialed his number. My heart stopped when I heard the recording saying that his number had been disconnected. Now I was worrying. Telly had plenty of money to pay his cell bill.

What the fuck is going on? I slipped on my Melissa sandals and headed out my door. If he wasn't checkin' for me, I damn sure was gonna check for him. I was going to find my dick.

I pulled up on Parkdale, and wasn't a soul in sight. His niggas and workers usually held court in front of the spot, but not today. I checked the other spot on Vance. Once again, no one was out. Pounding the steering wheel, I was mad as a mutha. I needed someone to talk to. Without Telly, I didn't have a life. He had me sprung, and I didn't want any other man besides him. But that didn't cut off all my options.

Brooklyn picked up on the first ring. Answered her door-

bell on the second. I didn't know what I was about to get myself into. Whatever it was, I blamed Telly. Where his tongue
wouldn't lick, another would.

Her perfume was sweet when she embraced me. Her
touch was soft, running through my hair. We didn't speak.
Didn't have to. We both knew why I was there. She lowered
the lights and blasted the music. Took my hand and led me
to the couch. Massaged my temples even though I didn't
have a headache. Again, I closed my eyes, weakening under
her touch. She stopped, and I opened them. Saw her standing in front of me, her pussy all in my face.

"You all right, Star?" I watched as those words fell from
her sexy little lips.

"I'm cool," I whispered, staring between her legs.

"Good," she said, pushing my body back and stripping me
out of my clothes.

Before I knew it, her face was between my legs, tickling
my clit almost as good as Telly. Her sex was so good. I just
went with the flow, blocking out everything but the tingle
crawling through me. I gapped my legs wider as she lashed
me with a knowing tongue. I felt myself about to squirt, and
I tightened my pussy muscles. I hadn't been dicked down in
weeks. I wanted this shit to last.

"Ooh," I moaned.

"You like that, Star?" she asked, her whisper traveling
from between my legs.

"Yeah," I admitted.

Her dainty fingers opened my pussy lips, then slid in and
out of me.

I gripped the couch when she licked me, then stuck something inside me. *A dildo.*

"You like that, Star?" she repeated, this time her words drifted directly into my ear.

What the fuck? How can she be in my ear and sucking, and fucking me with a toy at the same time? Better not be that damn dog! My eyes shot open.

Telly smiled. On his knees, he was between my legs feeding my pussy with the head of his dick.

I jumped up. He pushed me back down. Brooklyn massaged my temples.

"The best of both worlds," Telly said. "Star, meet my wife."

Brooklyn kissed my cheek, then licked my earlobe. She laughed. "We already met."

I sat there, dazed, but not confused. I'd been set up, and it felt good as hell.

AYEESHA
Erick S. Gray

I woke up to my six-twenty alarm, only to hear my man taking a shower. I sighed and stared over at the empty space. *That man just doesn't sleep,* I thought. He came in late last night after doing whatever the fuck he did out on the streets, and now he's gettin' ready to bounce outta this house again. This niggah is up before me every fuckin' morning, and obviously makin' that money is more important than fuckin' his wife. But I kept my mouth shut about it. I didn't have to be at work until nine this morning, so that gave me time to play around and to try to get me some dick—for what it was worth. But instead of lying next to me in the sheets, he was in the fuckin' shower.

I'd had a crazy-ass dream last night, and I woke up with my pussy on fire. I'd dreamed that I was in a barn surrounded by huge black stallions that kept staring at me. I was encircled by at least a dozen long-dicked horses as I lay butt naked on a pile of hay. It was getting dark outside, springtime, and the wind softly skimmed my skin and sounded like it was faintly calling my name—*Ayeesha*—as it held me in my dream. I was in heaven for real.

That spot between my thighs was tingling in my sleep. I wanted to be touched. I was wet with excitement, so I rested my head against the spongy hay, then parted my legs and was just about to get it on with myself when something made me look up. Walking out of the circle of stallions came this tall, dark, and gorgeous guy. He had the physique of a well-sculpted ironman with a six-pack, buff arms, and firm thighs.

He was naked, and his dick hung down on him like an anaconda. Shit, he was packing just as much as those horses were. He didn't say a word, and I couldn't talk either. He walked up to me, then got down on his knees and parted my thighs, eating me deliciously while the horses watched.

His tongue swam around in me like he was trying to dig for something. I panted loudly as I fondled my breast with one hand and gripped his gleaming bald head with the other. I was loud, so loud that I began stirring up the horses as they watched this fine man eat me out on a pile of hay. The horses started leaping up in the air on their hind legs, but we kept going and paid them no mind. The guy ate me to death as he gripped my right leg strongly. He spread my legs wider as his head swirled between my thighs.

"Aaaaaahhh . . . aaaaaahhh . . . aaaaaahhh," I panted, feeling myself sinking deeper into the hay.

He lifted his head up and stared at me with this strange dim gaze. He climbed on top of me and positioned himself between my wet thighs. We sank deeper into the hay as he pressed against me; I felt the tip of his big dick touching against my warm and inviting lips. His huge erection opening me up wide, and he pushed inch by inch of his vast size up inside me. I cried out.

"Ahhh . . . Oh, God!"

My nameless dream-man thrust and thrust into me as I straddled him and dug my manicured nails into his bare skin. I felt myself sinking lower and lower into the hay as he fucked me and fucked me.

Then suddenly I heard a voice call out . . . *Ayeesha!*

I opened my eyes, surprised that my dream had seemed so real. The sheet between my legs was damp, and I was horny as hell. I heard my husband in the shower and wished he was next to me, ready to fuck, just like I was right now.

I lay my head back against the pillow, and slowly moved my hand between my thighs, pulling up my silk-and-lace pink slip as I touched myself lightly. My husband had come to bed last night without even noticing what I had on.

I began to masturbate slowly, thinking about my crazy dream. I couldn't see or remember the stranger's face, but I definitely remembered his body.

I panted as I slowly dug two fingers into my pulsating pussy, closing my eyes and trying to recall those hot scenes from my dream. I'd been handling myself for at least ten minutes when the water in the shower was cut off and Tears shouted from the bathroom, "Ayeesha! Get yo ass up!"

I moaned, ignoring him as I continued to finger myself rapidly. Fuck! He had messed up my flow. I wanted to cum this morning!

Tears walked into the bedroom wrapped in a blue towel.

"Baby, come here for a minute," I called out, my voice dripping with sex as I gazed at him.

"Yo, what you want, Ayeesha? I got someplace to be in an hour," he replied. "Don't you gotta be at work soon?"

I looked at him with disgust. Here I'm laid up in his bed fingering myself, horny as fuck and wanting some dick, and he's worrying about work?

I watched him dig around in his dresser drawers looking for some clothes to put on. I got out of bed, approached him from behind and wrapped my arms around his waist, kissing his neck tenderly. He acted all nonchalant to my affection.

"Yo, baby, chill . . . I ain't in the fuckin' mood right now. I gotta get dressed. I told you I got someplace to be."

"What?" I replied with an attitude.

He ignored me as he dug deeper into his drawer and

pulled out a .45 automatic. He checked the clip and laid it on the dresser.

"Tears, what's up?" I asked.

"Business."

"I need to be your business right now," I told him. Damn! I hadn't had no dick in over a week. Shit, I'm dreaming about barns, strange men, and horses, and this niggah was walking around our bedroom half-naked and ignoring me like I wasn't shit right now.

I sat at the edge of the bed and spread my legs to show him that I had no panties on. My pussy was shaved and throbbing and ready for some dick action.

Tears stared between my legs for a second, then his cell phone went off on the nightstand. He reached for it and started talking, and all I could do was sigh.

"Yeah . . . I got you . . . nah . . . not on the phone," I heard him say.

He quickly ended his call, and continued to get dressed.

"You just gonna sit around all morning and not do shit? Yo, get your ass dressed," he said to me.

I looked at my boo like, *Niggah is you serious?*

I sighed heavily. *Fuck him!* I stomped into the bathroom and slammed the door shut. My pussy was still tingling and craving some dick, but that was all right. I could handle mines. I dropped my pink slip to the floor and gazed at my reflection in the mirror.

I was petite with silky skin and shaped like the letter S. My hair was long and black, and men always told me I had some beautiful hazel eyes. All of that and my niggah didn't wanna fuck me this morning? What the hell was wrong with him?

I opened the bathroom door and shouted to him, "Tears, are you on the down low?"

"What you say?" he shouted back from the bedroom.

I said, "Do you like to take dick in your ass?"

"Bitch, what you say?" he shouted again. He must have been distracted by something, otherwise he would have heard me just fine.

I sighed and closed the bathroom door. *His ass was out there.*

As I stood in the shower trying to cool off, I thought about Tears and how we first met. We'd been together for two years and I was starting to wonder what was happening to us. Yeah, I loved the shit out of him, but lately he ain't been giving it to me right. I thought maybe he was fuckin' the next bitch, but why would he?

Tears knows I'm a freak—shit the niggah met me in a strip club and fucked me that same night. I was dancing topless at this club on Hillside Avenue called Dreams, and trying to get my Bachelor's degree at York College. I grew up in the Baisley Projects over on Guy R. Brewer and Foch. I'd always dated thugs and drug dealers, and Tears was no different. I knew he was hustling. He made frequent trips back and forth from New York to B-More, moving product with his boy Rondo.

It was after midnight, and I was onstage twirling myself around the pole with a dozen or so men screaming and waving dollar bills. I was glistening with baby oil and clad only in a baby blue thong and six-inch stilettos. I made about three hundred that night, and was looking to make much more by the time I retired and went home.

I knew that I was the sexiest bitch in the club, 'cause I got countless requests for lap dances after my segment, and niggahs wanted to take me into the VIP room and feel me up, and some were willing to pay a little extra just to fuck me. But I wasn't trying to fuck any of these dirty-dick niggahs in the club.

My song, "Honey Love" by R. Kelly played loudly in the backdrop, and I rolled around onstage, gleaming, moving around like I was making love to the floor.

"Damn, you sexy," this middle-aged man stated, as he tossed a ten-dollar bill onstage at me. I smiled, moved my hand slowly across his face touching him soothingly, and then I grabbed his hand and moved it steadily across my breasts. I felt him squeezing my tits and groaning during the process.

"That's enough," I softly said, showing him a slight smile and moving his hand away from my goodies.

"Marry me," he joked, looking content.

I continued my seductive routine onstage, and the DJ was doing me right by his selection in music. He continuously played one R. Kelly record after another. This time I moved my butt to "Bump N' Grind." I grabbed the pole and dropped down to the floor into a wide split—showing these mutha-fuckas my flexibility, and then I bounced my ass up and down against the stage.

"Oh shit!" I heard someone shout. Soon they were tossing tens and twenties at me like wild. I stood up on my six-inch heels clutching the pole, and moved to the beat with extreme passion, eyeing the crowd and looking at their reactions to my hot dance and fine body. I got excited just watching niggahs praise and rave over me in the club. I was the best.

I was about to end my dance segment, when I noticed Tears looming from the crowd. He was so fuckin' sexy. I had noticed him around the way a few times, but never got at him like that.

He stood by the stage, gazing at me, wearing a clean white tank top, baggy Sean John jeans, fresh new Timberlands on his feet, and his bald head gleaming. Adorning his neck was a thick platinum chain and a diamond encrusted cross. I glanced at his right hand, and also saw him sporting a diamond encrusted pinky ring.

"What's good, luv?" he said, pulling out a wad of bills from his pocket. "You know you look good, right? What's your name?" he whispered in my ear as he leaned over me.

"Ayeesha."

"I like that. You a shorty fo' real." He peeled off three C notes and tossed them at me. Ya know I had to continue dancing after that!

For the next ten minutes, I belonged to Tears on that stage. He had my undivided attention as he tipped me big, dropping fifties and hundred-dollar bills on me.

His touch was soft, confident, and enticing. He had me lying down on my back, with my legs spread wide as he ran his hands down my thighs. I felt his fingers brush against my pussy. I moaned lightly as I peered up at him.

Then he gave me this wicked grin, and I suddenly felt him tugging at my thong, trying to remove it.

I jumped, grabbing my thong and said, "Yo, chill, chill . . . we can't get naked in here. You about to get me kicked out."

He gave me an assuring look and returned with, "Don't worry about the house rules; they know me up in here, luv . . . I got you. This is my treat."

I was nervous and reluctant. *What the fuck he meant, I got you,* I thought. But Tears was persistent and continued to tug at my thong. I was on my back when he pulled it off and dropped it next to me. I was now butt-ass naked onstage in nothing but some stilettos, and I heard the crowd of men around me go stir crazy.

Tears ran his hand down my thighs and then pushed his middle and index finger deep into my pussy. I moaned as I glanced around nervously for the manager, and surprisingly I saw him looking on without barking or screaming on me. I guess Tears really did have connections in here, because usually if a girl flashed one pubic hair she got her ass chewed out later by Neo, the club manager.

Men started to crowd around the stage, as all eyes were fixated on me and him, and they watched Tears lean forward between my thighs and sink his full beautiful lips and tongue into my wet and throbbing pussy. I cried out with passion as he consumed my pussy like crazy. I was sprawled out on my back, had my legs straddled around him with my arms outstretched behind me, clutching the pole tightly and forgetting about who was watching.

"Ummmm . . . aaaaaahhh . . . ummm . . . ummm . . . shit, mutha-fucka . . . aaaaaahhh, eat that pussy, Tears," I cried out.

The DJ had turned the music off, and everyone heard my loud cries. Niggahs started to chant, "Tears. Tears. Tears. Tears. Tears. Tears. Tears."

That niggah went buck-wild between my legs, not missing a beat. He tore my ass up as he ate my pussy. He gripped both my thighs and pushed my legs back, and dug his tongue deeper into me. I felt his wet tongue swimming around in me, and I continued to clutch the pole. I just couldn't let go.

Money was raining down on me like crazy, but that was the last thing I was worried about. I think I fell in love with Tears that night. He was raw and just didn't give a fuck. And I loved that about a niggah.

After five minutes of putting a sistah in bliss, he finally stopped. He looked down at me with this content grin, and said, "Yo get dressed. We outta here."

He didn't have to tell me twice. I collected my things and walked offstage butt naked. I didn't bother to put my thong back on. I just strutted through the crowd not giving a fuck, clutching countless big bills in my hand.

I made it to the changing room and quickly got dressed. I heard one of the girls in the room say, "That bitch is wilding. I don't know why Tears picked her for."

It was hate talking, but I ignored her jealous ass and threw on my shit and met up with Tears outside the club. I had counted up twelve hundred dollars, and most if it had come from him.

Tears stood outside in front of the club, leaning against his gleaming black Escalade that was parallel parked next to a few cars out front. I smiled and strutted up to him in my short denim skirt and heels and gave him a hug like I'd known him forever.

"You ready?" he asked.

"Yeah."

I jumped into his truck and he drove off. It was like we connected. We went and got something to eat, and I ended up fuckin' him in the backseat of his truck. We were parked by a grassy area and I straddled him in the backseat with my skirt pulled up to my waist and feeling his dick steadily moving in and out of me.

A month later, unexpectedly, he asked me to move in with him and I accepted. But before we hooked up like that he said to me, "Yo, when we do this . . . you my wifey forever, you feel me? I'm gonna take care of you, Ayeesha . . . you know what I'm sayin'? But if you ever cheat on me, I'll fuckin' kill you. I mean it. Ain't gonna be no conversation neither. I'm just gonna pull out my gat and your life will be over."

He was so serious!

But I knew I loved him, and cheating on my boo was far from my mind at the time.

Tears promised to take care of me, and he did, without missing a beat.

Because of him, I finished paying for school and got my

degree. A year later I was driving a brand-new Lexus. We might have been living in the projects but our apartment had everything money could buy. From a flat-screen TV, Gucci, and Donna Karan, to imported furniture and a Jacuzzi in the bathroom.

．　．　．

I stood in the shower thinking over my two years with Tears, some good and some bad. Surprisingly for me, I had never cheated on him. I really loved him and I was trying to make things exciting for us. But lately Tears had been making that impossible. He was too caught up in the streets, grinding, hustling, and forever across state lines moving weight. When we first got married Tears used to dick me down every fuckin' night. Now I'll be lucky if I get it once a week.

"Ayeesha, I'm out," Tears shouted, knocking on the bathroom door.

"Ayyite, baby . . . be safe," I shouted back. But I was still frustrated and still fuckin' horny.

It was Thursday morning, and I was ten minutes late, but my boss always gave me some leeway. He'd had an innocent crush on me since the day I started.

I worked in Brentwood, Long Island, far away from my home in the Baisley Housing Projects in Jamaica, Queens. I had to travel, but I loved going to work every day, because it was a change of environment for me. I'd lived in the inner city all my life, and working in Long Island was the best. It was so tranquil out there that it made you forget that you were still in New York. And I enjoyed driving the distance to work. For me, it was the only way to escape the bullshit that I was putting up with at home. In the projects I was constantly surrounded by thugs and drugs. But at work, I was surrounded by white America, especially the corporate men who kissed my sexy ass every day, lusting for some dark chocolate.

I rushed into the office and Patty, the receptionist, told me that Mr. Robinson wanted to see me in his office right away. I was a bit nervous. I put my stuff on my desk and quickly headed for my boss's office.

Mr. Robinson was a black man holding down a very lucrative position in the company. He was in his mid-forties and still fine as hell.

I knocked on the polished wood-grain door to his office and immediately heard, "Come in."

I walked into his plush corner-view office and immediately noticed a man seated on the stylish imported-leather green couch near Mr. Robinson's desk.

"Ayeesha, I've been waiting for you," Mr. Robinson said, peering at me from his lavish leather chair. "This is Raheem Mitchell," he introduced me to the man.

Damn! I thought, gazing at this fine specimen of what a real man should look like. He was tall, dark, sporting a gray three-piece business suit, and had a trimmed dark goatee. His lips were full, his head was bald, and his posture was strong and positive.

He stood up and shook my hand firmly saying, "Nice to meet you." I held his gaze for a moment. I couldn't take my eyes off him, because he was definitely eye candy. I noticed the diamond-studded watch on his wrist, and I knew he had money.

"Ayeesha, I need you to draw up the deposition for the Clemens account soon as possible, and work with Mr. Mitchell here. We might have him as a new account to this agency," Mr. Robinson said, smiling from his chair. "And before you start anything, can you please get Mr. Mitchell and myself some coffee?"

"Not a problem," I said.

I slowly backed toward the door, staring and smiling at Raheem Mitchell with my flirty ass. His eyes never left mine and I walked out of Mr. Robinson's office with that same tingling sensation between my legs that I'd had this morning.

I worked with Raheem all morning. He was thinking about bringing a new account to the agency, which would be worth forty-five million dollars, and Mr. Robinson was kissing his ass.

We talked and got to know each other, and all I knew was there was a serious attraction between us.

Raheem asked me all kinds of personal questions like he was dying to know my business. I told him that I was hooked up, with no kids, and had been with my man for about two years. I left out the part about how I was dancing onstage when I met Tears, and how wild I was.

Raheem said he wasn't with anybody and didn't have any kids either. He was so damn fine he made my panties melt. With all of his money he still had a deep gangsta voice, and I loved the way he talked.

"Your man is lucky," he told me. "You're every damn thing a black woman should look like."

I smiled real big and the flirting between us went back and forth. He made me feel hot. He made me feel wanted. And after that incident with Tears, he made me feel like he wanted to fuck me.

Hours passed, and it was soon time for my lunch break. I glanced at my desk clock and saw that I had fifteen more minutes until my one o' clock lunch. Raheem was in the office with my boss, and I was dying to see and talk to him again.

A few minutes later the door to my boss's office opened and Raheem came walking out. He looked like a male model striding toward my desk. I waited for him to say something, but instead he dropped a note on my desk and walked away without uttering one word.

I picked up the note he'd dropped, and it read: *Meet me at the Sheraton Hotel, room 825, during your lunch hour.*

I was shocked. I read the note three times, and then stuffed it in my purse. I had a devilish smile on my face as I wondered what he wanted with me. I was definitely gonna find out!

The Sheraton was a few blocks from my job, so it wasn't a problem. I jumped into my Lexus and made it to the hotel in five minutes.

I walked into the lobby strutting in my brown A-line boot-length skirt, black leather boots, a white blouse, and my light denim jacket draped over my forearm. I had never been in this hotel, but the lobby was beautiful. It was vast, with a large crystal chandelier suspended above marble floors, antique Georgian mahogany carver chairs with scroll arms and saber legs, and a swanky seating arrangement.

I strutted past the two female clerks and went straight for the elevators. I pressed 8 and waited. I was burning with anticipation and wondering what Raheem had planned for me.

I rode up to the eighth floor in silence. That threat Tears liked to make about me cheating on him came to mind. *Fuck him!* I said to myself. *He should've taken the pussy this morning.* I got off the elevator and continued down the posh, carpeted hallway. I looked for room 825 and my heart beating like crazy the closer I came to the room.

"825, it's a suite," I said to myself in a whisper.

The door was slightly open and I took a deep breath and slowly made my way inside. The room was dim with the shades pulled down and it was quiet. I glanced around the suite and didn't see Raheem. I stayed my ass near the door, and moved no further into the room.

Behind me, the door slammed suddenly, and out of the blue I felt a pair of masculine arms reach around my waist and pull me closer into his embrace.

"I'm glad you came," I heard Raheem say behind me. "You nervous?"

"Yeah. A little bit," I admitted, but pressed my ass against him anyway. "I gotta be back at work at two."

"Don't worry, we have enough time."

He slowly began undoing my blouse, and then I felt his hand reach inside my bra and cup my breast. I moaned with pleasure as he pulled up my skirt. His hand moved between my moist thighs and rested against my throbbing pussy. I shivered as he pushed my panties to the side and slid two fingers into my wet pussy.

"Oooh, ooh," I moaned, feeling him dig into me. I clamped my love muscles around his fingers and continued to squeeze.

"Um, your shit feels so tight, Ayeesha," he whispered in my ear. His breath was warm and smelled like Winter Fresh gum. I turned my head, facing him slightly, and he turned too, and we tongued each other down as he continued to finger my pussy tenderly.

His tongue was long and hot and he tried to push it down my throat. He kissed me like he loved my ass. His strong hands fondled my breasts, then continued to molest that part of me down low.

I finally turned all the way around and saw that he was in a thick white terry-cloth bathrobe. I wrapped my arms around him and continued to kiss him hotly, just like I used to kiss my boo.

It was already 1:25 P.M. and I didn't have much more time for my lunch break. I took off my boots, and began unfastening my skirt, giving Raheem a little show. I dropped my skirt to the floor and stood in front of him in my white blouse, bra, and some lacy pink panties.

"Damn! You are the bomb, Ayeesha," he stated.

I continued to strip, shedding my clothing gradually until I stood stark naked in front of him. I smiled, moving my hands across my flawless brown skin. "Your turn," I said.

He didn't have much to take off, so he removed his robe from his broad shoulders and let it fall to the floor around his ankles.

He stood butt naked in front of me and my ass was in awe. He had a BIG dick. It hung down like a snake from a tree. He had a rock-hard six-pack, some thick masculine biceps, and his whole body was very muscled and shapely.

Ohmygod, I thought, my eyes fixated on him from head to toe. He was built just like the stranger from my dream last night.

Raheem took my hand and led me toward the bedroom.

"You want me to show you a trick?" he asked as he stood near the king-sized bed.

"What trick is that?"

He scooped me off my feet and into his arms, then boosted me up over his shoulders until I was straddling his neck. He held me in the air and started eating out my pussy, devouring me like a lion.

"Touch the ceiling," he joked. His speech was a bit muffled 'cause his face was deep in my pussy.

"Aaaaaahhh . . . Ohmygod . . . Ohmygod . . . Ohmygod . . . Aaaaaahhh . . . Shit, Raheem . . . Fuck!" I cried out as my legs began to quiver from his intense tongue action. I grabbed his bald head. "Shit, you're a strong man."

He walked across the suite as he ate me as out. I was still hoisted up on his shoulders as he buried his tongue deep in me and my body shuddered with satisfaction.

He moved toward the bed and lowered me down until I was on my back. I peered up at him with a contented grin.

"You like that?" he asked, climbing onto the bed. He spread my legs, then pushed them over my head—good thing I was flexible—and continued where he left off.

I moaned out loud and clutched the green bedsheets as Raheem sucked and licked every inch of me with his expert tongue.

I glanced at the clock on the wall and panicked. It was 1:45. "Shit!" I muttered. "Fuck me, Raheem, right now," I begged, itching for his big black dick to penetrate me.

He rose to his knees and grabbed both my legs and pulled me closer to him. He pushed my legs back a little as he situated himself, then palmed the head of his big dick and slowly pushed inch by inch of his erection into me. I gasped, gripping the sheets so tight, then biting down on my bottom lip as his thick penis opened my pussy up like whoa!

I wanted to feel that dick raw. I cried out as he began thrusting about ten inches into me, hitting spots that no man had ever hit before. I mean, fuck the stomach! I felt his dick in my chest! I had to push against his stomach because the weight was too much for me to handle.

Raheem continued to pound and pound into me, and with each hard thrust that niggah heard how loud my vocals were. I'm surprised the whole eighth floor didn't hear my screaming and raving, but I'm sure the people in the next two rooms did.

"Raheem, I'm cumming!" I screamed out. "Oh shit, you making me cum!"

Raheem continued to fuck the shit out of me, until my whole body quivered and went limp from the strong orgasm he put on me. I lay motionless for a moment, trying to collect myself, until I glanced at the time again and yelped, "Oh shit!" It was five minutes after two. I jumped out of bed and quickly collected my things.

Raheem stayed in bed, grinning at me.

"What time do you get off?" he asked.

"Five," I said, fastening my skirt.

"I wanna see you again."

"Not a problem." I quickly buttoned my blouse.

"How about tonight, after you get off work? I have a ranch in Riverhead."

"Not tonight. But tomorrow night is cool," I told him.

"Okay. So I'll see you in the office tomorrow morning?"

"Yeah." I ran out the door and rushed to my car.

I got back to the office at 2:20 P.M., but surprisingly no one noticed I was late. I sighed with relief, sat down at my desk, and grinned inside as I thought about what I had just done and how much I couldn't wait to do it again.

.   .   .

That night I got home tired and hungry at around six, only to see a bunch of niggahs chilling in my crib smoking, drinking, and making a mess out of my living room.

I got agitated and asked, "Where's Tears?"

"What up, ma . . . he in the bedroom," one of his goons said, looking high as fuck.

I strutted into the bedroom and saw Tears sitting on the bed in a black tank top, with the phone clutched to his ear.

He glanced up, but never acknowledged me—it was like, Whatever, you home. I sighed and closed the bedroom door.

He finally hung up the phone and took a pull from the burning blunt he had between his fingers. His .45 was resting on the nightstand and I noticed about a pound of marijuana on my bed.

"Tears, why you got niggahs in my crib like this?" I asked in frustration.

"Them my peoples. We just chillin', baby," he said. He grabbed my chin between his fingers and placed a kiss on my forehead. "How was work?"

That shit was good! But I was scared to look at him. Scared that he might see the truth in my eyes so I muttered, "Fine."

He walked out the bedroom to go get high with his goons. I let out a sigh and plopped on my bed.

After spending countless hours with his niggahs in the living room, Tears finally decided to bring his ass to bed. It was after midnight when he crawled in and snuggled next to me in his boxers and a T-shirt.

"Baby, roll over on your stomach," he said, rubbing my legs gently.

"Tears," I said, feeling him kissing on my neck, and grabbing places that I didn't want him to grab at that moment.

"I wanna fuck you," he said, fondling my breasts.

"Tears, I'm tired. Can it wait?" I asked, moving my butt away from the erection he had in his boxers.

"What? C'mon . . . let me just get a quickie. You ain't gotta do shit but just lay there," he tried to reason.

"No. I'm tired." I was serious.

"Fuck you!" he cursed, and got out of bed. "I'm out."

"Whatever!" was all I said. I closed my eyes and went to sleep, hearing Tears move around in the room as he got dressed to go run the streets. *You should have took it this morning when I was throwing it at you!*

I woke up the next morning after having almost the same crazy dream with the horses! I wasn't into fucking in the presence of animals, and yeah the dream ended with the fine man eating my pussy real good again, but the dream really bothered me. This time I had been riding on a stallion butt naked, as the horse galloped through the grassland. Suddenly, I'd felt this entity behind me, and he was naked also. He wrapped his arms around my waist as he rode on the stallion with me gripping my soft naked ass from behind. He began fingering me as I moaned, then the horse leaped and the man's finger went deep inside me, causing me to cry out. I had never felt anything like it before. He grabbed my pussy and fucked me with his fingers.

I woke up in a slight sweat, and this time Tears wasn't even fuckin' home. *Fuck that muthafucka*, I cursed to myself. I glanced at the time and it was 6:45 A.M. I fell back against my pillow. My dream had seemed so real.

I went to work in a loose-fitting skirt, a blouse, and some sexy heels. I admit it took me longer to get ready for work than usual, knowing that Raheem was going to be in. I wanted to look my best for him today.

I strutted into the office beaming. I sat at my desk and

glanced around looking for him. I was hoping maybe we could do that hotel suite again. God knows I wanted to.

But two hours passed, and there was no sign of him. I started to get discouraged. I sighed, trying to do my work and get my mind off his dick. *Maybe it was only meant to be a one-time thing with him,* I thought.

I was going over a few spreadsheets for my boss, when I heard, "You busy?"

I looked up and it was Raheem smiling down at me, looking so fine in his suit and wearing a pair of sunglasses.

"Hey you," I cheerfully greeted him, feeling my pussy throbbing just at the sight of him.

"When's your next break?"

"I can take fifteen minutes right now," I told him.

"C'mon, then." He gestured.

I looked around, then told my friend Carol that I was taking my morning break. She nodded and I walked off with Raheem.

I followed him toward the men's bathroom.

"I'll wait for you," I said.

He gave me a sinful grin and said, "Inside, you and me."

"Are you crazy? I can't walk into the men's bathroom."

"Why not? We only got fifteen minutes. And besides, I already checked and no one's inside."

It was tempting, and my hot pussy was telling me to go ahead and get myself a quickie at work. Raheem gently pulled me into the men's bathroom, which was empty and— thank God—clean. I followed him down to the handicapped stall at the end of the row.

"I love what you have on, Ayeesha," he said, his hands sliding up my skirt and gripping my ass. "You look real good."

I rammed my tongue down his throat as I unbuckled his pants and pulled out his huge erection. I stroked him gracefully as I backed him against the wall. I wanted to taste him, and feel his big dick sliding in and out my mouth.

I squatted down with his dick still in my grip. I peeked up at him and he looked content already. I leaned forward and slowly sucked on the tip of his dick. He let out a slight moan. I bobbed my head back and forth as Raheem moaned with pleasure. I tried to deep-throat it, but I was only able to push about eight inches into my mouth without gagging. But no lie, his shit felt so good in my mouth.

A moment later I stood up and he sat down on the toilet seat with his pants and boxers around his ankles, and his hard-on looking like a flagpole.

"Come ride this dick," he said, stroking himself.

"Ssshhhh," I whispered, placing my index finger near my mouth. "We gotta keep quiet and listen out for the door."

"My badddd."

I pulled off my panties, keeping them in my hand, and hiked up my skirt as I walked up to the dick. I straddled him little by little; gradually bringing my pussy down on his dick. I groaned as I felt him penetrate me. I gripped the handicap railing near the toilet and started to ride him.

Raheem grasped my ass and brought me down harder on the dick, I let out a loud scream as he pushed damn near the whole thing into me.

"You better stop," I whispered in his ear. "This is my job you fuckin' with."

He gave me that same sinful grin, and continued to thrust in me, pulling at my hair and fuckin' the shit out of me. I let go of the railing and wrapped my arms around him, clutching his body tight, feeling myself about to cum.

"I'm cumming," I whispered in his ear, rocking back and forth, up and down on his lap. I felt that dick in my chest again.

"I'm cumming too, Ayeesha," he cried out, but suddenly we heard the bathroom door creak open and my eyes widened. We both remained completely still. I listened carefully. We heard someone peeing by the urinals. Raheem smiled at me, and grabbed my ass and tried to continue fuckin' me as he sucked on my nipples.

"You better stop," I whispered to him.

I heard the urinal flush and then water running in the sink. And then I heard the guy fart as he washed his hands. Raheem and I laughed silently as the man walked out of the bathroom.

We continued to fuck. Raheem sucked on my hard nipples and repeatedly pounded some good fuckin' dick up in me. "I'm cumming," I cried out again. I felt my legs quivering, so I gripped the railing with my left hand and continued to ride.

I felt his dick get harder inside me as he grabbed my butt tightly, and his fingers gripped my butt cheeks as I felt him shuddering and exploding in me.

Moments later, he made me explode too. I remained

seated on his lap, panting and trying to catch my breath. I glanced at the time and saw that I only had two minutes left of my break.

"Damn, you always do this to me," I told Raheem as I dismounted him, wiped myself, and put my panties back on.

He smiled and said, "But you know it's worth it."

We quickly got decent again, and Raheem stepped out of the stall before me to check if all was clear. He signaled for me that it was okay to leave, and I strutted out of the bathroom running my hands through my hair.

I made it back to my desk, and sank into my chair with a pleased look plastered across my face. Even Carol noticed it when she looked at me and said, "Damn, Ayeesha, that must have been some break. You looking like a whole new woman."

I smiled and thought, *If she only knew.*

* * *

After work, I rode east with Raheem in his new 2007 S-Class, gleaming black Benz. He had his hand up my skirt finger-popping me as he did eighty miles an hour on the Long Island Expressway as we headed to his ten-acre ranch in Riverhead, Long Island. And of course I sucked his dick in the car for a good twenty minutes!

We got there around eight that evening, and I was in awe. His crib was all that. I stepped out of the car amazed. He showed me around, which took damn near an hour, but when we walked out the back of the house and into a barn, my mouth dropped open. It was the same barn I'd been seeing in my dreams!

"What's wrong?" he asked.

"Nothing. Nothing at all," I said, staring at his big black horses. "It's just funny, because I feel like I've seen this place before," I marveled.

"You hungry?" he asked.

We ended up having dinner, drinking champagne and having some real good conversation. He introduced me to his butler, Henry, who had been taking care of Raheem since he was in diapers.

But the exciting news came when Raheem told me that he'd made up his mind to let my agency handle his account. That would bring a lot of money into the office, and he admitted that he was giving his business to my agency all because of me. He also said that he was going to give Mr. Robinson some really good reports about me, and I was thrilled because his word could help me get a promotion.

Around ten that night I found myself in the barn with Raheem, fucking him once again. He had me bent over one of the stable doors, my skirt pulled up, panties on the ground, as he did to me what he did best.

Moments later, we were butt naked in the hay wilding the fuck out. I was in the missionary position, legs straddled around him, and screaming at the top of my lungs. He did me justice that night! It seemed like every time we fucked, it just got better and better.

It was so good that I passed out nestled against Raheem in the hay, and we slept butt-naked in each other's arms the whole night.

I woke up around ten that Saturday morning and knew

that I needed to call my boo. Tears was probably worried sick about me. I had lied and told him I would be home late because I was accompanying Mr. Robinson to an important business meeting in the city, but that was no excuse to stay out all night long.

I sat up in the hay and was surprised that Raheem was not by my side. I figured he'd probably gone inside the house for a moment, so I quickly got dressed. When I walked out of the barn I saw Henry tending one of the horses.

"Where's Raheem?" I asked.

He looked at me like he never saw me before.

"And you are?" he asked.

"Ayeesha, remember? I came home with Raheem last night, and we had dinner together. We talked for hours."

"I'm sorry, I have no recollection of you," he stated. "How did you get here anyway?"

"Raheem brought me," I told him. I suddenly noticed that the Benz was gone. But I also remembered Raheem telling me that Henry was getting old and his mind sometimes came and went.

My ass had to take a cab home. I was pissed off that Raheem had left without waking me up or saying good-bye. But he was a busy man, making millions.

I got home around noon, only to get into a heated argument with Tears for staying out all night with no good excuse. I thought that niggah was gonna attack me—he was just that fuckin' furious. Over and over he threatened to kill me if he caught me fuckin' some other niggah, but eventually he calmed down after I lied my ass off about my whereabouts, then sucked his dick, swallowed his kids, and gave him some bomb pussy that made him shut the fuck up about me not coming home last night.

· · ·

Monday morning found me in my office bright and early. I was excited about Raheem's new account and my involvement in it. I knew it would mean some major shit for the agency. I looked around the office for Raheem, but he was nowhere to be found.

Noontime came, and I was getting anxious—still no Raheem. I sighed. I thought maybe he had come in even earlier than me, taken care of his business with the agency, and then had to leave on business.

I left my desk and went to Mr. Robinson's office. I knocked twice on his door and heard him call, "Come in."

I walked into his office and my boss was seated at his desk looking over some papers.

"Mr. Robinson, did we get the new account?" I asked, smiling tremendously about it.

He looked up at me and I saw his eyebrow arch. "New account?"

"Yes, with Raheem. He told me over the weekend that he wanted us to handle his account. He said that I was a big help in his decision to do business with us."

My boss leaned back in his leather chair and gave me this baffled look, and then he hit me with, "Who is Raheem?"

"You introduced me to him last week," I proclaimed, thinking my boss was losing his mind. "He was sitting right there on that couch." I pointed. "He was tall, dark-skinned, bald head, trimmed goatee—a very handsome man. He was in here talking to you about business."

"I'm sorry, Ayeesha, but I have no idea who you're talking about. I never met any Raheem, nor am I familiar with anyone with that name," he said.

I stood in my boss's office dumbfounded. Didn't anyone remember Raheem except me?

"You've got to know him. I met him right here. He's got to be real. I mean, we—" I stopped myself from blowing up my own spot in front of Mr. Robinson. "Raheem took me out to a ranch in Riverhead on Friday evening. He showed me his horses."

"Did you say a ranch in Riverhead?" Mr. Robinson said.

Suddenly, my eyes were drawn to a picture sitting on my boss's shelf. I'd never seen it there before, but it was familiar. It was a picture of Raheem.

"That's him! That's Raheem!" I shouted, pointing to the picture.

"My son?"

"Your son?"

"Yes. But his name isn't Raheem. It's Jerome, and he was killed three years ago. In fact, in Riverhead."

I looked at him like, *What the fuck!*

"If you don't mind me asking, how did he die?" I asked.

"Jerome loved horses all his life. A week after his twenty-

third birthday he was trampled by a stallion on a ranch in
Riverhead. In fact, today would have been my son's twenty-
sixth birthday," he proclaimed.

"Ohmygod!" I muttered, with my hand cupped over my
mouth. I felt like I was about to faint. *How could it be?* I
asked myself. My nipples were still sore. It had seemed so
real.

"Ayeesha, you sure you're okay? You need some time off?
You need to go home?" he asked.

"No, I'll be fine," I said, leaving his office.

I was spooked. Had I been fuckin' a spirit? A ghost? I
didn't know what to think. I made my way back to my desk
trying to come up with a logical explanation for all this shit.
The crazy dreams, the wild sex, and the fuckin' horses!

"Ayeesha, you okay?" Carol asked.

I nodded. I was starting to get a headache. I went into my
purse looking for something to take for my sudden headache.
That's when I pulled out the note Raheem had written me on
Thursday:

Meet me at the Sheraton Hotel, room 825, during your lunch.

I freaked straight out, falling out of my chair, hitting my
head on the desk, and making a loud thud as I landed on the
floor.

When I woke up again I was in my boo's arms. My co-
worker Carol must have called him to come get me because
Tears was looking down at me with big eyes. He had taken
me home and put me in our bed. At first I thought everything had been one crazy dream, until I saw the gun in

Tears's hand. He gripped me by my neck and pushed the note Raheem had written me up in my face.

"Bitch," he said with the barrel pressed to my forehead. "You met a motherfucker in room 825 at the Sheraton Hotel? Ain't no way you can fuckin' explain this shit!"

I opened my mouth to tell him it had only been a dream, but then I heard the trigger click, and just like Tears had promised, my life was over.

LIFE OF SIN
Joy

"What's your pleasure?" I purred into the phone. Being the sex kitten that I am, I knew I had the dog on the other end of the phone with his tail standing straight up.

"Shit, you. You my pleasure, ma," Papi said with his heavy Cuban accent.

It was 12:01 A.M. Even before answering the phone I'd known it was Papi calling. He made sure that he was always the first man to call me upon the dawn of a new day.

He loved being my first.

"You know I hate sloppy seconds," he always says.

"I'm your pleasure, huh?" I asked. I wanted to hear him say it again. Well, actually, I wanted him to think that I wanted to hear him say it again.

"Umm, you, *puta*. You're my pleasure, you fuckin' *puta*."

"I'm your *puta*, Papi. I'm your cunt," I said, sticking my index finger in my mouth and sucking on it. I knew damn well he couldn't see me, but he could hear my wet tongue slurping on it. The visual alone had his hands yankin' off on his *chilito* by now.

"What do you want to do to me, Papi? What do you want to do to this cunt of yours? Fuck it, huh? Is that what you want to do? Come on. *Oooh*, come on, Papi and just fuck it. Fuck it good for me, huh."

By now I had a smile a mile long on my face. I could hear Papi beating that stick like it was Rodney King and he was Five-O. It had been less than one minute and this nigga was 'bout to bust. This was a record-breaking time for me. I must say that I felt proud. But it was too premature to cele-brate. So just to make sure that his call to me would be worth it, I decided to go hard in the paint.

"I feel you inside me. I feel you inside me, Papi," I said, finding myself picking up on his accent. It was a force of habit. After only hearing Papi say a few words to me, I found myself replying to him with a slight accent myself. He never took it as though I was trying to imitate or make fun of him, though. As a matter of fact, it made him even more excited. I think he probably pictured a nice, coconut-complected, clammy Boriqua, with her hair sweated out, sprawled across her bed, him plunging his dick inside her pussy and bustin' a nut deep up inside of her hole instead of inside his fist.

"You feel it? You feel that shit, *puta*?" he moaned, breathing heavily into my ear.

"You're hurting me, Papi. Not so hard."

"Shut the fuck up and take this shit like a real *puta*!"

"Oh, Papi!" I let out a screech that sounded as though it was on the verge of pleasure and pain.

"Yeah, that's right. See, it hurts so good, don't it?"

"Yes, yes, yes. It hurts so good, but I can take it. I can take all of it. Give it to me, Papi. Give it to me harder!" I began damn near yelling at the top of my lungs.

"Oh shit," he yelled. I could hear the thumping of him jacking off. "Oh yeah." He got louder. I knew it was time.

"Oh, Papi, I want you to pull out and nut all over me. I want your babies all over me. I want to rub it in like lotion, Papi. Come on, Papi. Now! Now! Now!"

"Oh shit," I heard him yell. I then heard a large thump, the phone dropping. Because of the distance Papi was now away from the phone, his muffled tone informed me that he was cumming. Over and over he screamed it. "I'm cummin'. I'm cummin'. Oh, you fuckin' cunt, look what you made me do!"

"Here, listen to this," I said in a whisper as I took the phone off my ear and put it next to Sam's, who was sitting right there next to me in the bed, butt naked, and working on a crossword puzzle. I watched Sam's eyes light up at the drama going down on the other end of the line. The laughter that wanted to burst out of Sam's mouth had to be contained, and I quickly placed my hand over those gorgeous lips.

Sam looked at me with sparkling gray eyes, bright and full of life, listening in amusement at how I had just made Papi nut all over himself with my bomb-ass phone sex skills.

I'd sometimes let Sam listen in on the calls I received on my 900 "What's Your Pleasure" line. Anyone else's lover might have gotten jealous sitting there listening to their mate verbally fuck someone on the phone. But Sam knew that every last one of those men who called me up for my phone sex service was named Bill; Water Bill, Gas Bill, Light Bill, Phone Bill, Cable Bill, etc. . . . No man could do for me what Sam did for me, so they were no threat to our relationship.

I removed the phone from Sam's ear and placed it back on mine.

"Papi, oh, Papi." I panted lightly, as if I had just cum myself. "See what you do to me? Why do you do this to me all the time?"

"Whew-wee," he said, as if he was trembling from the aftershock of his earthshaking explosion. "It's not what I do to you, Mami. It's what you do to me."

"And you know you like it."

"That's where you're wrong. I love it." We both laughed in each other's ear.

"Same time next time, Papi?"

"Same time next time, my little *puta*."

"Adios," I said, ending the call.

Upon hanging up the phone I looked over at Sam, who

looked over at me. Sam slowly took the crossword puzzle and the pen and laid them aside. Then, like a fiery wild little panther, Sam arched on all fours and slowly crawled toward me. My clit immediately began to swell and throb like it was a dick. It got to the point where I stuck my hand down the black lace panties I was wearing and grabbed hold of my crotch, just double-checking that God hadn't played some cruel trick on me and grew me a dick out of nowhere. I rubbed my sensitive, moist knob as Sam kneeled on all fours over me. I leaned back on the stack of three soft head pillows and allowed my hand to play with my wet patch.

"I like finger food," Sam informed me. "Let me taste."

I smiled, catching the hint Sam was throwing, and removed my hand from my panties. One by one I slowly let Sam suck my juices off my fingers as I crooned my hips at just the thought of Sam doing to my pussy what was being done to my fingers.

"Ummm," Sam said, inhaling my entire middle finger then spitting it out and heading straight for my croonin' jungle.

Sam slowly slid my panties down my long, slender legs, the color of a tootsie roll, sniffing the crotch before tossing them onto the floor. "Smells like a rose," Sam said, before diving headfirst into my pool of chocolate thoughts.

"Oh fuck," I said as Sam licked at my clit like the momma kitten would lick a baby. I couldn't help but grab Sam by the hair and start humping.

"Ummm," Sam hummed on my clit, making me spread my legs like I was pushing a baby out.

252 | From the Streets to the Sheets

I held my legs open by my ankles. I was open wide, signaling Sam that I was ready to be finger-fucked. Not a moment too soon, Sam plunged one finger in after the next, dipping all in and out of my Kool-Aid, trying to figure out the flavor.

"Come here," I said to Sam.

I could feel Sam's middle finger inside of me while at the same time I felt Sam's body lay upon mine. Sam brushed my bangs to the side to join the rest of the strands of my dusty brown shoulder-length hair. She then looked into my dark brown china-shaped eyes, inherited by my half-Chinese, half-black father.

"God, I love you so fuckin' much," I said with tears in my eyes as I pumped up and down on Sam's fingers. I was crying because it felt so good. I was crying because I really did love Sam. It felt good to be made to feel so damn good. It felt good to be in love.

"I love you too, baby," Sam replied with such deep sincerity. That's when I decided that I wanted to fuck Sam too. So I took my middle finger, maneuvered it through the soft hairs leading to Sam's jungle, and entered my finger in one thrust.

As if Sam was trying to upstage me, I felt two fingers massaging the inside of my walls, in search of that G-spot, while a thumb pressed against my clit, providing the ultimate sensation.

"Oh, Sam," I said, lifting my head up and shoving my tongue down Sam's throat while we plunged our fingers in and out of each other's pussy as we smacked our bodies up against one another. "My sexy Samantha."

Samantha was my foxy little project chick. With her soft gray eyes, smooth, vanilla-wafer Cover Girl skin, a short cut, showing off her curly loops, tinted with gold-rush blond hair, and standing at only about four feet nine inches, she looked like a short double for that Eva chick from *America's Next Top Model*.

"Move your hand," Sam said, pulling her fingers out of me. "Open your lips," she ordered me, referring to my pussy lips. I took my thumbs, placing one on each lip, and moved the skin back so that my throbbing clit was exposed like a dog's dick when he's in heat. Sam did the same with hers as she brought her pelvis down against mine tightly and our clits pressed together. I closed my eyes at the feeling of pure ecstasy. The feeling of being like one with Sam was amazing. I felt like we were connected as she began sliding her clit up and down mine. "Hold on to me tight," she ordered me.

I placed my hands around Sam's size-four waist and pulled her tight against me as we fucked the shit out of each other's clits, banging coochies like it was arma-ghetto up in that bitch.

"Fuck me, Sam. That's right, fuck me," I said, sticking my tongue out for her to suck on it. She took the bait and began to suck on my tongue as she started to whine.

"Uh, oh, uh, oh," she cried, the uhs and ohs growing louder and louder. "Cum with me. Cum with me, baby."

"Fuck that clit. Fuck that clit. Nut on it, damn, nut on it," I begged Sam as I felt our juices brewing down below.

Sam's clit felt so warm, so soft, and so precious as it pleased itself against mine. I planted my fingers deep in her ass checks as she rose up and arched her back. Tightly, I pulled her against me as we humped and grinded. Sam's head was thrown back. All I could see was her perfectly arched neck and her brown titties, nipples hard and beautiful. She was mine. Any nigga, any dyke bitch, would kill to be getting a piece of a pussy so sweet. But it was mine, all mine. After all, I had made it what it was. Before me, Sam had allowed dick after dick to try to fill that emptiness she had inside of her. It was an emptiness that only pussy could fill—my pussy, and my gentle fingers and caressing lips. All her life she had been waiting on me, a woman, she just didn't know it, or just didn't want to admit it. But now the obvious was being displayed as I brought her to the climax of her life.

"I am nutting on you," Sam assured me. "I'm cumming, I'm cumming on you now."

Just those words sent me berserk as both our bodies trembled as we glazed one another with our special sugary coatings.

"Oh yes," Samantha said as her petite body collapsed on mine, her chest moving up and down from breathing so heavily.

"Umm, you came a lot," I said as I reached between Sam's legs and felt her sticky cream. It was so warm and smooth, just like her. Slowly she began grinding on my hand, just to get one last nut off before retiring to the shower.

Watching her shiny, sweaty ass walk away to the bathroom only made me want to get one more in myself. So I was forced to replay in my head the last few minutes of fucking

Sam, and masturbate to the vision, pleasing myself in less than a minute. Sam just had that affect on me.

If I hadn't discovered by the time I was thirteen that I preferred to play hide-and-go-get-it with little girls over little boys, after taking one look at my sexy Samantha I would have definitely lost my appetite for dick and taken on a new craving for pussy. But lucky for me, I never had to even entertain the thought of fuckin' around with a bunch of hood niggas only to discover that no-sized dick is worth putting up with them and their bullshit. All it took was growing up with Naomi Kensington—aka, my moms—and living the life she subjected me to, to know that I preferred pussy over dick any day.

"Honey," I heard Sam call from the shower. "Come join me. Wash my back."

I loved washing Sam's back, from her shoulders to the small of her waist. I loved it. With me standing a little under a foot taller than her, towering over her made me feel so protective of her, like she was mine, really mine, unable to function without me. I know damn sure I'm unable to function without her. I love me some Sam, and not just because she was my first and only piece of ass, the woman I learned how to please a woman with, the woman I learned how it felt to be pleased with. It was because she was there when I was sixteen, out on the streets and needing that mother figure, any mother figure, to show me love.

Being five years older than me, Sam was twenty-one when I was sixteen, and she was living with some thug-ass nigga named Detail who didn't do nothing but beat her and fuck her, and usually in that order. He would clock on her over any little thing. If the toast was too brown, if the bed wasn't made right or she missed a spot when she dusted, he'd get all up in that ass. He demanded perfection. That's how he got the name Detail.

He was meticulous about everything. His car had to be wiped down just right. The bed had to be made to his standard, tight like a hospital bed. Towels had to be hung in a tri-fold manner. I mean, nothing got past that fucker's eyes. He was a real stickler for detail, to the point where, if you ask me, it was a sickness.

One day I came in from hoopin' at the court in the projects where we lived, and before I could even open the apartment door I heard the thumps of his fists hitting her. I don't remember a whole lot after that. But I do know that on that day Sam and I fucked that nigga up. That was the last time he ever put his hands on her. He was out of her life for good. From that day on there was this eternal bond between Sam and me. I just remember us holding each other. I was crying so hard that I was trembling. There was blood all over Sam. I just held her, held her for what seemed like forever.

"Did you hear me?" Sam called again from the shower. "Honey?"

"I'm coming," I called as I sat up in the bed. Before I could put a foot on the floor, though, my 900 line rang. "Damn," I said under my breath. "I can't, Sam. That's my line."

I knew she was disappointed. I was disappointed. Oh well, there were bills that needed to be paid and that ringing phone meant that there was money to be made. So pushing pussy to the back of my mind, Sam's pussy, I sat up and answered the call. "What's your pleasure?"

Whore's Daughter

I don't know what the fuck my moms was thinking when she named me Sin. No, it's not short for Sindy, Sindiana, Sinammon, or any other name black people come up with and think that just because they spell it different, that makes it different. Don't matter how you spell it. When you say it, the shits all sound the same. So it's just plain old Sin.

No pun intended, but it was hell growing up in the projects full of Shaniquas, Keishas, and Tahjanays. Them kids let me have it about my name every chance they got. That's how come I can brawl like Antonio Tarver to this day. I might lose the first fight, but I'ma damn sure prove myself in the second one. My moms had to know I was going to get teased endlessly about my name and have to defend myself with my dukes. So I figured either that bitch was just trying to be funny when she named me Sin, or she wanted me to be a reminder of what her life was full of. And Lord knows what the life of Naomi Kensington was full of, and I know people expected me to turn out just like her.

What I do for a living, running my own phone-sex line, is legal. It pays the bills and I get to keep Sam laced. Morally, I guess muthafuckas would have some ol' negative shit to say. But hell, I could be out there doing the worse of the two evils. Instead of selling just the fantasy of my twenty-three-year-old ripe pussy for $3.99 per minute, I could be just outright selling the pussy. But that's a profession Naomi mastered.

The word was written about my moms before she was even conccived. God knew exactly what kind of woman she was going to be, even before my grandfather's nut clashed with my grandmother's egg. And it must have been a rotten egg at that, to produce someone as foul as Naomi. That wayward girl, that prostitute in the Book of Proverbs, that would be my moms. As far back as I can remember, Naomi has been saucy and pert, always dressing seductively. She had to. How else could she get married niggas, single white men, non-English-speaking Puerto Rican men, rich Jewish men, and any other species of men to spend their last cent on just the idea of her black cunt?

Granted, Moms was a fine-ass ho, and you really couldn't tell she was a ho outside of the neighborhood. But in the hood, everybody saw the tricks coming and going out of our apartment. Even our blind neighbor, Miss Bee, saw that shit. If no one saw it, they sho nuff smelled it. I think my moms wore a dab of pussy behind her ear the way men flocked to her. Fuckin' walking hard-ons is what men are. All them rat bastards ever thought about was getting their fuck on, or their dick sucked. They didn't even care that a little girl was right there in the house. Hell, they used to sit lined up on the couch next to me while I played Ms. Pacman on my Atari, just waiting to be consumed by the spirit of the Jezebel.

Naomi knew just how to make these men feel like they were the only one to ever be inside of her, lacing her bed with lovely colored sheets made of the finest linen that she got from Gold Circle department store. They weren't exactly imported from Egypt, but with the myrrh, aloes, and cinnamon freshener she sprayed on them, who could tell? By the time she whipped that pussy on them cats they felt like they were in a whole nother goddamn world, let alone country.

One time, when I was thirteen going on fourteen, I came home from school early because I got sick during gym class. The nurse tried calling my moms to excuse me, but couldn't get a hold of her. Because I literally lived about a two-minute walk from the school and there was only an hour left in the school day, they allowed me to sign out and walk home.

When I walked into the house I could hear voices coming from upstairs. I climbed to the top of the steps where my mom's bedroom was. Her door was open and immediately I realized that was where the voices were coming from. There was my moms, and she had left her bedroom door open not thinking that her little teenager would be home early, and I watched her. I stood there and watched her.

At that particular time she just happened to be tricking with two men at the same time. If one was in her mouth, the other was in her cunt. If one was in her cunt, the other was in her ass, or some type of sexual combination. One would have thought my moms was made out of rubber the way they had her stretched and positioned all over the place. The shit looked like it hurt the way they were blowin' her back out. I don't know why, but I just continued to stand there watching. I couldn't move. Then all of a sudden my mother turned around and faced the door. I guess she just had a feeling that someone was watching her. Someone *was* watching her. That someone was me, her daughter.

I'll never—I mean, *never*—forget the look in her eyes when they locked with mine. By then I think the tears that had welded in my eyes were running down my cheeks. Without saying a word, I curved around to the left, where my bedroom was, went into my room, and slammed the door behind me. I made it over to my trash can just in time to throw up. I had already thrown up twice at school. But then it was because my stomach was sick, this time it was because my heart was.

Of course, Naomi continued fucking those two men. She had to. Everybody knows if dem niggas don't bust a nut, a ho don't get paid. Once the two trick niggas finally left, I heard the front door close, and then I heard Naomi come back upstairs.

Please don't come in my room, I remember thinking. *Please don't come in my room.* I was embarrassed for her. I knew my moms was a whore, everybody knew she was a whore, but to see it with my own eyes was just too much for me to take. My moms didn't come into my room, but I could have sworn I heard her standing outside my door. She never came in, though.

After a minute I heard my moms draw a bath. She soaked for what was hours, I bet. I could hear her weeping. I don't know if she was weeping because of the pain, the physical pain, or if she was weeping because of the pain, the mental pain. All I do know is that that night when my moms laid down and went to sleep, she never woke up. Whatever kind of pain it was, she ended it with an overdose of prescription pain pills. I was so fuckin' mad at her. How could she leave me like that? What the fuck did she expect me to do? But I just said, "Fuck it." Although my moms had quit on me, she had been living her entire life on her back anyway, now she was on her back permanently.

From that moment on I knew I never wanted to have anything to do with a man for as long as I lived, not even my father, who was given custody of me when my moms died. He didn't want me. He just pretty much didn't have a choice but to take me. I hadn't seen him in the six years since he abandoned me and my moms in the hood to take up with that honky bitch he had married.

I tried living with him for a minute, but that bitch-ass white wife of his looked at me and saw my moms, I guess. Why else would she be jealous of me unless I was just a constant reminder of the other bitch he had fucked? I tried to hang in there, but it was two years of living hell. I was invisible in my father's life with his wife, especially once she got pregnant and they had a child of their own together.

I ended up running away, back to my hood. The hood was all I knew. I hung out, sleeping over a couple of my peep's houses, here and there until Sam, who was a friend of one of my peep's mom, told me I could stay with her and her dude when she found out that I was pretty much homeless. At the time, there wasn't anything sexual between Sam and me. Sam was just good people and felt sorry for me, is all. The two of us had no idea that we would fall so deep for one another. We were truly just friends until after the big fight with

Detail. When it was over between them two, Sam and I became lovers.

For a minute there, Sam and I were so caught up experimenting with each other's bodies, that we didn't realize that Detail was the muthafucka who made all the money. But when the bills became due, it was a quick reminder. Detail was a small, very small, dope pusher, so when Sam called herself going to some of the cats he fucked with to try and get put on or flip a lil' somethin' somethin', all them niggas wanted to do was fuck, and after a minute I could tell Sam was only one more rejection away from actually deciding to trick with one of them hood niggas. I could tell by the look in her eyes, by how worn down she was from trying. It was that same look my moms had had in her eyes after my father left us and she kept getting turned down from jobs. Finally, my moms decided to just start fuckin' the bastards who weren't giving her the jobs. That became her job.

"You thought Detail beat your ass," I remember telling Sam as I held her by her wrist. She was older than me, but I was bigger than her. "I swear to God, Sam, if you even think about it—"

"Then how the fuck we supposed to live, Sin?" Sam spat as she yanked her wrist away from me, knocking some of the items off of the dresser we were standing by. "I can't keep this place if I don't have no money to pay the bills. You thought *you* were on the streets. We both gon' be on the streets. Then what we gon' do, huh?"

I thought for a moment. Here I was only sixteen, but feeling like a grown woman.

"Samantha, I put it on my life that I'd rather be out there on the goddamn streets homeless with you than under a roof where you got to lay on your back to keep the roof over us."

By then I started to break down just thinking about how my moms went out.

"Sin, I'm sorry. I'm so sorry," Sam cried as she comforted me. "I didn't mean to . . . I just don't know what to do. I'm sorry, baby."

Sam began kissing my tears away, and then slowly I tasted the salt of my tears on her tongue. I lifted her up and placed her on the dresser. She was only wearing a T-shirt and some panties. I moved her panties aside with my hand and as I tongue-fucked her, I finger-fucked her at the same time. Her ass scooted back and forth on the dresser as she pleased herself with my three fingers that were inside of her.

"Oh, Sin," she moaned. "This isn't right. I shouldn't be—"

"Shhh," I quieted her as I felt her pussy muscles squeeze around my fingers with the pressure of a boa constrictor. "Something that feels this good has to be right. Age ain't nothin' but a number," I assured her. "I know what I'm doing. I know what I want, and right now I want to make you feel good, Sam. Am I making you feel good, Sam?" By then I was all up in her shit, pumping my ass like I actually had a dick up in her soaking-wet pussy.

"Oh, Sin, baby," Sam said as she grabbed me by my head. That was the prelude to her about to nut, so I quickly pulled away and tasted her creamy stream of sugar water. It was crazy, but I think I actually nutted on myself too. My panties were so wet and sticky that it was unbelievable. Just the feeling of making Sam feel so good actually made me cum. I knew I had to take care of her, take care of our situation, and that's when I got the idea to start the phone-sex line. It only made sense. Niggas loved pussy, and this was the next best thing, and it proved to be a good money-maker. Within a few months we were able to move out of the projects and into the nice little condo we lived in now.

In the beginning, Sam and I would alternate taking the calls, then eventually Sam got a "real" job, according to society's standards, working in a check-cashing place. Within two years, we each owned a car. I started placing ads in the back of magazines, and my business shot through the roof. Just last year I bought Sam and me matching motorcycles, and paid for us to go on a Carnival Cruise that ported in Mexico and the Bahamas. While in Mexico we got someone to perform a civil ceremony, which, of course, isn't legally recognized in the United States, but in Sam's and my eyes, we are married.

Out of the blue I drove Sam to New York and took her on a shopping spree. We stayed at the Waldorf Astoria, just because, while we were there. It only took me about a week of phone calls to replenish what I had spent on our weekend getaway.

Something inside made me buy my moms a really nice headstone to replace the little cheap one the state gave her. I got her one of those huge marble ones that stands about three feet tall, with a crystal vase for keeping flowers. I guess it was just my way of saying that I forgave her, and at the same time a way to let her know that, to be whore's daughter, I wasn't doing that bad at all in life.

Keep It in the Closet

"Yes, yes, that's right! Fuck me! Fuck me in my ass," I yelled to the down-low homo-thug on the other end of my 900 line.

He was some guy named Braw from the West Coast. Pussy-ass nigga done been in that California sun too damn long. I could always tell a homo-thug from a straight dude no matter how hard they tried to keep it in the closet and pretend to be all hardcore and shit. On the first phone call, right away they'd start out with just wanting me to pretend to be getting fucked in the ass, no getting their dick sucked, no nothing. They'd jump straight in the ass, no foretalk. By the second phone call they wanted me to talk them through my make-believe boyfriend watching him fuck me in the ass. By the third phone call they wanted me to talk them through me watching my make-believe boyfriend fucking him in the ass. So with Braw, unlike Papi who would visualize that I was some Latino *Mami* that he was stickin' it to, Braw visualized I was some big black nigga with a big black dick to match the one he was getting stuck by.

"Same time next week?" Braw asked after I sold him the fantasy of my watching him get fucked in the ass.

"Damn, Braw, my man doesn't even want to fuck me anymore because he's so into you. But what the hell, same time next week." I then ended the call.

"That is some nasty shit," Sam said. She had been sitting there listening to the thirteen-minute phone conversation.

"You got some nerve seeing how we bump coochies every night," I replied. "You are such a fish."

"I don't know, it just seems different with women. Dudes are so big and beastly, and to be sticking their dicks in each other's asses . . . I don't know, man."

"We stick our tongues in each other," I said, slithering my tongue in and out like a serpent.

"Oooh, baby, don't do that to me," Sam said, watching my tongue and quivering as if just the thought of me eating her out sent chills up her spine.

"Don't do what? Don't do this?" I said as I playfully continued slithering my tongue in and out of my mouth, while moving toward Sam.

Instead of playing along and trying to move away, she spread her legs open, revealing the fact that she wasn't wearing any panties under her chemise. Just the sight of her waxed triangle-shaped hair, with her clit peeking out at me, got my body hot. I immediately attempted to dive in with my tongue, but Sam stopped me by putting her hand out.

"Let me stir it up for you, baby," she said sensually, licking her lips and then sticking her index finger in her mouth, sliding it out slowly and then placing it into her pussy with one push. "Oooh, uhhh, ohhh," she moaned as her finger went in and out of her. She closed her eyes and slowly her hips began to move, keeping pace with her finger.

I laid in front of her watching before I followed suit by licking my finger and placing it inside her as well. Her wet pussy took in both of our fingers.

"Sin, Sin, I love you," Sam said as she opened her eyes and looked deeply into mine. With my finger still pleasing her, I sat up and began kissing her passionately. Sam took her finger out of herself and placed both hands on my face. "I do love you so much, Sin. You just don't know."

Sam's voice cracked and before she could hold back, as the cum filled my hand, tears filled her eyes.

"I love you too, Samantha," I said. "I love you too."

The next thing I knew Sam was in my arms, weeping. Without her saying a word I knew what was going on in her mind. She was thinking about Detail.

"You saved me," Sam said. "I could never repay you, Sin. You saved me from a life of hell when you—"

"Shhh," I said, placing my index finger, the same finger I had just fucked her with, over her lips. She then stuck her tongue out and began licking my finger up and down like it was a dick. I pulled her to me by the finger that was in her mouth and tongued her down. The harder I kissed her the more she cried.

I knew what it was like to love someone so much that just thinking about that person stirred up uncontrollable emotions. I knew because I loved Sam that same way. I loved her so much that I would die for her. I would kill for her and she knew it. She knew it because I had proven it when I put that ten-inch butcher knife into Detail's back. I don't know what came over me that day. I just walked in the apartment and saw Detail beating Sam to a pulp, and she wouldn't fight back. She just wouldn't fight back, so I had to fight back for her.

I was a project chick, and used to throwing them blows. After all, I'd fought muthafuckas over my stupid-ass name all the time. But even fighting over my name became secondary to all the blows I had to throw because of kids talking about my mother. You know how it was back in the day—you fight one sibling and you had to fight them all. But you best believe I caught them hoes slippin' one by one and beat their asses. But the one time they caught me, I got suspended and sent home with a black eye and a busted nose. My moms had the nerve to fuss me out, talkin' about all I ever did was fight and that I was out of school more for fighting than I was in school for learning.

"Maybe if you go get on welfare like every other mother around here instead of laying on your back to feed us," I spat at my moms, "then maybe I wouldn't get into so many fights trying to defend you when the kids call you tramps and whores and stuff. I don't even know why I'm fighting. Why should I get mad at them when all they spittin' is the truth?"

Even when I saw my moms laying in the casket at her funeral I thought about the slap she gave me after I said those words to her. I remember rubbing my right cheek, the one she slapped me on, as I stood over her casket crying. I'll never forget the pain—not the pain of the smack, but the pain that was in my mother's eyes when I said those words to her. I think deep down inside that's why I stayed so angry with her for so long. If I stayed angry with her, then I didn't have to be mad at myself for the life I chose to live. But no matter what life I chose to live, I knew that I wanted it to be with Sam and I wasn't about to let Detail take her away from me.

I hardly remember actually putting the knife into his back ten times. I remember dropping it, though. I sometimes have nightmares of the knife dropping down onto the white sheets. I see Sam's hand picking it up and finishing what I started. Every time Detail moved, she stuck him. She had so much fear in her eyes, fear that if Detail got back up, he'd surely kill her, kill us.

Once he finally stopped moving, I remember looking at Sam. She was covered in blood, but not her own. It was Detail's blood. At that moment I lost it and just went into complete shock. I didn't talk for weeks, ironic, because now I talk for a living. Sam was the levelheaded one. She's the one who thought of taking up the floorboards in the closet of that cheap-ass bottom-floor apartment of ours. Together we dug, and we dug, and we dug, and we dug, until the hole was big enough to stuff Detail's corpse into it. If we had hit a pipe or gas line or anything, we would have been fucked.

Sam went to Home Depot and bought some lime and a couple of bags of quick cement. We mixed it in this five-gallon bucket and poured it over the body. I vomited until I was so dehydrated that Sam had to force juice down my throat.

Sam replaced the floorboards. We stayed there for a few more months, hoping and praying that a stench would never surface or else we'd have to come up with a Plan B. Years from now, when they end up condemning that place, maybe they'll find his body—but nine times out of ten, just like every other murder in the projects, it will be written off as gang related. But until then, just like Braw's homo-thug lifestyle, Sam and I will keep our little secret in the closet and continue our life of sin.

TRAINING DAY
Kweli Walker

Have you ever . . . you know . . . fucked?" Dushawn
asked softly, licking his fingers until they glistened in
the last orange and lavender rays of the sun. Before I
knew it, he had my jeans unzipped. "If you ain't, you
need to holla cuz I got a big, long, thick-ass dick, and if
you ain't used to dealin' with that I'm gonna have to
break you in easy."

It took every brain cell in my skull to help me nod
my head yes.

I said, "Uuuh . . . yeah."

I almost said no, cuz on a scale of one to ten, what I had really experienced was a fuckin' zero. The guy I was with had been a straight fuckin' zero. Zero skills, zero dick, and zero holdin' power. The one time I gave it to him that fool had pulled outta me like a little bitch and squirted cum all over his mama's fake-fur seat covers. The worst part was how long he had sweated me, and how much his ass had bragged on his skillz. I coulda done better with my own two hands. I really shoulda told Dushawn no. I'd said yeah just to keep it real.

But Dushawn must've figured out by the look on my face that this was going to be my first *real* ride. He laughed and shook his head, "He wasn't shit, huh?"

"Unh-unh." I shook my head, kinda laughin'.

"Don't worry, La La, I'm going to teach you how to ride Big Black, but first I'm gonna polish your phat saddle of an ass for the ride. Come 'ere, girl."

I strolled over to him, trembling in excitement. "Bomb fuck" rumors spread through the ghetto like wildfire about Dushawn Lambert. Rumor had it that he was a guy who could get the job done. I couldn't wait to see if the rumors were true. The shit was on!

I gasped, "Sssshh . . ." as his cigar-like fingers slid down deep inside my panties, through my slippery pussy lips, and curled way up inside my body. *Oooh!* Having Dushawn's hands strokin' my soft cunt hair with his big fingers digging all up in my pussy was in-fuckin'-credible. After a couple of minutes of the ultimate massage, I spread my legs for more. Suddenly, he trapped my swollen clit on both sides with his knuckles and started kissing me again. Every kiss was longer and deeper than the next. The whole time he was kissing me, he was popping my slippery clit between his knuckles like a clit-popping machine. I felt myself bloom inside, wider than the Grand Canyon. I could barely catch my breath. Dushawn was breathing like a bull.

"Lemme just look at it," he gently commanded, with his soft deep voice. "That's all, baby. I just want to see it."

I knew this was the tippin' point. I knew that if I said yeah, wasn't gon' be no turning back. Outta all the men in the world, I was falling for the brother of my best friend, and the son of my mom's worst enemy. I thought about that for a long, hard second. Unfortunately, my pussy overruled all that loyalty shit. I had fantasized about Dushawn for years, and now was the time for my first toe-curlin' fuck.

"Sure, take a look." I smiled. Seduction at this level has a way of brangin' out the bold in a sista—even a trainee. I had been feeling chilly just a few minutes earlier, but now I peeled out of my jeans and then *BAM!* I was standing in front of Dushawn feelin' like it was the Fourth of July. I had on a lime green crop-top sweater, but was butt naked from my waist down to my lime green ankle-tie spikes. If it was cold outside I sure couldn't feel it no more. I was straight on fiyah!

Dushawn kept his word and just looked. It was late Friday afternoon. A dope beat was blastin' from this apartment across the alley on Indigo Street, so I served it up for him to the music, nasty-girl style. I may not have fucked an army, but I could definitely slow roll my ass to the beat.

"What you know 'bout shit like that, girl? Turn 'round and let me see you bounce that bubble."

You know I did.

The longer he watched the hotter and juicier I got. He was feelin' fire too. I could tell by the bulge in his jeans.

He tossed his head back gently, and signaled for me to come over to where he was sittin' against the wall. I strolled over to him slowly. He kept signaling me to come closer until my pussy was just 'bout an inch from his lips. I could feel the heat of his breath spread across my thighs. He crawled to his knees and this . . . is when I almost lost my whole goddamn mind.

He had me spread my ankles apart, wider and wider, until I stood in a wide upside-down V. The cool air blasted in between my legs and up the crack of my ass. He pressed his nose into the soft damp curly fur surrounding my throbbing pussy. He took a few quick deep breaths of my spicy scent. All of a sudden, his hands went buck-the-fuck wild. They roamed up and down my body, from my ankles, and back up into the deepest folds of my ass and thighs.

He said, "Damn yo shit is tight, li'l mama! Turn around and let me see that pretty ass you got, girl." He was talkin' straight to my pussy. His deep voice sank into my bones. I turned around with a quickness. He grabbed my ass cheek between his pretty white teeth and gave it some sexy love bites while he massaged my clit—wigglin' his fingers up my split, over my clit, and then sliiiiiidin' 'em back down real slow.

"Let me see them nice big titties," he said, turning me back toward his talented tongue.

I was too ready to ride by now, but I obeyed. I was hoping he was as ready to fuck as I was, but he took his time. His hands worked their way up into my titties, but he didn't miss nothin' in between. He stopped and popped my bra loose. I pulled my tee-top back behind my neck and let 'em swing. He pulled me down and gave my big titties all his attention. He gently rolled and chewed my dark chunky nipples until I whimpered and moaned with pain and pleasure. Dushawn tenderly licked and sucked spots I never knew were hot. His large dark brown hands slid back down into my deepest pussy folds.

He slowly spread my thick outer lips apart, and exposed my stiff clit from all shelter. At first he barely brushed it with the moist insides of his lips. When it was slick with his moisture and my own, he started tenderly sucking my whole clit, pushing back the hood with his skillful kisses and plunging it into ecstasy with his powerful tongue. When Dushawn started circling the hot mouth of my cunt with the tips of two thick fingers, my legs started to rattle violently in the extreme pleasure of my pre-cum climb. I held his strong neck to steady myself. The rapid rippling of his jaws sent chills through me. He stopped for a few seconds, to unleash his big hard dick from his pants. I couldn't take my eyes off it. It was thicker and longer than I imagined. While he devoured my clit, I ran my fingers all over his well-shaped head and muscular neck. His freshly cut hair pricked the tender skin of my palms. Finally, I came. I came longer and harder than I had ever come in my life. *Yes-s-s-s!!*

Dushawn lightened and slowed his sucks and kisses from a storm to a gentle breeze. He didn't stop until I completely stopped shuddering. I begged him to fuck me. If his dick had gotten any harder it would have shattered. It looked like a big black satin pole. His eyes were crazy but he igged my pleas. He pulled me down into his lap, sidesaddle, on top of his bulging thigh.

"Don't turn down my gift, Dushawn," I whispered into his thick sexy lips.

"Z'hat whatchu really want, Nailah?" he whispered. I looked him dead in the face. He was still smiling but he looked kinda worried.

"What's wrong?"

He said, "We fixin' to cross the line. You know that, right?"

"Yeah, I know that."

"I like you way more than you think I do, La La. I been checkin' you just like you been checkin' me but . . ." He paused.

"But what?" I snapped.

"I don't wanna hurt you."

"Hurt me how?"

"You know this can't really go nowhere right now. I mean . . . my mom and your mom had *serious* beef."

His words cut me to the bone but I shook it off with a quickness. I wasn't gon' let him fuck up the mood with other people's bullshit . . . especially some *old* bullshit drama.

"My mom been dead for two years, Dushawn. Your mom need to let it go. That mess was between them and we both know it was over some shit that *never* even happened."

Back in the day, when our moms were friends, me, Dushawn, and his lil' sister, Camille, used to walk to school together. Me and Cami were tighter than tight. We did er'y-thing together. Sometimes in middle school we even dressed alike. We had matchin' diaries when we were teens. Some kinda way our diaries got mixed up. Her nosy-ass mama called herself snoopin' through Cami's diary and ended up readin' mine. At the time, I had a King Kong crush on Dushawn. Every page was covered with fuck fantasies about him and me, but we hadn't even held hands. Mrs. Lambert invited my mom by—*to talk*. She was cool with her conversation at first, but she started dropping nasty lugs on my mom about gettin' pregnant in high school and never gettin' married, and living on the "rough" side of Compton. She ended up tellin' Mom that if I was tryin' to trap Dushawn the same way she had tried to trap my father, it wasn't gonna work.

Momma snapped into bitch mode and called her every kinda bitch/cunt/ho she could think of. When we left, Momma slammed their door so hard it sounded like a bomb went off, and it cracked their big front window. So much for the "nice" long talk to smooth things out.

From then on, we weren't supposed to see each other anymore, but me and Camille were like sisters. We did a lot of sneakin' and we never lost friendship. Dushawn would wave but that was it. Back then, I lived just to see him wave from across the street. When Cami told me he got shot in a drive-by at Campanella Park, I snuck by to see him every day on the way to school for two weeks. After that, whenever he saw me he would stop and talk if his mom wasn't around. Whenever we talked, I could tell he was really feelin' me. For the longest time, I waited for him to make a move and here we were—ready to finally get our fuck on—and he brings up that shit. I was pissed—actually more hurt than anything.

I choked back a lump of disappointment the size of Texas and said, "Look, I don't want *no* muthafucka who don't want me. Either you want me—or ya don't."

"You know I want you. I just don't want you to get things twisted."

I threw up my hand. I spoke slow and clear. "If you want this pussy, you better jump the fuck on in this bitch! I'll deal with tomorrow when it get here. Who knows, *you* might be the muthafucka that gets sprung."

That made him laugh. His hands was running all over my body again. He asked if I had some lotion. I quickly dug a tube out of the side pocket of my silver and lime green camouflage handbag. He gently scooped his hand between my legs and gathered the juice from my pussy and thighs. He mixed it with a big blob of lotion. He started stroking his dick until it stood out so stiff that it looked like a lethal weapon. It glistened in the amber glow spilling from a streetlight. "Work the tip for me. That's where I can really feel it," he said, climbing to a stand and leaning against the wall with his pants around his ankles. I grabbed him a little too tight at first. He scolded playfully, "Hold up, Killa!" At first I was embarrassed but we started laughin' again and then he started showing me exactly how he liked it rubbed and stroked. I caught on quick. I could tell he liked my touch by the look in his pretty dark brown eyes—all sexy and dreamy-like.

"You ready to ride Big Black?"

"Been ready," I said with much attitude. I crouched down into a squat right over his long thick dick. He was definitely ready to fuck. His dick was hard as a baseball bat, but he looked so cocky I promised myself that once I swallowed that big muthafucka up inside, I was gonna give him some'm to think about . . . with his cocky ass.

After I got used to bouncin' his tip in and out of me, I started takin' it deeper and deeper. It felt like too much at first, but after I slid up and down awhile, my pussy was like, "Thank! You! Laaawd! This what a dick is spoze to feel like!"

Not only did Dushawn keep a hard dick, he knew how to r-r-r-rock that muthafucka! When I'd go down, he'd come up to meet me! Then he'd grind his coarse dick hair back and forth across my clit. I had never even made my own self cum twice, but round two was 'bout to jump off with Dushawn.

As good as it felt, I didn't want that to happen yet. I wanted to make his cocky-ass lose control. I didn't know what the fuck I was doin', but I had watched enough of my uncle Ray Ray's pornos to fake it. I stopped for a few seconds, came back down, and commenced to workin' my tight pussy up and down Dushawn's dick like a wood chipper. My braids were flappin', my hips were snappin', and my back was crackin' like a whip.

I'd take it up to the tip and then spiral down, like a merry-go-round. As soon as I started talkin' shit—tellin' him how much I liked the way he tossed back that big black dick—his eyes rolled back and his body started to buck.

Mission accomplished! Dushawn let out a loud groan that echoed through the large empty building. On his last stroke, he tried to plunge his big-ass dick up through the roof of my pussy. I felt like I was 'bout to bust wide open, but I kept ridin'. He moaned and kept grindin'. I threw my ass into overdrive and bounced on the leftovers until I finished my second hard cum.

. . .

We got dressed in the purple light of night. Just before we climbed out of a secret third-story entrance, Dushawn hugged me tightly and gently devoured my lips and tongue. He gave me one last sweet deep kiss and said, "Let's bounce." Holding hands, we left the old abandoned factory where we'd played hide-and-seek as kids, and started walkin' back to Alameda to where we had parked our cars by Angel's Doughnuts. We figured it was safe there cuz it's always some old guys on the patio playin' dominoes and takin' bets.

As we got closer to Angel's, the streets got noisier and more crowded than usual because it was Friday night. All the soldiers lined the sidewalks and steps of their apartments, laughin' and plottin' capers. Pook and Dre were at the curb slippin' dimes of Chronic, and a slick song was blastin' from the windows of a big tan-and-white apartment building on Willowbrook. A couple of young moms were sittin' out front, bouncin' their babies to the beat while they kicked it and cut it up.

"Hey, gurrrrrrrrrrrl!" It was this bitch named Nakisha. She knew me and Cami from Willowbrook. I could tell she was shocked to see me holdin' hands with Dushawn. Life had not been kind to her. She was fat as fuck, with a kangaroo pouch in the front and two grocery bags of ass in the back.

"Camille never told me you and her brother was kickin' it."

"Did I miss something? When did you and Cami start kickin' it? We talk er' night and she never mentioned *yo* ass." I shut that shit straight down, but I knew I'd have to talk to Cami right away. Dushawn never said a word, but he never let go of my hand either.

A little further down, somebody was fryin' the hell out of some chicken. It was smellin' up the whole block. TVs were flickering through every other window.

Dushawn was quiet and I was pretty quiet my damn self. My pussy was still clenching and throbbin' from being broke off proper. I thought about Camille. I wondered how she'd act when I told her about me and Dushawn. She used to haaate the bitches that tried to get to Dushawn by tryin' to strike up a fake-ass friendship with her. I knew I had to tell her before Nakisha blurted it out just to see the look on her face. You know how foul bitches do it.

◆   ◆   ●

When we got to our cars, Dushawn gave me one last strong hug and kiss I'll remember 'til I die.

I blurted, "You think Camille's gonna hate my ass?"

He looked at me like I had sprouted another head and said, "Naw. I'll talk to her. She used to tell me all the time how cool you was. She told me I needed to dump them skank-ass hoes and get wit a girl that really cared about me. She knew that meant you, La La."

We hugged and kissed again. It wasn't the XXX hug we had shared in the old factory but I could feel it was real. When I tried to let go, he tightened his hold and gave me a long deep kiss that reached down to my seriously satisfied pussy. I didn't want it to end.

I said, "I got one question."

He said, "Ask."

"When the shit went down about my diary. Did your mama talk to you first?"

"Yeah."

"Didn't you tell her we wasn't doin' nothin'?"

"Yeah."

"She didn't believe you, or what?"

"Prolly not, 'cause she had caught me with my draws around my ankles more than a few times," he laughed.

"Come on, Dushawn. I know you had to tell her some'm else for her to be that mad. What'd you tell her?"

"I'll tell you if you promise to see me again," he teased.

"Promise!"

He pulled me closer and whispered, "The truth—I told her you was wifey material and that when I was ready to settle down, you was definitely on my list."

All I could say was, "Mmph! Mmph! Mmph!"

*   *   *

The next year was the best and worst in my life. Me and Cami got tighter than ever. Her mama still hated my ass but bein' that we was grown-ass bitches on our own, it wasn't nuthin' she could really do. I finished cosmetology school and got my license. Camille had a baby with Tarik Jackson and moved to North Long Beach. We still talked every day, but her baby girl slowed her way down. I was by myself. Breast cancer had taken my momma after I graduated from high school. We barely had a chance to say good-bye. One minute she was complaining of a little bump under her titty, and a few months later she was gone. I was lonelier than I'd ever been in my life. I hadn't heard shit from Dushawn since the day we kicked a hole in it. Camille told me that he moved up north to go to school. I didn't hold it against him too much. He had already told me what the deal was, besides, I had all kinds a men steppin' my way, if I wanted them. I looked good, I smelled good, I dressed good, and I had my own thang poppin' at my hair and nail shop called Tight.

•   •   •

I thought about Dushawn a lot, but I went on with my life. I ran across a thirty-two-year-old guy named Mike Gray who had done a dime in San Quintin but came out doin' the damn thang. He got much gold from fixin' up old houses and sellin' 'em quick. He had bank and didn't mind sendin' a sista to the mall with his credit card. He was the bomb in bed, but I still thought about Dushawn every time we hit it.

We kicked it for almost a year but Mike told me he could tell I was *somewhere else,* and I was glad Cami was there for me when me and Mike crashed. A few weeks later she told me that Dushawn had asked 'bout me. My eyes lit up like Creshaw Blvd. after the Rodney King trial.

"Dushawn told me to tell you that he's coming home." She handed me a slip of paper with his phone number on it. Then she said, "He said he'll call you if you don't call him." I didn't want to get my hopes up, and I was still salty about the way his ass dropped the fuck off. Sayin' that to say this—if I called Dushawn first, Kanye West is white.

One day about a week later, I got home late from work and noticed the blue light pulsing on my answering machine. I figured it was some bitch needin' to have her head hooked up for some emergency club night or something. But when I heard Dushawn's voice coming outta the phone my knees got weak. He asked me to meet him in Santa Barbara for the weekend—so we could catch up. He left the address, directions, and room number to the Seaside Suites.

He said, "I can't wait to see you and hold you, Nailah."

I flew into a blind rage for a few minutes. I started slinging things and cussin' until I lost steam. After I cleaned everything in my house, I flopped down in my overstuffed chair and dozed off. I had a triple-X dream of me and Dushawn, fucking like we was the last two muthafuckas on earth. When I opened my eyes I started digging through my sexiest shit to pack for my trip. I called Breanne to ask if she could take all my clients. She said yeah.

That Friday, I rode up Pacific Coast Highway with the top down on my electric blue 350 Z. I decided that if Dushawn could forgive me for movin' on, I could forgive him for droppin' off. What's wrong with a good fuck between friends?

The sun felt good on my bare, dark copper skin. I wore a "barely there" silver kidskin bikini with matching leg-strap heels and a white suede baseball cap that said PLAYER 69 when I went to meet him. No point in beatin' around the bush when I wanted him to beat the bush up. My trainin' days were long gone.

I saw Dushawn from a mile down on the highway. His mouth dropped and his dick pointed to the left like a traffic cop when I hopped out my ride. The eighteen months had been good to me. I was thicker and curvier than ever. I had figured plenty of things out about men and sex and seduction. What I hadn't read, I'd learned from experience. When my heels hit the asphalt, they clicked with absolute confidence. One look and Dushawn knew I wasn't the nervous little girl he had sucked and fucked out of her mind in the factory.

When we got inside the room he must have said, "Damn..." ten times in a row. He asked, "You wanna get some'm to eat?"

I said, "Sho! . . . after we fuck!"

He pulled the drapes open wide and sat me in a cushioned chair facing the ocean. He ran both hands through my braids and across my scalp and gave me a kiss that made me know how much I had been missed. I bent the dial when I slapped it back on him. He praised my new skillz, "You've learned a few things, huh, La La?"

"I sure have. Thanks for that bomb first lesson, Dushawn." He slowly untied each strap on my bikini until it fell away from my body, revealing all.

He asked, "This one?" as he dove tongue first into my juicy cunt, joined by his big thick fingers. This time he reached deeply and twisted his fingers in and out of me while he sucked and tongued my clit with a hot new rhythm. He picked me up and sat me on top of the dark wood dresser on the other side of the room. I dug my heels lightly into his shoulders and gapped my thighs wide for him. Dushawn took slow deep fuckin' to the Olympic Gold level. Just when he was starting to lose it, he put me back in the chair and sucked my pussy like a pro. I was more than ready to come, and when I did I shuddered and let loose an animal-like grunt as Dushawn tongued me back down to earth.

"Your turn, Mr. Lambert."

I twirled the head of his slippery dick in my mouth and popped it from side to side until he called out my name. I stroked his dick from the tip to the back of his thick shaft—

soft and slow, and then wild, fast, and hard. Suddenly I stopped and made him sit in the chair. I knelt in front of him and let him look out at the ocean. I sucked him into a wicked pulse and ran my fingers through his curly black hair. He was just about to pop, but he pulled away just in time and said, "Let's fuck watchin' the ocean together, La La."

I asked, "How we gon' do that?"

He moved me into the doorway of our spot and climbed on doggy-style. He started sliding his thick dick in and out of me from behind. My clit was on swole again. He reached up front and started whippin' it from side to side, plunging deep as he could and every now and then he'd freeze . . . Mmph! Holdin' it all the way in . . . filling me up. I wanted more. I told him to hol' up and I went and unpacked my toys. I gave Dushawn the honor of inserting my li'l red devil tail ass plug for me. That and Big Black drove me outta my mind.

"Where you learn to freak like that?"

I said, "Maybe you haven't noticed, but I haven't asked you shit about where you been and who—oops! I mean, what you been doin'—now have I?" We laughed a little and then took turns fuckin' the shit out of each other until the sun started to go down.

Later, we decided to get some'm to eat on the pier. It was still warm outside so I threw on a scandalous burgundy suede halter and low-riders set. I pulled my hair back into a ponytail and grabbed my nicest shades.

He held my hand while we walked. It felt good but I couldn't help but think about how he had held it this way be-

fore, and then turned around and left without even sayin'
"Fuck you, bitch!"

Dushawn was reading my mind. "Don'tchu wanna know
where I been and why I didn't get in touch?"

I said, "Not really. I ain't got no way of knowin' if that shits
for real. Let's just do what we do best—fuck and forget about
it."

. He laughed at how I point-blanked his ass.

"Anybody ever tell you how sexy you look when you mad?"

"Cut the bullshit and tell me what's up, Dushawn."

"'Member when I got popped at the park?"

"How could I forget? Yo ass like to died."

"I found out who did it."

There was a lot that coulda been said, but it didn't need to
be said. That changed everything. I thought back to when
Dushawn left and who came up missin' before that. That
told me all I needed to know. The Lambert brothers didn't
really bang, but they hung and slung with guys that did. If
somebody fucked with any of 'em, it wasn't over until it was
done. Dushawn was a Lambert.

After he spilled the details, he told me that he'd been
chillin' with his cousins in Sacramento. He said he had
learned how to do electrical work from this O.G. named
Jerry, and that he was 'bout to buy a house outside of Sacramento. That's when the convo got serious. Dushawn asked
what my plans were.

Truth be told, my plan was to come up to Santa Barbara,
get freaked proper by my first good fuck, and then take my

ass back to Compton. Things had swung serious though, and I knew Dushawn wasn't just askin' shit to be askin'.

I told him I needed to think about that.

"Take your time, baby. I got plenty a shit to keep me busy 'til you hit me back with your answer. I just need for you to know that I can't ever come back to Compton. I did some serious dirt before I left."

"You askin' me to move up here?"

"That depends on whatchu got planned."

I felt like my brain was 'bout to bust. Everything had flipped so fast.

I told him, "I need to come up here for a few weeks and take a look and see where I fit in. I can't come up here blind, Dushawn. I gotta be able to take care of myself. I got a business to think about. I mean . . . every couple thinks they gon' make it forever. Know what I mean?"

He said, "If I say forever, I mean forever. Splittin' up ain't a option. I want some kids. Don't you want kids, La La?"

That shit blew me away. He was talkin' marriage and family.

I asked him, "Where the ring, fool?" I was just jokin' but he went to the bedroom and started diggin' through his suitcase. When he came back, he hit the floor and grabbed my hand. What he slid on my finger was some'm that would make the ladies say, "Oooooh!" It was at least three carats and slangin' fire all over the room.

There was a lotta shit I coulda said, but I kept it short and sweet. I said yes.

Me and Dushawn spent our last day together fuckin' each other's brains out. We talked about er'ything—friends, family, work, old times, and times ahead. I felt like I was dreamin'. We talked about his moms. I saw her from time to time in the streets, and nothing had changed between us. She turned away when she saw me, just so she didn't have to speak.

Dushawn said, "Don't worry about her. She's down there and we'll be up here."

I said, "That sounds all good and shit right now, but how do you think she'll feel when she knows we're gettin' married?"

He said, "She'll get over it—or she won't. My pops thinks she will."

We had a good laugh about his dad dick-whuppin' his mom into acceptin' me as her daughter-in-law. We talked until we fell asleep in each other's arms. We woke up to the sound of the ocean crashin' on the shore. That last day we spent together, we got up before sunrise and walked out to the end of the pier. It was empty. We stood behind the little bait house and food stand and watched the seagulls fight over scraps. Dushawn was behind me with his big arms wrapped around me.

I wondered if we could beat the odds. Most people ain't up to forever. Suddenly he pulled up my jacket and my mini skirt, and moved the crotch of my panties to the side. He slid up inside me and started workin' me slow while we watched the tide crash against the pier. I thought, *Maybe it won't last forever, but as long as he fucks me like this, it will.*

Shit. I pushed back on that big dick and stopped worryin' 'bout whether or not it would last. As my man squeezed my ass and made my juices run down my leg, I squeezed my pussy muscles and started worryin' 'bout how to finish my business in Compton and get back to Dushawn as soon as possible.

2 CAN PLAY
K'wan

"Whassup," I said, standing in the doorway of her midtown apartment. She was a little on the plump side, but had a cute face. From the moment I saw her I knew her type. One of society's misfits. They're all one type or another. I know, it's a chauvinistic statement, but what do you expect from a nigga in my line of work?

"Hi," she said, sheepishly. "You must be Chocolate?"

"True," I said, stepping into her apartment, not waiting for an invite. Her place was plush to say the least. Fifty-eight-inch television, plush carpet, and original paintings lining the walls. Shorty was obviously sitting on a few dollars, which suited me just fine. I mighta been a tramp, but I was no ho. To get a taste of this chocolate, you had to pay like you weighed. In Ms. Thang's case, she'd be breaking the bank.

"I'm Chandra," she said, extending her hand. I didn't take it, I just stared at her.

Chandra was a big-boned sister, but she wasn't fat. Give it a few years or a baby or two, and she would be. She had smooth caramel skin and a round face. Her hair was rich and black, just tickling her shoulders. I could tell that she had the potential to be a very attractive chick, but lacked the self-confidence to step it up.

"Can I use your bathroom?" I asked, giving her my most innocent smile.

"No problem. It's down the hall to the right."

I gave Chandra a playful wink and headed toward the bathroom. Once inside, I closed the door and locked it. I proceeded to ramble through the medicine cabinet, garbage pail, and even peeked under the toilet seat looking for piss stains. I made it a rule never to roll into an apartment or house that a woman shared with a man. That was sure nuff asking to get got. I'd learned over the years that what a chick says and what's *real* can often be two different things. I had broken this rule once, and ended up getting stabbed in the back by a hater boyfriend. That's the reason why I started carrying a gat when I went to see a trick. I use the term trick, as opposed to client, because that's what I did. I tricked women into believing they needed what I was selling. Most of these women should have realized that they were fine and strong enough not to need a man like me, or any man, to make them feel good. The thing was, the majority of them never really looked deep enough within themselves to find that inner strength. Relying on a man for strength or happiness was a shortcut. This worked for me, because it insured that as long as my dick could get hard, I'd never be pressed for cash.

After making sure that there wasn't a dude either living there or squatting, I went back into the living room. Chandra was standing in the spot where I had left her, rubbing her hands together nervously. From the look in her eyes she probably knew what drill I had really conducted in her bathroom. I gave her a sexy grin to set her mind at ease, and took a seat on the couch.

"Would you like something to—?"

"Take your shit off," I cut her off, totally catching her off guard. Chandra stood there with her mouth open. She tried to read my face to see if I was joking, which I wasn't.

"I figured you might'a wanted to talk for a minute. You know, get to know each other a little bit?" she said, trying to buy herself some time.

"What's there to talk about? We both know what time it is." My cinnamon brown eyes ensnared her, causing her to turn away. "Time is money, love. Come up out that dress."

She hesitated for a quick second, then started to undress.

Chandra began undoing her black Versace dress. Her pudgy hands fumbled with the clasp at the shoulder, but finally managed to unclamp it. I admired her full breasts, pushed up by the black Victoria's Secret bra. The formfitting dress gave her some trouble coming down over those wide hips, but slid off smoothly past that point.

"Turn around," I said. Chandra folded her arms across her chest and began to turn slowly. *Nice,* I thought. Her skin rolled over the waistline of her panties a bit, but she had a deliciously phat ass. I had always been a sucker for a phat ass.

I could tell by the way that she was covering herself that she was ashamed of her body. Just the type I figured on. Chandra was your classic case of a beautiful, full-figured woman who had been brainwashed by white fuckers in society to be ashamed of carrying a few extra pounds. When I guessed someone's type, I was hardly wrong.

"Come'ere, Chandra," I beckoned her. Once she took that first step in my direction, I knew I had her. See, most guys believed that if you put a good fucking on a woman it made them yours. This was not true. Any fool could conquer a woman's body, but only the most skilled playas could conquer their minds.

When I reached up to take Chandra's hand, she jumped back. I gave her a warm smile, letting her know it was all good, and pulled her down on the couch beside me. Using just my thumb, I stroked the back of Chandra's left hand. My trained eye spotted just what I was looking for, a tan line. So, she was married. That meant this wasn't her house. One of her girlfriends probably let her use the crib to fulfill her nasty little fantasies. That was fine by me, as long as I didn't have to put lead to some crazy nigga trying to rush the place, tripping behind his girl being a jump off.

Somewhere Chandra had a man who probably had no idea that his wife was about to give away his goodies. The thought of this turned me on even more.

Men like Chandra's nigga came a dime a dozen. They played the game until they had their chicks trapped, and once the thrill faded the relationship went stale. The woman who was once a trophy piece on the arm of her man found herself spending a lot of time alone in the house. This is where I came in. I enjoyed fucking honeys in general, but there was something about fucking some other nigga's pussy that made it that much sweeter. As I looked at Chandra sitting beside me damn near naked, I thought of how her man's face would look if he could see her. I had to bite off the laughter that was trying to bubble out of me.

I was a predator on two legs. The worst kind, if you asked my opinion. I preyed on the insecurities of women and bent them to my will. I didn't do it out of malice, or because I liked hurting people. It was more of an addiction than anything else. It was my drug of choice, so to speak. I got high from the hunt and the conquest of women.

Chandra opened her mouth to say something, but I silenced her with my tongue. Her breath was sweet, with just a hint of the wine she had been sipping as she prepared herself for the sinful act she was about to commit. I inhaled deeply, as if I could share in the drink with her. Chandra's body went stiff when my fingers traced a line down her back. When I went to slip my fingers between her pussy lips, Chandra pulled back.

"I've never done this before," she said, slightly out of breath.

"Yeah, but I'm sure you'll like it so much you'll be calling for me again."

Sometimes I can be a little arrogant, but chicks got off on a confidant man. I think I surprised Chandra when I scooped her in my arms and stood up. I must admit, my knees felt like they might give out on me, but it was all for effect. I gently laid Chandra back on the leather sofa and took a step back. She just lay there looking up at me, wondering what I had in mind. Well, I was just about to show her.

I slipped out of my leather jacket and tossed it onto the love seat. I could tell she was impressed at how the tight wife-beater hugged my muscled chest and arms. As cool as I could, I ripped the T-shirt down the middle. I could see Chandra's eyes light up, but the best was yet to come.

Kneeling beside Chandra, I kissed along her thighs and knees. Her skin was streaked with stretch marks, but I pretended not to notice as I licked her navel tenderly. A low moan came from somewhere deep within Chandra. My nimble tongue darted in and out of her navel then worked its way down to the rim of her panties. Her hands tried to cup the back of my head, but I moved it. As a rule, I didn't allow tricks to play in my hair, especially when my braids were fresh.

I pulled Chandra's panties down over her thick hips and

admired her stuff. Her pussy had been recently shaved, but bore signs of new growth. Using just my fingers I spread her lips and found them soaked. Chandra squirmed, but didn't pull away. "Take it," she panted, but I wasn't quite ready yet.

I stood up so that Chandra could take in all that I was packing. Her eyes hungrily moved from my six-pack to the bulge in my baggy jeans. "You think you ready for this?" I dared.

"Hell yeah," she whispered.

Chandra was looking at me like I was a baby deer and she was a hungry lioness. Weighing in at a chiseled 220 pounds and just a hair over six-two, I knew I had it going on. I stepped closer to where she lay and placed her hand over my crotch. She ran her palm up and down the front and smiled at what she felt. The warmth of her touch, even through the jeans, only made me harder. Chandra tried to unzip my pants, but I wouldn't let her. As another rule, I had to be in control at all times. I purposely took my time unzipping my pants while she looked on in anticipation. When I pulled out my just-under-ten-inch dick, she almost fainted.

I stood directly over the nearly drooling woman and licked my lips. I had one hand on her cheek, while my other hand stroked my dick. "You like what you see, Chandra?"

Words had escaped her so she just nodded.

"Then suck it like a good little bitch."

Chandra looked up at me as if she wanted to be offended, but she knew better. Here she was, a married woman about to pay cash money for the next nigga to fuck her. Crazy, right? But you'd be surprised at how many women pay for sex. Be it with cash, jewelry, or favors, they pay. The next time one of you cats who leave your women at home while you tip out see a hunk of a withdrawal from y'all joint bank account, just think of me. 'Cause I might be runnin' up in your bitch and taking your money at the same time.

When Chandra took my dick into her mouth, I was immediately turned off. She tried to jump right into the blow job, but only ended up scraping me. She gave me that old, "Sorry, but I ain't never done this before" look, but I knew better. If a woman doesn't feel confidant about her body, then nine times out of ten she won't know how to use it properly. Judging by her shyness at me seeing her naked, I knew she'd given out more than her fair share of blow jobs to try and keep a man around.

Without warning, I grabbed Chandra by the back of the head and yanked her free of my dick. Saliva ran down her chin as I barked, "Bitch, stop playing with me and suck it with some fuckin' emotion!" She nodded dumbly and went back to the task. This time she handled her business properly.

Chandra sucked me at three different speeds, licked my balls, and tried to lick my ass. I stopped her before it got too crazy and moved on to the main event. Slipping on a Magnum condom, I got back into my kneeling position in front of Chandra. I spread her big thighs and tickled her clit with the head of my dick. Chandra tried to squirm onto my dick, but I backed away. *My show, my way.* "Beg for it."

"Please," she whimpered, pawing at my dick. Chandra had a look in her eyes that went beyond want or need. Her eyes was filled with the desperation that you see in a junkie who needs a quick fix. There was no doubt in my mind that if I didn't break Chandra off, she was gonna try her best to *take* the dick.

I ran my fingernails along Chandra's thighs, barely touching her skin. Chandra sighed as a tremble went through her body. I started out just slipping the head of my dick inside her. I can't even front, Chandra's pussy was tight. Even with the lubricated condom, and her pussy now running like a faucet, I had a little trouble getting the head in. I began stroking her slowly, careful not to let her feel the whole thing just yet. By the time I got my dick halfway in, Chandra was hissing like a viper.

"Yeah, this pussy is tight," I huffed, keeping a steady rhythm. I hadn't had a pussy that tight since high school. There was even a moment that I had the urge to cum prematurely, but you know I was too cool for that. Chandra's husband either had a little dick, or he wasn't hitting it much. I slipped my dick about three quarters of the way in before I hit her vaginal wall. Chandra let out a yelp, but made no attempt to stop me.

"You like this dick, don't you?" I whispered into her ear.

"Yes," she sobbed.

"Tell me you love this dick, bitch. Tell me you love it." I demanded.

"I love it. Goddammit! I love this dick!" she shrieked.

I continued to give it to Chandra, alternating from a slow grind to a rapid pounding. She cursed and grunted, throwing it back at me. I knew she was about to cum because I felt the walls of her pussy start to tighten around my dick. Just before she reached her climax, I pulled out. Chandra looked at me as if she could strangle my ass, but I paid her no mind. "Turn over," I ordered, and she flipped onto her stomach real quick.

Cocked up in the air, Chandra's ass looked like a giant heart. A thin line of sweat ran down her back and into the crack of her ass. This time when I slipped inside her it was a much easier fit. I proceeded to dig as deep as I could into Chandra's guts, slapping her hard on the ass. She grunted like an animal and dug her nails into the soft leather of the couch while I worked out on her. After ten minutes of hitting it from the back, Chandra's juices began to run down my thigh. A lot of niggas could make a woman cum, but your cock-game had to be boss to make them squirt.

Feeling myself about to cum, I spread Chandra's ass cheeks so I could get deeper into the pussy. Chandra's pussy felt like a warm spring day, clinching and unclinching on my dick. "Yeah, I'm 'bout to cum," I panted.

"Cum in my mouth," she pleaded. "Let me taste you, Chocolate."

Never being one to deny a woman her sexual thang, I gave Chandra what she wanted. Right before I came, I pulled my dick out of Chandra and snatched the condom off. Chandra spun around and knelt before me on the couch, mouth open, eyes wide. With a few good strokes, I busted my nut. Cum shot from the head of my dick and splattered across Chandra's face and chin. She moved my hand and began to jerk me off, catching the excess cum in her mouth. Chandra wrapped her lips around my throbbing dick and sucked out whatever was left. By the time she was done, I was winded and dizzy.

• • •

I took a quick shower at Chandra's and slipped on a fresh pair of boxers and a white T-shirt. I always kept a spare set of underclothes in my gym bag, right next to my Glock. Normally, I wouldn't bother showering at a trick's house, but I had to meet my boys uptown and I didn't want to ride all the way back to Brooklyn.

Chandra was stretched out on the couch, wrapped in a lavender bathrobe, staring at me though glassy eyes. I knew that look all too well. See, being a brilliant lover had an up and a downside. The upside was; the woman would always remember you and chances were you could fuck her whenever you felt like it. The downside was, a lot of chicks wanted to try and turn a good fuck into a potential relationship. I knew what was running through Chandra's mind, and I wasn't with it.

"You leaving?" she asked, twirling a lock of hair around her finger.

"Yeah," I said, flatly.

"I was thinking maybe you could spend the night, and I'd hook you up with some breakfast in the morning?"

"Nah, baby. I'm cool. I just need you to lay that bread on me so I can get going."

Chandra's face took on a look of disappointment, as if I gave a shit. She got off the couch and headed toward the bedroom. Watching that phat ass move under that silk robe made my dick hard again. Shorty did have some good pussy, but I was straight about my cheese. Pussy would always come. Chandra returned a few moments later and handed me an envelope. I quickly thumbed through the contents and found five crispy hundred-dollar bills.

"The extra hundred is for making me squirt." She smiled. "I'd heard about it happening, but I've never experienced that shit until tonight. Thank you."

"Not a problem, baby." I tucked the bills into my inside pocket. My work was done and it was time to head out. Chandra walked me to the door and I could tell by the look on her face she had something else on her mind. I tried to dip off before the situation became awkward, but had no such luck.

"Chocolate, I'd like to see you again," she finally blurted out.

"Sure, honey. You know my rates, holla at me."

"No, not like that. I mean, the sex was the bomb, but I like being around you."

"Chandra, you got a man, shorty. I don't rock like that."

She folded her arms and balanced on one hip. "My man didn't stop you from fucking the hell out of me, did he?"

"One thing ain't got nothing to do with the other. You paid for a service, and that was that," I said coolly. "Don't complicate things, hon." I could see the hurt all in her eyes, but I had my money and Chandra's feelings weren't my concern.

"So, it's like that, Chocolate?"

"Afraid so, shorty. My show, my way."

"I shoulda known better. You ain't nothing but a ho!" she shouted. She was trying to get a rise out of me, but of course I was too cool for that.

"I might be a ho, but being that your money is in my pocket, I guess that makes you a trick, doesn't it? Give your man a big old kiss for me."

She shouted a few more crazy insults at my back as I headed for the elevator, but I couldn't hear shit she said over the roar of my own laughter.

*   *   *

I steered my Dodge Charger up the Westside Highway, bumping the new Jim Jones CD. I fucked with the Diplomats. Though they weren't the nicest rappers in the game, I respected their hustle. These kids had come from the same streets I was from and started a movement that was spreading like wildfire. I rested my head in Brooklyn, but I was still a Harlem nigga to the heart.

When I heard Teddy's "Love TKO" coming from my cell, I knew who it was without looking at the caller ID. "What's up, boo?" I said into the tiny microphone of my earpiece.

"Hey, baby," Keita replied in her sultry voice. "I miss you, lover man."

Keita was my boo. My down-ass chick that I held above all the others. Now, I was a stone-cold dog, but even a dog needed a main bitch. For me, that was Keita. I had met her about a year ago at All Star Weekend in Denver. She was with her girls and I was with my niggaz, but when our eyes met there was no one else in the room. We got to politicking and

306 | From the Streets to the Sheets

I found out that she was from the Bronx. We spent the whole weekend together and by the time we got back to New York I had already decided that I was gonna make her my wifey.

"I miss you too, my one and only," I said, sounding like a real clown-ass nigga. I was a lion at heart, but when it came to Keita, I was a pussycat. As hard as I was, Keita was my only weakness. The bastard in me warned against it, but the heart makes you crazy.

"You still at work?" she asked.

"Nah, baby, I got off early. I'm on my way uptown to meet Benny and them."

"I'm glad, sweetie. Sometimes I don't understand you, Dante. You make good money at the car dealership, so why do you continue slaving for UPS at night?"

By now, you're probably confused, so let me explain it to you. Chocolate is what my niggaz and these tricks call me, but my given name is Dante Burton. The part about me working at a car dealership during the day was true, but I had quit my night job at UPS months ago. I never bothered to tell Keita, because it was a good alibi for the odd hours I kept with my tricks. I've found that I could make way more money slinging dick than loading trucks.

"I know, ma, but you know a nigga gotta hustle. How else are we gonna get that big house?"

"Baby, you're too sweet. I'm lucky to have a man like you," she said in a most sincere tone. Sometimes I felt bad about misleading Keita, but whenever a bitch broke me off a wad of cash, my conscience flew out the window.

"You know it's all about us, Keita. What you got going on tonight?"

"Nothing much. Me and my girls might go to Envy."

"You better not be in there letting them scumbag niggaz grind all up on your ass." I said seriously. I was very possessive when it came to Keita.

"Boy, stop acting crazy. You know I don't know how to do nothing but the two-step." She laughed. I loved to hear Keita laugh. It always reminded me of bells, and all things happy.

"I hear that hot shit. You just remember what the fuck I said."

"Okay, Daddy," she sang.

"You want me to pick you up afterward so we can go get something to eat?"

"No," she said, hurriedly. "I'm the designated driver tonight. Tell you what, though, why don't you meet me at my place and we can eat each other."

"Sounds like a plan," I said, thinking of her warm mouth on me.

"Okay, so I'll see you later, Daddy. I love you."

"I love you too, ma." With a great deal of reluctance, I ended the call. I loved Keita to the point where it sometimes hurt me physically. Damn this thing called love for making me so fucking weak!

My boys thought I was bugging for falling for a chick so quickly, but they didn't understand. I had been with a lot of bitches in my day, but none of them ever quite measured up. They were always lacking in one area or another, either not being pretty enough, or smart enough. My baby girl was the total package. Keita was five-four, with medium-length black hair that she usually wore in a wrap, and honey-colored skin. Whenever she smiled, you couldn't help but to smile back. She just had that effect on people.

Keita was an independent woman who got up and went to work every morning, and hardly asked for anything other than my time and affection. She was hood, but she wasn't ghetto. I could have just as much fun with her at a black-tie affair as I could at a Rucker's game in the summertime. She could move in either circle. My girl liked to go out and have a good time, but she knew how to conduct herself. Though I was insanely jealous, I never had to worry about her stepping out on me. It just wasn't her way. Keita's mother was heavy into the church and had instilled that in all four of her daughters. Hell or high water, my boo was in service every Sunday morning.

Having Keita in my corner made me feel like the luckiest dude on earth. Most of you are probably wondering: If this girl is so special then why the hell do I step out on her? To put it simply, it's just the nature of my species. Sometimes the thrill of the hunt is even greater than the prize.

•   •   •

Mochas was our spot. It had been since they opened their doors about four or five years ago. It was a small but cool lounge on Eighth Avenue in Harlem. During the week you could go there for drinks and possibly a comedy show, but on the weekends they brought in the DJ and everybody got their groove on.

It was a Friday night and there was a line of people outside waiting to get in. The bouncers were very picky about who they let in on weekends, and would send your ass home if they thought you weren't dressed the right way. I gave a bouncer named Freddy dap and proceeded through the glass door. Though I was *technically* properly dressed, the normal rules didn't apply to me. I was a regular at Mochas. Everyone knew Chocolate.

It was just after one in the morning so the spot was in full swing. There were beautiful women, single and in groups, scattered around the lounge, and thirsty men trying to pump them full of alcohol. I paused by the bar and scanned the crowd for my partners. It didn't take long for me to spot them; sitting on a love seat near the DJ booth, trying to charm a group of young ladies out of their panties. These niggaz thought they had game, but they knew who the real Don was.

As I made my way across the room all eyes were on me. I nodded to a few of the guys I knew and flashed smiles at some of the bitches I had fucked. A time or two I caught sight of some nameless female that I'd probably slept with but hardly remembered, trying to get my attention, but I acted like I didn't see them. I didn't feel like the headache. All I wanted to do was have some drinks with my boys and chill.

I had almost made it over to where my friends were sitting when my path was suddenly blocked. The brazen young thing had yellow skin, and wore her hair in a straight weave. I knew her angelic face, but for the life of me couldn't remember her name. Her ass was plump, but not large. Just enough to where it looked good. She stared at me with her bright green eyes and waited for me to say something. Since I knew that's what she wanted, I remained silent.

"You can't speak, Chocolate?" Ms. Green Eyes asked. The sound of her sweet voice reminded me of a string quartet.

"What's happening, baby?" I grinned, but was careful not to give her a full smile. Though I would've liked nothing more than to take her in the bathroom and slam her pussy, I couldn't seem too thirsty. I was Chocolate, and like the rest, this bitch would recognize.

"Oh, you on it like that? You can fuck me in a park, and then act like you don't know a bitch?"

My groin tingled as my mental Rolodex finally placed her.

Shorty's name was Harmony. I had met her on the side of the New Jersey Turnpike one night on my way back from seeing a trick in Philly. It was pouring raining and her car had broken down on the side of I-95. At first I was gonna keep it moving, but as I passed I caught a glimpse of those eyes and almost caused an accident slamming on the brakes.

She couldn't thank me enough for coming to her rescue. A quick look under her hood told me that her alternator had conked out. Harmony found herself in a bind, but looking at that ass and those juicy breasts, of course I had the ideal solution. Placing a quick phone call to a guy I knew in Camden, I made arrangements for her car to be towed to his shop to see if he could get it running. The job was going to take at least a couple of hours, so I offered to keep her company.

I took Harmony to a restaurant I knew of located inside the Hotsheet Hotel in Camden, while we waited on my buddy to fix her ride. We made small talk, exchanging information about each other's backgrounds and places of residence. Harmony was a registered nurse at Mount Sinai Hospital, and like me, a native of Harlem, 118th, if I remembered correctly. She had a quick wit about her and was very well read. It felt good to be able to spar with someone intellectual after having spent most of the day with my not-so-smart trick in Philly. Though we kept the conversation neutral, occasionally making flirtatious remarks, there was an obvious attraction.

After about three drinks I could tell that Harmony was beginning to feel it. It would still be a while before my buddy would be finished with her car, so I suggested that we go for a brisk walk to clear our heads. The rain had stopped, leaving behind a humid night.

I frequently came through the area so I was somewhat familiar with the layout. I led Harmony to an out-of-the-way park that was in walking distance of the hotel. As we strolled up the stone path, Harmony looped her arm in mine. She fronted like her balance was off from the alcohol, but her eyes were hardly glassy enough for her to be that drunk. I already knew what time it was, even if Ms. Harmony didn't.

Our walk led us to an arrangement of rocks that were off the main trail of the park. The way the rocks were situated, there was a nook that had been protected from the rain. Harmony and I sat there and talked over a blunt of haze.

"So, what kind of name is Chocolate?" she asked, expertly blowing the smoke through her nose.

I shrugged, and said, "It's a nickname that I got in college. All the girls used to joke about how sweet I was."

"I'll just bet." She smiled, pinching my cheek playfully. "With the rain gone, it's nice out now," she remarked, looking up at the clearing sky.

"A night for lovin'," I replied, tracing my fingers along her arm, barely touching her skin. I felt that telltale shudder run through her and knew that the gauntlet had been laid down. There was a moment when all sound ceased and Harmony and I just stared at each other. She opened her mouth to break the silence, but I hushed her with a finger over her lips. Harmony kissed it softly then began sucking on it. Feeling her warm mouth on my finger I imagined what her lips would feel like on my dick. My vivid imagination caused a small pup tent to rise in my jeans.

"Let me find out about that lovin'," she said, looking down at the bulge.

"That's what I'm hoping," I said, placing her hand on my dick so she could see what a nigga was working with. I thought she'd pull away, but she didn't. Harmony firmly pressed her hand against my crotch and gave a smile that said she was pleased.

"Let me see it," she asked, playfully.

"Shame on your ass, girl," I laughed. "We don't even know each other."

She laughed back. "Stop fronting, Chocolate," she said, gripping my dick through the jeans. "I seen how you was looking at me all night. You're just as curious about how wet my pussy is as I am as to how deep your dick can go. We're both grown, so ain't no need to play games."

I was a little thrown off by her directness, but turned on at the same time. There was nothing I liked more than a chick who knew what she wanted and wasn't afraid to ask for it. I leaned in and kissed Harmony deeply. I usually didn't like kissing, but her full lips were so sexy that I couldn't help myself. As our tongues performed a mating dance I let my hand roam up her sundress. Even through her thong panties I could feel the heat radiating from her pussy. I slipped my middle finger inside her and began to explore her love nest. Harmony breathed deeply and slid further down onto my finger. It was like dipping my finger into a warm pie. She was so wet that I could feel the moisture building in my hand like a thin film of sweat.

Harmony undid my belt and began fondling my dick as we continued to try to suck the breath out of each other. I could tell that she was surprised at my length as she stroked me. Running my hand up her back, I began playing in her soft hair. Before she knew what was going on I was guiding her head down to my lap. She didn't seem to mind as she ran her tongue along the head of my dick. My eyes rolled back in my head as she worked her lips down the side of my shaft and tickled my balls.

She sucked on my sack like she was trying to get the last bit of meat out of a snow-crab leg, drawing a low moan from me. Gripping a fistful of her hair I began fucking Harmony's mouth. Her warm breath felt like heaven on my throbbing cock. She bobbed up and down on me expertly, letting a stream of saliva run down my dick and settle on my balls.

"Damn, you really do taste like chocolate," she gasped, before continuing to suck me off. I let her continue with her little show before pulling her head up and gazing into her pretty green eyes. Behind those eyes I saw a hunger that matched the one building up inside of me.

"Fuck this pussy, Chocolate," she demanded, laying back on the rock and hiking her sundress up. I pulled Harmony's thong to the side and admired her bush. It was hairy, but she kept it neatly trimmed. I watched carefully as she began sliding her finger in and out of her pussy, inviting me to take the plunge.

I was so thirsty to run up in this little tender that my hands were nearly trembling as I ripped the condom wrapper open. Gripping her ass cheeks, I lifted her slightly off the rock and slid her onto my dick. I had no problem running up in Harmony's soaking wet pussy. She winced a little when I reached her rear walls, but that didn't stop her from trying to pull me deeper. Her small hands gripped the collar of my shirt, almost popping the buttons off as I pounded her.

"Ooh, get this pussy you black muthafucka," she grunted, throwing it back at me. My face contorted into a mask of something hideous as I appreciated her hot box. "Yeah, that's what I'm talking about. Fuck me, Chocolate. Fuck me!"

Now, I had always considered myself as somewhat of a pussy wrecker, but Harmony was no slouch. For as hard as I tried to dig into her, she threw it back equally hard. I placed Harmony on her side and spread her legs into a scissor. She braced one foot against the top of the rock and let me go as far as I could into her.

While I fucked Harmony's pussy, she fingered her ass and barked for me to go deeper. At one point I had gone so deep that I almost hurt myself against her walls. I proceeded to flip her onto her stomach and enter her from behind. One hand balanced on her back while the other gripped a fistful of her hair. I went to work on Harmony's pussy, slapping her buttercup ass on command. The slaps sounded like thunder in the still night, but this only seemed to excite her more. She wailed like a cat as I thrust myself into her over and over. I was glad that she was on her stomach so she couldn't see the ugly-ass face I was making when I exploded into the condom. I came so hard that the muthafucka almost came off. Even when I was empty, Harmony kept pumping. For a moment I thought I would blackout waiting for her to cum, but she had finally reached her climax and lay under me, trembling.

"Damn, Chocolate, the way you throw dick, I'd think you did it for a living," she joked. Harmony thought I was laughing at how witty her joke was, but I was really laughing because she had no idea how close to the truth she was.

Once we had caught our breaths we proceeded to clean ourselves with some sanitary napkins she had in her purse, and headed back to my car. By the time we got across town to my buddy's shop, Harmony's car was ready. As we prepared to go our separate ways I promised to keep in contact with her, and at the time I really meant it. But once she was gone, Harmony became just another faceless pussy.

* * *

"Harmony, what's good?" I hugged her close to me. I inhaled the sweet smell of her skin and felt the throbbing in my groin. Harmony had truly left an impression on me.

"Yeah, act like you know." She squeezed me back. "Nigga, I thought you were gonna call me."

"My fault, ma. I lost my phone not too long ago," I lied.

"Yeah, right," she said, noticing the very same Nextel I had used to call my man in Camden clamped to my hip. "You ain't gotta lie, Chocolate. I'm a big girl."

"Anyway, what you been up to?" I asked, trying to change the subject.

She shrugged. "Same shit, different day. You know how it goes."

"For sure. Oh, congratulations," I said, noticing the rock on her finger.

She self-consciously covered her hand. "Thanks. Listen, Chocolate—"

"No need to explain," I assured her. "Shit happens, ma. I ain't mad at ya."

"You never called."

"I got tied up."

"For six months? Chocolate, you know how long I sat by that phone hoping you'd ring it?"

"Like I said, I got tied up," I said, sounding very uninterested.

"So tied up that you couldn't even call and let me know what was good. I'm not blind, Chocolate. I've seen you and your girl spinning around town. You could've told me you were involved."

"You didn't ask," I said, sarcastically.

"Chocolate, you broke my heart when you played me to the left. I don't just go around fucking niggaz I meet on the highway."

I raised a mocking eyebrow.

"Don't play ya'self, a'ight? I thought we had some kind of connection?"

"We did. That was one of the best shots I ever had," I admitted.

"So that's all it was, a fuck thing?" she asked, trying to hide the hurt in her voice.

"Nah, baby, I was really digging you, but you know how it goes. It was the heat of the moment."

Harmony's green eyes flared. "I don't believe this shit. You know, I prayed that if I ever ran into you again that you'd have a good reason for not calling. I hoped that the stories that these girls tell about you weren't true, but I see they are. You ain't nothing but an egotistical whore."

"If that ain't the pot calling the fucking kettle black." My gaze went to her engagement ring. "It wasn't that long ago that you were sucking my dick in the park, and I know that engagement didn't happen overnight. Right after you gave me head you probably went and kissed that nigga in his mouth, so don't try to hang no fucking labels, dig it? Granted, yours was some of the best pussy I ever had, but the fact of the matter is, we both had someone we were going home to. It was a brilliant fuck, but don't try and make it more than that."

A lone tear ran down Harmony's cheek, and her jaw muscles tightened. "I fucking hate you, Chocolate!"

"Good, then that's one less bitch I gotta worry about trying to get in my space. Now, if you'll excuse me, I've got some people waiting on me," I said, brushing past her. I never even bothered to look back at Harmony, but I could feel the heat on my back. If looks could kill, I'd have probably dropped dead on the spot. I didn't give a fuck though. It was my show and my way.

• • •

By the time I got to the table where my partners were sitting, I was greeted by hearty laughter. Apparently they had watched the whole exchange between Harmony and myself and gotten a kick out of it. Though we were all pushing thirty or had recently passed the mark, we were just big kids at heart.

"That chick sure looked pissed," Max said, slapping me five. Max was a high-yellow cat who still wore his hair in a fade. He and I had played on the same JV team in high school and been friends for years.

"You know Chocolate be having these bitches acting all out of character," Hog added. Hog had gotten his nickname because his nose resembled a pig's snout. He looked like a slightly more handsome version of the Notorious B.I.G., with a shaved head.

"Y'all niggaz always got jokes," I said, plopping down on the chair closest to Max. "Where the fuck is Reggie?"

"He dipped out about twenty minutes ago. He went to see that stripper bitch he met last month," Max informed me.

"Sucker-for-love-ass nigga," I laughed. "I know a lot of niggaz who done paid for pussy a time or two, but Reg is making that shit a regular occurrence. What is that, like the third time he's seen her this week?"

"Fourth," Hog said. "Silly muthafucka took off work the other day to get a shot of that."

Max shook his head sadly. "That boy is gonna take himself to the poorhouse."

"Anybody ever seen this chick?" I asked.

"Nah, we weren't with him when he met her. He was fucking with Tay and them niggaz from the hill," Hog said. "She must have some bomb-ass pussy, because she's got this nigga acting like a schoolgirl."

"Let him tell it, she's got fairy dust tucked in her twat," Max joked. "This dude told me that she licked his ass cleaner than Martha Stewart's kitchen."

"Shit, I wouldn't mind getting a shot of that," I admitted.

Hog pushed me playfully. "Nigga, your hands are full enough. You got a girl and you're still fucking everything on two legs. One day your dick is gonna fall off."

"You know these hoes can't get enough of Chocolate," I said, referring to myself in third person, as I was known to do. "They pay like they weigh, my dude."

"You pop that shit now, but what you gonna do when these females get together and try to burn your ass at the stake?" Hog said, in his gravelly voice.

"I wich the fuck they would. My dick is like crack, and these chicks know who got the best product in town. They all pay homage to the king," I boasted.

"These bitches got you gassed," Max said. "Chocolate, I ain't never met a nigga as stuck on himself as you."

"Stop hating, fool, you know how I do. My show, my way. Recognize!" We exchanged high fives and ordered another round of drinks.

Though my niggaz loved me, I know that sometimes they got a little jealous. I was young, fine, and doing me in a major way. I got more pussy on a weekly basis than some of them got in a month, and still I had a bad bitch who was madly in love with me. My game was on a million and it was only gonna get tighter, or so I thought.

•   •   •

It was about three-thirty when I finally left Mochas. I wasn't drunk, but I had a damn good buzz going on. Max and Hog were gonna shoot down to the Strand to get a bite to eat with some chicks that they had met. One of them was a fine, light-skinned girl that was looking at me like she'd suck the life out of my dick. They wanted me to tag along, but I had to decline. The dog in me had wagged its tail enough for one day, and I was anxious to get back to my boo.

It took me about thirty minutes to get to Keita's. She lived in a nice little two-story house, right off of West

Fordham. I let myself in, using the key she had given me two months prior. My boys thought I was tripping for giving her keys to my pad too, but that was just the hater in them coming out. If I loved her enough to give her the keys to my heart, it was nothing for me to give her the keys to my pad.

Keita wasn't home from the club yet so I decided to doll myself up for her while I waited. I took another shower, scrubbing my skin with some scented wash that Keita had bought me. My boys would clown me for using those kinds of products, but fuck that. I was a pretty nigga and liked to smell good too. After my shower I slipped on a pair of thong underwear, another gift from Keita. They were the kind of joints that had the tubular pouch that your dick slides into on the front. When all that was done, I settled down in front of the bedroom television to wait.

Halfway though whatever dry ass movie I was watching, the television and lights blinked out. I tried to cut them back on but they weren't working. *The fuse must've blown,* I thought to myself. Grabbing the flashlight from Keita's closet, I made my way down to the basement to replace the fuse.

Keita was one of those people that didn't believe in throwing shit away, so the basement served as a makeshift storage facility. Bags of clothes were strewn throughout the basement and every wall was lined with boxes. The fuse box was located in the far corner, just above a stack of storage bins. To reach the box I had to stretch over the bins, and even then I was still barely able to reach it. I guess that's why

Keita called me every time one of the damn things blew. I had successfully removed the burnt-out fuse and was about to put the other one in when it slipped out of my hand. I tried to catch it, but it bounced behind the bins.

"Fuck!" I shouted. That was the last fuse in the house, so that meant that I'd have to move the bins and retrieve it. After a bit of struggling I had finally managed to move the bins enough to squeeze behind them. As I was shining the flashlight back there I noticed a space in the floorboards. It was so small that I wouldn't have noticed it if I hadn't been looking for the fuse. It might've been nothing, but my curiosity wouldn't let it go.

I slid the bins away from the wall entirely and crawled behind them to investigate the space. That shit was barely the width of my pinky finger, but I could see something underneath. Using an old paint stick, I pried the floorboard loose and found what appeared to be several hatboxes hidden under the floor. I had no idea why the hell Keita would be hiding hatboxes under the floor, but best believe I was about to find out.

One at a time, I removed the hatboxes and sat them in the corner. After replacing the fuse, I turned on the basement light and sat down on the floor. When I opened the first box I was surprised to find that there were clothes in it. The box was filled with thongs and bikini tops made from all different kinds of materials. There was even a small whip curled up at the bottom of the box. At first I thought that it might be old shit, but nothing felt dry-rotted. Upon further inspec-

2 Can Play | 323

tion, I could smell the faint scent of Keita's perfume and musk. This sparked my interest and prompted me to move on to the next box.

Like the first, this box with filled with items that I couldn't understand why Keita was hiding. There were things ranging from handcuffs, to different-sized vibrators. I even came across a leather mask. My mind reeled trying to figure out what was going on, but it would be the last box that would alter my life forever.

The third box was filled with adult movies. I knew Keita watched porn because we often watched the films together, but this was some hard-core shit. There was everything from guy-on-guy movies to animal snuff films. In addition to these, there were mini DVDs, with dates on the labels. Determined to see what the fuck was going on with my boo, I carried the box upstairs.

After hooking up the mini-cam I had bought her for Christmas, I popped one of the tapes in. The first scene was taken at strip club called the Wedge Hall. I knew the spot because I had been there a few times with Hog and Max. There were nude girls performing onstage and giving lap dances. One girl was familiar to me, but I couldn't see her face because she was wearing a mask. The very same mask I had found in one of the hatboxes. My pulse quickened as the pieces began to fall into place. The woman who I had given my heart and soul to was leading a double life as a stripper.

I leapt from the bed and screamed at the top of my lungs.

I knocked over lamps, and smashed mirrors, but it still didn't quench my rage. A wave of heat shot from my toes and washed over my face as I watched my beloved baby girl bounce her ass while men threw dollars at her. Keita performed tricks on that stage that she never had in our bedroom, and the crowd loved her. My heart felt like it had shattered into a million tiny pieces. I thought I had seen the worst, but I was terribly wrong.

The camera faded out of the strip club, and faded into a dingy motel room. There was a man sitting on the edge of the bed talking to someone I couldn't see. I prayed that it wasn't my Keita, but by this point I knew I was reaching. She came on camera wearing a thong and some thigh-boots. Tears stung my eyes and I wanted to turn away, but I forced myself to keep watching. She began by licking this cat down his chest, then taking him into her mouth. Now, with me Keita always fronted like she really didn't know what she was doing when she gave me head, but she sucked dude off expertly. I thought it couldn't get any worse until I saw another man come into frame and start pounding her from the back while she continued to suck his partner.

I cried like a baby, watching as my woman fucked and sucked other men. To say that she got nasty with them would've been an understatement. Keita performed tricks on these men that you only saw in porno movies. They even double-teamed her, with one cat beating the pussy while the other one fucked her in the ass. Through it all Keita spewed obscenities and reveled in the fuck-fest. As I watched a trio of well-hung studs take turns cumming in her mouth, I thought about all the times I had kissed her lovingly, and I threw up all over the carpet.

By the time I got to the last tape my eyes were swollen from crying and my throat raw from screaming. During the very last scene, Keita was kneeling in front of the camera, waiting for God knew who. A tall cat with piss-yellow skin came into frame, totally naked. Keita proceeded to lick up and down the shaft of his dick, while running her nails across his ass cheeks. His back arched in ecstasy as she sucked him like a peppermint stick. Dude grabbed her by the wig she was wearing and began fucking her mouth like a jackhammer. She began jerking his dick while she licked under his balls and made her way around to his ass. I wanted to throw up again, but I didn't have anything left in my stomach!

As if the knife hadn't been driven in deep enough, the dude's face came into frame and what little bit of breath I had left in my body escaped me. It was my man Reggie. So, Keita was the freak-ass stripper that he had been spending so much of his time and money with. I sat there and watched helplessly as my man fucked my girl in every single hole. When he was done, he came all over her face and proceeded to wipe what was left onto her waiting lips.

I was a man defeated. For all the running around on Keita I did, it never occurred to me that she might be doing the same. Not my love-goddess. Never in a million years. I thought I knew all the tricks, but apparently she knew one that I didn't. Keita had put one over on the infamous Chocolate.

Seeing my woman fucking all those guys on tape took something out of me. The fire that had only hours prior burned within me was gone. I no longer had the strength or desire to live. I crawled—yes, crawled—to where my gym bag lay and retrieved my gun. The iron felt cool yet comforting in my hands. I placed the barrel in my mouth and prepared to leave this cruel world behind, until I heard the sound of the front door opening.

"Baby, are you here?" she called up. "Dante, why are all the lights off? Are you being nasty?"

Hearing her voice enraged me. Here I was about to check out over a no-good, low-life bitch. The more she talked, the madder I got. At one point I felt like I had completely taken leave of my senses, and for the kind of shit I was thinking about, I guess I had. Suddenly, a plan began to form in my mind.

"I'm up here, baby," I called down in my sweetest voice. Pressing myself against the door, I listened for the sound of her footsteps on the stairs. That bitch must've been outta her mind to think that she could put the move on me. I was Chocolate muthafucking Burton. This bitch would recognize like all the others.

I waited patiently for Keita to make it to the second floor and down the hall to the bedroom. She was the first bitch to ever run game on me, and she'd damn sure be the last. It was my fucking show, and my fucking way. And when she crossed the threshold, I gave her my warmest smile before pulling the trigger.

Show's over.

My way.

ACKNOWLEDGMENTS

As always, all props go to the Father above for blessing
me with the ink that flows from my pen. I'm also thankful
for my sense of humor and my patience because I wouldn't
have survived the knife wounds without them.

Thanks to Missy, Jay, Ty, Nisaa, Black, Man,
and my girl Aretha Temple for having my back and
brushing the dirt off my shoulders.

To those of you who stay hungry for my original
urban erotic tales and send me mad e-mails full of love,
I love the hell outta y'all right back. You might have
crowned me the Queen of Urban Erotic Tales,
but it is me who bows down to you.

STAY BLACK.

NOIRE

Noire's
URBAN EROTIC RIDERS

Noire is the number one *Essence,* Black Expressions, Black Issues Book Review, and Borders bestselling author of the urban erotic tales *G-Spot, Candy Licker, Thug-A-Licious, Baby Brother* (with 50 Cent), *Thong on Fire,* and *Hood.* With the publication of *G-Spot: An Urban Erotic Tale,* Noire burst onto the literary scene with fire and street credibility, and caused the tongues of veteran authors to wag in a million different directions. Noire's debut novel quickly became a nationally bestselling title with over 100,000 copies in print, and that number continues to climb. Noire's short story "That Bitch Juicy" is the first in the series of "G-Spot Teasers," which are short stories to be published in future urban erotic quickie anthologies. Noire promises that each "teaser" will bring the reader closer and closer to the explosive climax they've been waiting for: *G-Spot 2: Juicy's Revenge.*

As the editor-in-chief of NOIREMagazine.com, an original

332 | Urban Erotic Riders

source of street elite urban entertainment, Noire is riding the urban erotic train into new frontiers. NOIREMagazine.com is dedicated to exposing new authors in all genres and boasts Da Beautiful Mind's Noirotica poetry corner, Reem Raw's Urban Music Shelf, Angie's Monthly Book Picks, an Urban Altar column by E. N. Joy, and a gully column filled with urban entertainment news, called "Ree-Ree Got the Scoop." Noire continues to parlay the urban erotic dream into new realms with NOIRE Music Group, in collaboration with Reem Raw and N.J.S. Entertainment, and with upcoming film projects for *G-Spot, Candy Licker,* and other titles. Noire's first urban film, *Hitting the Bricks,* starring Alexandra Merejo, Ness Bautista, and Texas Battle, was recently shot in Los Angeles and is scheduled for release in 2008.

**Plea$ure,** a St. Louis, MO, native and resident, made her mark in the underground hip-hop music industry before transitioning into the urban fashion scene, and now the literary industry. A self-proclaimed princess of the streets, Plea$ure accentuated the negativity of the hard-core streets that raised her, turning it into a positive by utilizing the lessons and lifestyle in her raw, edgy tales. This is her first story. Look out for her debut novel, which will be released by Urban Erotic Tales by Noire Publications.

Euftis Emory is a graduate of Howard University with a degree in Computer Based Information Systems. Founding Dominion Publishing in 2005, Euftis has quickly become one of the most daring and raw black erotic authors on the market today. When he is not writing, Euftis presides as the chairman of the Dominion Corporation, a management information systems consulting company. Euftis can be reached at *Euftis_Emery*@yahoo.com. Or visit his website at http://groups.yahoo.com/group/OffdaChain/.

Andrea Blackstone attended Morgan State Univesity and is the recipient of The Zora Neale Hurston Scholarship Award. After a two-year stint in law school, she later changed her career path and earned an M.A. from St. John's College in Annapolis, Maryland, with honors. The self-published author of *Schemin': Confessions of a Cold Digger*, and the sequel, *Short Changed*, Andrea's inspirational story, *My Mother's Shoes*, was published in *Chicken Soup for the African-American Woman's Soul*. In 2008, she completed her first book deal with Q-Boro Books. *Nympho* was well received by erotica fans, and *Sexxxfessions: Confessions of an Anonymous Stripper* became a Black Expressions bestseller. Andrea has appeared on *Real Sports with Bryant Gumbel* and *E! True Hollywood Story.*

Gerald K. Malcom, author of *The Last Temptation*, has reached thousands of readers, and now flexes his literary prowess in the film industry. With a screenplay, *The Maskerade*, complete and ready for filming, he continues to push forward through joint ventures in Los Angeles and on the East Coast. He recently co-founded a T-shirt company, www.twistedrealities.com. His initial shirt, *You Can Call Me the Inward*, has caught the attention of several key components in the entertainment industry. Malcom educates youths and adults through creative writing courses for those who are interested in learning the craft. After ten years in the literary business his writing continues to be comedic, sensual, and realistic. With several other literary, television, and film projects in the works, he finds solace in a quiet game of chess or by spending time with family and friends. He can be reached at www.geraldkmalcom.com.

Thomas Long is the author of the urban fiction smashes *A Thug's Life* and *Cash Rules.* He is also a contributing author in the bestselling anthologies *Around the Way Girls 2* and *Around the Way Girls 3.* Long's latest novel is *Papa Don't Preach.* The versatile and prolific author's book *A Thug's Life* has been adapted into the recently released DVD *4 Life,* starring Wood Harris and Elise Neal. For more info on Thomas Long or the movie, go to www.athugslife.com or www.watchmenowfilms.com.

Jamise L. Dames is the nationally bestselling author of *Momma's Baby, Daddy's Maybe* and *Pushing Up Daisies,* and is a contributor to the anthology *On the Line.* A public speaker and published songwriter, Dames holds a B.A. from the University of Connecticut, and is pursuing a master's degree. Dividing her time between the West Coast and the South, Dames looks forward to hearing from her readers at www.jamiseldames .com and www.myspace.com/jamiseldames.

Aretha Temple knew she had a talent for writing in the seventh grade, when she started writing poetry. People enjoyed it so much, they asked her to write their wedding vows. As Temple got older, she discovered that her passion for writing expanded beyond poetry. She began writing erotic and urban short stories, sharing them with her various online groups, as well as on her MySpace pages: www.myspace.com/twothick4you and www.myspace.com/arethatemple.

Temple wrote a short story with a couple of other members of UrbanEroticNoire@Yahoogroups.com; titled "The Prison Chronicles," it caught the eye of the Queen of Urban Erotica. Temple was then recruited by Noire to write the column "Ree-Ree's Got the Scoop" for Noiremagazine.com.

Temple's first novel, *A Hustler's Ambition*, will be released this year. She is currently working on her second novel, as well as on her second anthology. Temple resides in Toledo, Ohio, with her two sons, Dominique and Da'Jaun. "You have a choice to say something or shut up."

Erick S. Gray, founder of Triple G Publishing and author of the urban sexomedy *Booty Call*, has been writing seriously since 1997. Born and raised in the south side of Jamaica, Queens, this thirty-one-years-young gifted author introduced himself on a high note with his first endeavor, *Booty Call*, which was published in 2003. Gray continues bringing good stories as he shows in his collaboration with Mark Anthony and Anthony Whyte, *STREETS OF NEW YORK VOLUME 1*, *Ghetto Heaven*, and his most recent smash, *It's Like Candy*, along with *Flexin' & Sexin'*, *Nasty Girls*, *Booty Call *69*, *Money Power Respect*, and the much anticipated novel, *Crave All, Lose All*.

Gray continues to illustrate that not all young African-American males fall into the categories of drug dealer/thief/statistic. His future is filled with promises of more intriguing and diverse stories for the masses to digest. Don't judge the book by its cover!

"Life of Sin" was the last literary work **Joy** completed before making her transition from secular works to Christian, children's, and young adult fiction. Other past works by JOY include *If I Ruled the World, Dollar Bill,* and *Mama I'm in Love with a Gangsta.* You can visit Joy at www.JoylynnJossel.com or e-mail her at joylynnjossel@aol.com.

K is the sexxxy alter-ego of author **Kweli Walker.** Born and raised in South Central, Los Angeles, Kweli attended CSUN, majoring in Afro-American studies and biology. She also attended Loyola University, majoring in Fine Art—painting and drawing. **K** kicked off her Afro-erotic career with a collection of short stories called *Walkin' Pussy.* She was featured in Susie Bright's *Best American Erotica,* and will also be featured in the *Mammoth Book of the Kama Sutra.* Her latest novel, *Fire Blue,* is scheduled to be published in 2008.

In 2002 **K'wan** hit the scene with his debut novel, *Gangsta,* published by Triple Crown Publications. What started as an argument went on to become a part of urban-lit history and an *Essence* bestseller, as well as drawing rave reviews internationally.

After penning his second novel, *Road Dawgz* (2003), K'wan drew the attention of St. Martin's Press. The literary powerhouse quickly signed K'wan to a three-book deal, the first of which was *Street Dreams* (2004). K'wan's titles also include

Hoodlum (2005), *Eve* (2006), *Hood Rat* (2006), *Blow* (2007), *Flexin & Sexin* (2007), *Still Hood* (2007), and *Gutter* (2008). With these, as well as several yet-to-be-published Dark Fantasy pieces, K'wan has proven himself to be among the elite of the literary game.

Since his emergence into the publishing world K'wan has been featured in *Time* magazine, *Vibe, King, Felon, Pages, Big News, Time Out New York,* and the *New York Press.* He was also interviewed on MTV and BET, and was a guest on WBLS and Power 105. K'wan is also a motivational speaker, freelance writer for *Men's Health* magazine, and CEO of Black Dawn, Inc. The Harlem native is currently at work on his next novel. Please visit his website: *www.Kwanfoye.com.*

Coming Soon!

Noire's
STREET SCRIPTURES

Urban Erotic Quickies
Volume 2

NOIRE